DEMON'S ADVOCATE

STACIA STARK

For Petra. This one's for you.

CHAPTER ONE

Samael

Finvarra lounged in front of my desk, a glass of whiskey in his hand. He sipped at it, his expression inscrutable as he narrowed his eyes at me.

"Our alliance is on shaky ground," he said.

"And yet everything Danica did led to our survival. I wouldn't be here if not for her strategic thinking."

Finvarra snorted. "Strategic thinking?"

"From what I heard, you took the opportunity to negotiate your own deal." I couldn't blame the unseelie. Like us, they struck at the first sign of weakness. While I was sure Finvarra wasn't happy that Danica had given his enemy the one sword with the power to kill him, he'd been quick to–

A jolt of terror shot down my bond with Danica, and I shot to my feet.

"What is it?" Finvarra asked, his expression bored.

I tuned him out. Even with everything that Danica had faced since we'd bonded, I'd never felt such bone-deep fear from her before.

My little witch was *terrified.*

I strode toward my balcony, automatically reaching out to my bondmate.

"What is wrong, little witch?"

"Samael, it's Cellen. You need to—"

Nothing.

Sudden nausea threatened to drop my knees to the ground. I fought it, thinking past the instinctive reaction. Danica was alive. I could still feel her at the end of the bond. But it was excruciatingly faint.

My phone signaled. I was vaguely aware of Finvarra using his magic to float it to me, and Evie's voice was suddenly screaming at me over the speaker.

"Cellen took them, Samael! Danica and Kyla. Even Keigan."

I launched myself off the balcony, arrowing toward Danica's office.

Evie was slumped in the office on her knees, tears rolling down her face.

I could still scent my little witch, could still sense her, but she wasn't *there* anymore.

Unconscious. She must be unconscious. If she was dead, I would know.

I repeated the thought over and over again as another part of my brain automatically responded to Evelyn. I was dimly aware of my people arriving, voices tight as they talked.

But the majority of my conscious thought was devoted to reaching for Danica. Feeling my witchling at the end of the bond was the only thing keeping me sane.

Agaliarept clutched my shoulders. "She's alive."

I didn't ask him how he knew that. If I'd felt my little witch die, this city would be in ruins.

There was no longer terror radiating from the other end of the bond. I could feel Danica now, awake and confused. But something was suppressing our bond. For every second that passed, I could feel her less and less.

"Danica. Answer me. Please."

Nothing.

Just minutes ago, if someone had asked me if magic could interfere with our bond, I would have denied it, so confident that no power could touch something so intrinsic to us.

But Danica couldn't hear me. When I reached for her, there was… nothing.

My breaths sawed in and out of lungs that felt like they were filled with cement.

I threw my head back and roared.

Danica

I took a bite of my dessert. I wasn't sure what it was, but it was rich and sweet.

"More wine, my love?"

I glanced up. Pischiel was watching me with his dark, inscrutable eyes. I smiled at him. "No, thank you."

He reached out and took my hand, playing with the bone bracelet on my wrist.

"This doesn't suit you."

I narrowed my eyes at him. "I like it."

He sent me a slow smile. "I bet I can convince you to remove it."

My cheeks heated and butterflies danced in my stomach at the promise in that smile.

Wrong. This is wrong.

I frowned.

Pischiel squeezed my hand. "Are you okay?"

"Yes. Just... Déjà vu, I guess."

Pischiel glanced at my grandfather, who was deep in discussion with Daimonion. I barely refrained from sneering. I couldn't remember a time when I *hadn't* hated Daimonion. Ever since I was a little girl...

Pain stabbed into my temple and my hand tightened around my spoon. I slowly laid it on the table next to my plate and reached for my water goblet.

My grandfather's concubine sat on his right, her own bracelet gleaming in the candlelight. My chest ached with a strange kind of *want* at the sight of it. Hera smirked at me, and I forced myself to pull my gaze away from the gems, which sparkled with internal fire.

I'd never been particularly avaricious before. I felt like I was losing my mind.

Then I got to my feet. "I think I'll take a walk in the gardens," I said.

"I will walk with you," Pischiel said.

What I wanted was some time alone. My grandfather looked up and met my eyes, sending me an encouraging smile. My lips trembled as I shook my head at him. He'd long hoped that I'd fall in love with Pischiel—was already planning our bondmate ceremony.

The long, midnight blue gown I wore trailed across the ground as I rounded the table. I leaned down and brushed grandfather's cheek with my lips on my way out the door.

"I know what you're doing, you romantic fool," I whispered.

His eyes sparkled as he grinned at me. "Enjoy your walk."

I ignored Daimonion's sneer and nodded at grandfather's other advisors before taking the arm Pischiel held out to me.

We strolled out of the dining room and toward the royal gardens.

I'd placed my hand in the crook of Pischiel's arm and he covered it with his.

"It's a nice night," he said.

"Yes," I smiled, shaking off my weird mood and surveying the beauty of the night-blooming garden. "It is."

Samael

"He's here," Agaliarept murmured behind me.

I nodded, my gaze still on the city below us as we stood in my penthouse. My fists clenched and unclenched with the need to find my little witch. With the need to hold her close.

I could barely speak, my rage battling with a wild sorrow that spread through my chest. My power was unsteady, and it took every ounce of my willpower to hold on to it, to prevent my fury from breaking free.

If I leveled this city, Danica would be grief stricken when I finally got her back.

And I *would* get her back.

I could feel Agaliarept hesitating behind me.

"Speak," I ordered.

"It may be a good idea to leave the city. If your power breaks free…"

I slowly turned. To his credit, he met my eyes. But whatever he saw there made the blood slowly drain from his face.

I suspected I knew what he was seeing. The few times I'd caught sight of my reflection, my eyes had been dead.

My little witch was all alone in the underworld. With my greatest enemy. Lucifer knew if he killed her, he would be protecting himself from the threat she represented.

That fucking prophecy.

I cursed it once more. Without the prophecy, there would be a much greater chance of Danica staying alive. Lucifer may be playing with Danica now, but the moment his granddaughter proved to be too much trouble, he would slaughter her without a second thought.

"Samael?"

I was staring into the distance, still mentally reaching for my witchling. I glanced back at Agaliarept, who was closely studying my face. What had he asked me?

"No," I said. "I will not leave this city. This is Danica's home."

Ag narrowed his eyes. "We can all feel your power. If it breaks loose, the loss of life will be unimaginable."

I took a single step closer. "Are you insinuating that I do not have enough control?"

He gave me a look that said the way I was acting spoke for itself.

"I apologize," I gritted out.

"Accepted." He sighed, and I realized he looked exhausted. My people were pushing themselves to their limits to find any hint of what Danica was facing in the underworld.

Ag was still talking and I forced myself to focus. "No one could blame you if your control did falter, Samael. The fact that you can't contact her…"

Grief welled, tightening my throat. Distantly, I could feel blood slipping from my palms as my claws cut into the skin. There should be nothing that could prevent me from speaking to my little witch through our bond. I suspected Lucifer had harnessed the underworld's power in order to do such a thing.

My witchling was alone, without her ability to even speak to me. She must be so scared.

The tower shook. Agaliarept sent me a telling look, and I took a deep breath. Then I strode toward the door as he stepped aside.

The seelie king stood in my penthouse, surrounded by guards. He dared to nod at me, as if *I* were beneath him.

The tower rumbled and groaned, swaying around

us, and one of Taraghlan's guards tensed, reaching for a weapon. I glanced at him, and he froze. Prey.

"Leave," I said.

The guards glanced uncertainly at their king. Taraghlan studied my expression, then angled his head, his eyes narrowing. "Go," he said.

The guards turned to file toward the elevator. One of them leaned closer to mutter something in the king's ear and he shook his head, gesturing for him to leave and meeting my eyes.

"If you attempt to kill me here, it will mean war," Taraghlan said. The guard finally left the room, sending me a warning glance that almost got him killed.

I smiled. "Do you think I have any hesitations about such a thing? Do you imagine I care about warring with you? No, the only reason you are still alive is because I have a use for you."

"I would like to make it clear that I had no idea what Cellen was planning."

I didn't respond to that. Both of us knew that every ruler was responsible for their people and the choices those people made.

"Samael." Ag spoke quietly behind me. I frowned, coming back to myself. My power had crept out, surrounding the seelie king. His shields were strong, but from the look in his eerie eyes, he knew it was only a matter of time before I broke them.

But if I killed him, I wouldn't get what I needed.

Focus.

"Meow."

Lia had nudged open the door and strolled in, tail

swaying. She jumped onto the table next to me and pushed her head into my hand in clear demand. I petted her, and both of us eyed the seelie king.

I gave him a grim smile. "This is the problem with having someone swoop in and remove you from the slightest danger for centuries. I could snap your shields with a thought. What *will* you do without your little portal maker?"

Taraghlan's jaw tightened, and I forced myself to pull my power away.

Think of her.

"I know what you seek in your war against Lucifer," Taraghlan said. "I have ordered one of the pocket realms to be brought to this world. And I will give it to you for your use as my people's apology to yours for the loss of your bondmate."

I ignored the last part of his sentence. *This* was why I needed to keep him alive. Lilith had come close to securing one of the artifacts we needed, but we no longer had time for her to negotiate with her contacts.

Allow him to live until you have what you need.

"How long?"

Taraghlan swallowed. "The owners of the artifact are… unstable. I will keep you updated."

"*Who* are the owners of the artifact?"

His mouth twisted. "The bubaks."

"The bubaks," I drawled, coating the words with amusement. Taraghlan's eyes fired, but he said nothing.

Most people thought the bubaks were a subset of demons. In reality, they were just one of the light faes' dirty little secrets. Scarecrow-like beasts, which had once broken free of the seelie realm to terrorize Eastern Europe, they hunted in corn fields and kept to secluded parts of the forest, lurking along river banks where people were likely to stop during their journeys.

They liked to eat children, but could also mimic the sound of a crying baby, earning larger meals from the adults who investigated.

"How did the bubaks gain the pocket realm?"

"That is none of your business."

I tutted. The deal was likely made in an effort to keep the creatures far from any portals. The seelie so enjoyed pretending they were creatures of light.

"I want the realm within two days, or I start killing your people, one by one."

A muscle ticked in his jaw, and I could practically hear his teeth grinding, but he gave no other indication of his fury. "Impossible. Time does not move the same in all areas of my realm. The team I dispatch for the artifact will be traveling to a part of my realm where one day there is equivalent to eight in this realm. If they have to take the artifact from the bubaks by force, the trip will take longer."

My power began to escape me once more, dark as night as it twisted around the seelie king. He couldn't see it, but I knew he could feel it, poised against his shields and ready to strike.

"One day in this realm is equivalent to two in the underworld," I hissed. "The longer you take, the longer my bondmate is facing torture and *death*."

Sixteen days. If I was to use the pocket realm, Danica would be trapped in the underworld for sixteen days.

My little witch. Alone with my greatest enemy for more than two weeks.

To Taraghlan's credit, his gaze hardened, although color slowly leached from his face. I didn't need to tell him that if Danica died, I would make his death last for *centuries*.

One of the downsides of immortality was the body's ability to heal catastrophic injuries. Over and over again.

"Three of my people will travel with yours." I sent him a sharp smile. "I wouldn't want any of your people to betray me again."

"Impossible. If demons appear in that part of my realm, my people will fight. The bubaks will flee, and we will be forced to chase them deep into the territory that has been solely theirs for centuries. That will delay my people further."

The rage that ate at me was useless. The frustration that clawed through my gut entirely unhelpful. In this, at least, Taraghlan was outmaneuvering me. That made him an enemy. And I wouldn't forget it.

"Your people will leave today."

"As I have already ordered." The hint of a sneer crossed his face, and I tamped down on my power as it attempted to escape my control. I needed him alive. For now.

"Why haven't you taken the artifact with the pocket realm before now?"

"I have no use for it. And I chose not to create a rift between myself and subjects I have a treaty with.

We have given much to convince the bubaks to keep to their territory. Some of them have been alive for as long as the demigods."

"Bring the artifact to me within eight days in this realm, or I begin slaughtering the people you value most."

It took everything in me to keep my face neutral as Taraghlan nodded. His shoulders were tight as he stalked toward the elevator. Lia gave him a casual hiss and jumped down, wandering out of the room as I strode to my balcony.

Tendrils of dread wound their way through my body. *"Little witch?"* I reached for her once more, even though I knew it was useless. For now.

But I would never stop trying.

The silence hung between us, and I could feel the cavernous hole where she should be. Our bond was still there, but it was… frayed.

I jumped off my balcony and extended my wings, landing on the 45th floor, which was now entirely devoted to our planning. The balcony door was open, and I stepped through, conscious of Ag shadowing my every move. He was the one who was most likely to be able to contain some of my power if I lost control.

The long table in the meeting room sat thirty people, and more were gathered, leaning against the walls. My demons had broken into groups and were currently speaking in low voices. They noticed my presence and those voices turned silent.

Evie stood, her face ashen, dark circles beneath her eyes. Soon, we would have an ugly little scene as

I made her rest. Not something I had planned with my witchling's sister, but Danica would be displeased when she returned if Evie had run herself into the ground.

I leveled a stare at the werewolf leaning against the wall behind her. Nathaniel stared back, unrepentant. One would think he would have ordered Evie to go to bed by now.

The Alpha obviously followed my thoughts, because his lips peeled back from teeth as he snarled at me. Those teeth were looking longer than usual.

The first sign of true aggression I'd seen from him. Interesting. Perhaps having one of his wolves taken was making it difficult for him to keep hold of his own control. I automatically glanced around the room to see if Danica had noticed, and my entire body turned cold as her absence gnawed on me with sharp teeth.

My brain knew she was gone, but my body kept forgetting, kept searching for her.

"What did Taraghlan say?" Evie asked. The rest of the room seemed to hold its collective breath.

"We will have the pocket realm within eight days, or I will begin killing his people."

"Eight days?" Her voice cracked and Nathaniel's hands fisted. Next to her, Vas stood as well, slinging an arm around her shoulders.

"Sixteen for Danica," I bit out.

Evie looked as if she wanted to go hunt for the pocket realm herself. I gave her a warning look, and her eyes darted away. I made a mental note to put an extra guard on her. Danica's sister was sneaky.

Vas forced a grin. "If anyone can last that long in

the underworld, it's Danica. By the time she's done, Lucifer will be begging to return her."

A few faint smiles broke out. Evie merely watched me.

"Time moves differently in that part of the seelie realm," I bit out. It was unlike me to explain myself to anyone who wasn't Danica, but when my little witch returned, she would be upset if I had completely alienated her sister. "It will take us that long to form our army and strategize our attack." I surveyed the room. "Thoughts."

Lilith slowly unraveled her body, lazily getting to her feet. "We have options for smuggling the pocket realm as close to Lucifer's palace as possible. The issue is going to be communicating with our spies. All portals have been locked down and are being heavily guarded. And Lucifer has new spells in place—likely placed by the traitor witch."

Gloria.

"I believe I can help with that." A thin, reedy voice called out. Demons parted to reveal the black witch Danica liked. Hannah.

"Speak."

She smiled at me as if I amused her.

Do not kill her. For whatever reason, Danica likes this witch.

I ground my teeth. Her smile widened.

"My power grows with negative emotions," she said, sitting back in her chair as if she was at a fucking luncheon. "That means that simply being in this room for the past four hours has given me everything I need to perform a simple communication spell between realms."

Four hours. Was that how long it had been? Something that felt a lot like panic twisted in my stomach and I shoved it down.

"A few more hours in your presence, and I will reach my full capabilities," she said.

Because my misery, rage, and grief were feeding her, and she would grow powerful on them the same way a leech grew fat on blood. Good. I needed all my people at their best. And like it or not, the black witch was now one of my people.

"Make it happen."

CHAPTER TWO

Danica

I woke, frowning into the dim light. My dreams had been full of people I didn't know. At one point, I'd jolted awake, sure I could hear a male voice calling my name. When I sat up, my face had been wet, and I'd stumbled out of bed, wandering through my rooms in a bid to see if anyone was there.

When I'd opened the main door to my rooms, a guard had been walking down the hall.

"Can I help you with something?" he'd asked.

"No," I'd murmured. "I just thought I heard a noise."

His eyes were intent as he studied my face. Finally, he'd smiled, but it hadn't come close to reaching his eyes. "Best get back to bed, princess."

I'd frowned, but he'd already reached out and closed the door between us. For the life of me, I couldn't seem to remember his name.

A knock sounded on my bedroom door, jolting me from my thoughts.

"Come in." My voice was hoarse, and the maid bustled into the room, heading straight to the thick black curtains, which she pulled open.

"Good morning." She beamed at me, and I attempted a smile. Her dark eyes were intent as she studied my face. "Would you like to take your breakfast in your rooms? On the balcony, perhaps?"

"The balcony would be great, thanks."

I swung my legs out of bed and my long black nightgown tangled around my calves. Distaste suddenly roared through me, and I frowned.

"Your royal highness?"

I jolted. The maid was holding out a thick, matching black robe.

"Thank you." I allowed her to help me into the robe and tied the cord myself, opening the door and striding out to the balcony so she wouldn't see my expression. Her wings rustled as I passed her, and I wracked my brain. The maid had attended to me for years, and yet I suddenly couldn't remember her name. What was wrong with me?

I took a seat at the table on my balcony and studied the kingdom below me. The sound of wings flapping above my head made me tense, and I glanced up. A lesser demon landed, perching on the turret above me. He bared his sharp teeth at me, and I turned away.

Someone knocked on the door to my rooms and I tuned into the voices.

"Breakfast will be on the balcony this morning," the maid murmured to whoever had brought the food.

"Of course, Yusilin."

Yusilin. That was her name. I sat back in my chair, relief making my muscles weak. I knew Yusilin. She woke me each morning, helped me dress, and occasionally gossiped with me about my grandfather's court. She also dried my tears when I wept in frustration each time my grandfather decreed I was to eat in my rooms while he was 'entertaining.'

I didn't know what it was he didn't want me to see on those nights, but banning my attendance was an insult to my rank.

The maid who'd brought breakfast smiled at me as a platter of food floated behind her. She made a quick gesture with her hand, and the plates slowly rose from the platter and glided through the air until they arranged themselves on the table in front of me.

"Thank you."

She studied me, much like Yusilin had. I attempted a smile. "Something on my face?"

Her cheeks heated, her wings rustling in obvious mortification. "No, your royal highness, please forgive me."

Was she… afraid of me? I couldn't remember a single time when I'd been cruel to her. Of course, I couldn't remember any interaction with her at all. Perhaps she was new.

"Nothing to forgive," I said.

She bowed her head and turned, walking back into my bedroom, where she whispered with Yusilin.

Loneliness crept up on me, sinking into my gut where it stayed. I picked at the fresh bread and cheese I preferred to start my day with, then switched to the tart pari berries, which I'd loved since I was a child.

Déjà vu again. I sighed.

"Your grandfather would like to see you when you're finished eating, your royal highness," Yusilin murmured behind me.

"Please, call me Danica."

Her silence spoke for itself, and I sighed, turning my head. Her eyes were wide with shock. "I understand it seems strange, but I would prefer it, at least while we're alone. Please."

All this time, and I'd never asked for something that would make me so much more comfortable? Yusilin finally nodded, a hint of a smile trembling around her mouth. "Okay. Danica."

A sharp, indrawn breath from the maid behind her. I smiled. "That goes for you, too."

From the way she rushed out the door, I had a feeling that wouldn't be happening. I pushed the food aside. "Well," I said as I got to my feet, "I suppose I should get ready to see my grandfather."

I dressed quickly, choosing a forest-green gown that matched my eyes. My grandfather liked me in green, saying it reminded him of my grandmother, who'd preferred the color. She'd died before I was born, and my parents—

"Ow!" My hand shot to my temple, where it felt like I'd suddenly been stabbed with a blade.

"Your royal high—Danica," Yusilin said when I opened one eye to look at her. "Are you okay?"

The pain was quickly fading, and I managed a nod. "Yes. I must just be tired. I didn't sleep well."

"I'm sorry to hear that. If you turn, I will tie your gown."

I complied, and her deft hands got to work. A face appeared in my mind. Delicate features, creamy brown skin, and bright blue eyes that had flashed with displeasure as she stared down at her own gown.

"Danica?"

"I'm sorry." I shook it off. "I… I'm not feeling like myself."

Yusilin attempted a smile, but her eyes were dark with worry. "You have been unwell."

"I have? Unwell how?"

"You… hit your head, and the healers had to work on you for a long time."

"How did I hit my head?" No matter how hard I tried, I couldn't remember the incident, although that probably wasn't uncommon with head injuries.

"You tripped and fell in the gardens. I believe this is why your grandfather wishes to see you this morning. So he can see for himself that you are feeling better."

I read between those lines. My grandfather may indulge me as his granddaughter, but he had no time or patience for anything he considered to be a weakness. If I couldn't prove to him that I had gotten past my injury, he would keep me from important meetings. The kind of important meetings that I needed to attend if I would one day rule with Pischiel.

Relief swept through me as I followed Yusilin to the vanity so she could do my hair. That was why I was having issues with my memory. A head injury. But I couldn't allow my grandfather to learn of those ongoing issues. I needed to convince him I was myself. Healthy, powerful, and once again ready to learn all he had to teach me.

I rolled my shoulders, ignoring the tiny voice that screamed at me.

This is wrong. Wrong. Wrong. Wrong.

"I wonder if Pischiel will attend court today," I said instead.

Yusilin beamed at the change of subject. "He never seems to miss an opportunity to woo you," she sighed. "It's so romantic."

Yes. *He* was romantic. So why was I being haunted by molten silver eyes?

I pushed the thought away, anger making my shoulders tight. I wouldn't allow a head injury to make my grandfather lose faith in me.

After all, all we had was each other.

Samael

I landed outside Finvarra's keep, conscious of the unseelie who were watching my every move. I could practically feel the enchanted crossbows trained on my back. If the unseelie king hadn't agreed to this meeting, I had no doubt that I would have been shot with poisonous arrows as soon as I'd gotten within five hundred feet of the keep.

It wouldn't have stopped me, but it would have hurt.

Ignoring the guards, I strode up the steps of his keep as if I owned it.

One of them made the mistake of stepping in front of me, his eyes hard.

My hand clamped around his throat, and I squeezed, enjoying the way his face changed color. Another guard leapt toward me, his sword swinging, and I glanced at him, my power sending him flying into the wall.

Cold burrowed into my stomach, arching out toward my limbs until I was encased in it. The violence felt good. I had been forced to suppress all my instincts to kill. Now, I could take the edge off, release some of the tension—

"He will see you," another guard announced.

I glanced at him. His expression was carefully neutral, but his gaze darted between my face and the hand I had wrapped around the other guard's throat.

I sighed and released my hand, ignoring the guard as he dropped to his knees. Several of Finvarra's men jumped forward, one of them calling for a healer as I strolled up the stairs.

I'd always approved of Finvarra's home. It was easily defensible, with one entire side built *into* the mountain, ensuring enemies had few opportunities to get close.

The same guard who'd told me Finvarra would see me gave me a distrustful look. But he waved his hand, and both of the huge black doors creaked open, revealing the entranceway. "His Majesty is in his office," he said stiffly. "I will take you to him."

Agaliarept had been… displeased at the thought of

me coming alone, but the unseelie king and I currently needed each other.

Finvarra hated the seelie king almost as much as I hated Lucifer. The enemy of my enemy may not be my friend, but he would do as an ally. For now.

The guard knocked on the door and it opened. Finvarra stood from behind his desk, nodded at his guard, and then glanced back at the door, which closed behind me as I stalked inside.

If I wasn't going out of my mind with rage and grief, I might admire the unseelie king's taste. His office was spacious and comfortable, with large windows on one side and a well-stocked bar.

"You've been taking your problems out on my people," he said, his voice carefully neutral.

"They got in my way."

Silence. I sighed. "I won't touch them when I leave." It was all I had.

Finvarra shook his head as if fighting amusement. "Drink?" he offered.

I shook my head. "Barely clinging to control," I admitted. "I don't think alcohol will help."

He studied me, and something that looked a lot like pity flickered through his eyes. "You'll burn it off before you leave here."

I shrugged, and he glanced at the bar. A few moments later, two glasses of whiskey appeared on the desk in front of me.

I took one and gulped at it. Finvarra watched me out of eyes that had always reminded me of Scylla's.

"I'm sorry for your–"

"If you say *loss*, I will forget that we are allies. For now."

He smiled, sitting back in his seat, but his eyes were hard. "Fine. I assume you are here to talk strategy."

"Yes." Also, because Bael was using Hannah in an attempt to contact some of our spies in the underworld, along with those we were attempting to turn to our side. He'd made it clear that any demons who were on the fence were unlikely to cooperate if they saw my shaky grasp on control. Then he had not so subtly hinted it would be a good idea for me to leave for a while.

"My forces can be mobilized within six days, your time."

"I won't have the pocket realm for eight."

Surprised flashed across his face. "And how did you convince Taraghlan to give you one of *those?*"

"It was his advisor who betrayed him. Who delivered Danica to Lucifer."

"Ah. And you threatened to wage war until he fell in line."

"He will betray me. I can smell it on him. The only reason he would do such a thing is if he was hoping I wouldn't be around to kill him for it later. I have no doubt his plan is to ensure I'm dead so he can attack you without risking my demons allying with you," I told Finvarra, and his eyes burned at my words. "Unfortunately, I have to play his game for now. But the moment he double-crosses me, he is dead."

I sipped at my whiskey and placed it back on Finvarra's desk. It automatically refilled.

"You believe if you go into the underworld, there

will still be someone left to save?" He raised a hand. "Don't attempt to kill me. The question is relevant. You had no plans to war with Lucifer yet, and we both know that being ill prepared for him means you risk *all* of your people. How do you know Danica will still be alive?"

"The same way she knew she could save my life."

"You are fortunate to have a woman so devoted to keeping you alive," he said. While his expression remained carefully blank, I could hear the truth in his words.

"More fortunate than I could have ever imagined," I agreed. "And I know she can keep herself safe, at least in the short term." It was that faith in her that allowed me to cling to the little control I did have.

Finvarra raised his own glass to his lips. "Our combined forces may be able to decimate Lucifer's people, but how, exactly, do you expect to kill the underking?"

I got to my feet. "Leave that to me. Just ensure your people are ready."

Danica

My grandfather's office was intimidating. His desk was a huge slab of black marble, mined from the quarries of Tartarus. Hades had an arrangement with my grandfather, and it was said that the evil souls who mined the marble empowered it with their blood, tears, and regrets.

I raised my hand to my head, suddenly dizzy. I knew *that*, but I didn't know the name of the woman who brought me breakfast each day?

I dropped my hand as grandfather glanced up. "Danica," he murmured. "Take a seat."

I sat, watching as he signed the paper in front of him before setting it aside. His eyes—the same color as mine—were intent as he scanned my face.

"How are you feeling?"

"Fine."

Silence.

I sighed as he waited me out. Another thing I should've remembered? Grandfather had spies everywhere.

"I've had a few… challenges," I admitted. "But I'm already feeling better. I should be back to my normal self soon."

Was I imagining the flicker of amusement in his eyes?

I really was going crazy.

"Good. I wanted to speak to you about a potential opportunity. I know you've been eager to prove yourself."

I flushed, and he laughed. "Ambition isn't a bad thing, granddaughter. Although why you feel the need to compete with Pischiel instead of uniting with him is beyond me." He grinned. "If you were to mate with him, both my granddaughter and my son would one day rule."

His gaze dropped to the birthmark on my wrist, his

expression hardening. I resisted the urge to cover up the gold mark. I'd had it for as long as I could remember, and it was the reason why I usually tried to wear long-sleeved dresses in his presence.

My grandfather was a kind, level-headed man, but for some reason, catching sight of the birthmark sometimes made him grow enraged.

"Remove it," Lucifer roared, spittle flying from his mouth.

"I'm trying," the witch snapped, but even I could hear the fear in her voice. "There's no way to remove it, Your Majesty. You'll have to–"

"Danica?"

I smiled, shaking myself from the strange nightmare I'd had last night.

"I told you I'd give him a chance, and I meant it. I'm even planning to take a walk with him this morning."

He smiled back. "Good. Now, about this opportunity. I need to send an ambassador to Heretix soon. Nacheran is pushing his limits, and he needs to be reminded that he rules only because I allow him to. You will be your usual sweet self, while also reminding him of what will happen if he displeases his monarch."

"Of course." Heretix was one of the largest territories in our kingdom. There were rumors that our enemies were courting Nacheran, attempting to sway him and his forces to their sides.

"When will I go?"

"When I determine that you have recovered from your little injury. You must be at your best in order to sway him. If I have to visit, the loss of life will be enormous."

I swallowed. No pressure. "Okay. I'm almost recovered," I lied. "I'll be ready."

"Good."

I got to my feet and rounded the huge desk, pressing a kiss against his cheek. "You can trust me, grandfather."

"I know. Now go take your walk with Pischiel."

I rolled my eyes at him, ignoring his low chuckle. But my mind was racing as I left his office.

Grandfather would never allow me to take the trip if he knew I could barely find my way around our home. If he knew I was having trouble remembering names and faces. If he found out about the déjà vu.

I'd wanted to make him proud since I was a child. So why wasn't my brain healing from my injury? His healers were the best in the underworld. If I was going to convince him I was healthy enough to be his ambassador, I would have to compensate for my own deficits. And that meant relearning everything I'd forgotten.

Starting with our home.

Pischiel was waiting for me outside grandfather's office. "To the gardens?"

"Actually, I thought we might walk inside today."

He frowned. "Inside?"

"Yes. I love this palace, don't you?"

"Of course, but–"

"And the weather seems like it might turn."

We both glanced out the nearest window to the perfection of the blue sky.

"Besides," I attempted a smile. "We can talk more *intimately* inside."

His gaze met mine, and he smiled back. "In that case, where should we begin?"

We began in grandfather's throne room, where I'd spent my early years playing with some of the lesser demons who were perched on the exposed beams far above us.

From there, I insisted on the kitchens, and Pischiel laughed at me as all work stopped the moment I entered. Servants bowed, while lesser demons seemed to quake with fear. I swallowed and backed out, a frown on my face.

"What's wrong?" Pischiel was watching me closely.

"Nothing." We walked down the stairs that led to the servants' quarters. The light was dimmer down here, and it was quiet—the servants all working. Torches of demon fire flickered every five paces or so, and our footsteps echoed on the stone.

Pischiel wrinkled his nose. "Really, Danica, why would you want to spend time down *here*?"

I shrugged. "You're right. Let's go to the gardens."

"Much better." His hand covered mine, where it was still clasping his elbow, and he turned me, leading me out a side entrance of the palace. We turned left, walking along the east wall.

I didn't know what I was looking for, but I wasn't going to find it—

That door.

Heavy, thick metal. And a large X stamped across

it, running diagonally from each corner. I *knew* this door.

Pischiel noticed my attention, and he laughed. "Let me guess, you want to drag me through the dungeon next."

The dungeon. Of course.

Strong arms carried me toward a metal door. I fought with everything in me, but the demon holding me merely ignored my struggles as Lucifer took a knife from the sheath on his side and sliced his palm.

He pressed it against the door, and it swung open. With a victorious smile, Lucifer gestured for the demon carrying me to follow him.

I swayed on my feet, swallowing around the sudden tightening of my throat. Pischiel seemed to be waiting for my reply. What had he said?

"Very funny," I croaked out. Pischiel merely grinned, steering me away from the door. His dark eyes danced as if he found me oh-so-amusing, and I had the sudden urge to punch him.

What was going on with me? I'd never hit anyone in my life.

"You look upset."

"Not upset," I attempted a smile. "Just a little tired."

"Walk with me for just a few minutes and I'll escort you back to your rooms." He studied my face, pausing as we approached the main gardens. "I want you to be happy, Danica."

I raised my eyebrows. "I am happy." It was difficult to meet his shrewd gaze. Did he know my mind was failing?

"I can protect you if you let me."

I blushed, and he angled his head as if he found me *charming.*

Wrong. This is wrong.

I pushed the voice away. Just because I was having a few issues with my memory didn't mean I had to ruin my relationships.

My chest tightened as I glanced back over my shoulder. The door waited for me.

I couldn't explain it–would sound insane if I tried–but seeing that door made dread walk icy fingers down my spine. Was this another example of my mind being impacted by my injury? If so, I needed to conquer it so I could serve as grandfather's ambassador.

I suddenly had an inescapable feeling of… *loss.* It tore through me, incinerating my lungs until I couldn't breathe. It took everything in me to smile up at Pischiel.

I had to get through that door.

CHAPTER THREE

Danica

I knew I was dreaming. That was my first clue that something was wrong.

The second? The dream had a strange, realistic edge to it. Even surrounded in white mist, I was too aware, too *engaged,* for this to be just a normal dream.

"Little witch."

I jumped about a mile in the air as a demon appeared out of the mists. He was tall—so tall he towered over me. And he was built like he could throw several of my grandfather's guards across the room—at the same time. His wings gleamed, and something about them made my hands itch.

But it was his silver eyes that stood out—even in a face that seemed as if it had been carved by the gods themselves. They almost *glowed*, and they looked at me with what appeared to be pure, unfiltered love.

I almost tripped over my heavy skirts as I backed away from him. Grandfather had warned me about people who dream walked. If you engaged with them, they could take your soul.

His expression tightened. "Danica?"

"How do you know my name?" A stupid question. Most demons knew of the underprincess.

Shock warred with grief and his hands fisted, as if he was barely holding himself back from reaching for me. He froze. And then an expression of such devastation twisted his features that my chest ached. He looked as if I were breaking his heart.

No, this is one of their tricks.

I'd also been warned about our enemies–and the lies they would tell in a bid to take my grandfather's throne.

The throne that could one day be mine. As long as I could prove I was worthy of it.

"Release me from this dream!"

The blood slowly drained from his face. It hurt me, for reasons I couldn't describe, to see this demon look… shell-shocked. But his jaw clenched, those lush lips firmed, and his brows lowered.

"What did they do to you?"

"I'm unsure what you're referring to." When in doubt, it was always a good idea to use my haughtiest court voice.

"Little witch–" He took a step toward me, and I backed up again. He froze. "You don't need to be frightened of me. I'd never hurt you."

"I'm not frightened. And I'm not a witch. I don't know who you think I am–"

"I think you're my bondmate. And somehow they got to you." His laugh was hollow. "Everything Lucifer has done and somehow, I never expected *this*."

I frowned at him. "I'm no one's bondmate." Except

maybe Pischiel's one day.

He took a deep breath and nodded toward my wrist. "That mark says differently."

"My birthmark?"

He held up his own arm, pulling back the sleeve of the strange white shirt he wore. "It's not a birthmark, Danica. This is the symbol of our love. You burned this mark into my skin when you saved my life."

My lips had gone numb. Grandfather had said these people would try to trick me, but I'd never expected anything like this. Replicating my birthmark, of all things. Few people knew of the mark on my wrist since grandfather had advised me to keep it hidden. Obviously, there were spies closer to us than we could have ever expected.

"Visit my dreams again, and I'll have my grandfather's witch cast you out."

He gaped at me. And then he laughed. "Gloria? If you can overcome your instinctive desire to kill her, I'll be impressed."

How did he know about that? I'd told no one how much I hated the witch. "Stay away from me."

"Never. You're *mine*, Danica. *Remember.*"

I turned and ran until the mist disappeared, and I woke, panting in my bed.

It was dark, the maids in their own quarters. I could pull a rope and have them bring me a nightcap, but I shook the thought off. I was the princess of the underworld. And I was going to visit my grandfather's dungeon.

Samael

I roared as I leapt from the bed. Demon fire poured from me, and Bael threw open the door, his ward protecting him from the flames that licked up the walls.

"Samael!" he screamed. "Pull it back."

I… couldn't.

The flames licked the ceiling now. If I couldn't gain control, my power would destroy this tower. And then it would move on to the city Danica called home.

"What happened?" Bael roared at me.

"He's taken her memories. She… *feared* me."

Evie appeared in the doorway, automatically enveloped in Bael's ward.

"He *what?*"

The sight of Evie… helped. It hurt, pulling back the power that wanted to tear every world apart until my little witch was in my arms. But I wouldn't harm Danica's sister.

The power slowly trickled back into me. The walls were destroyed. So was most of the furniture, although it was likely I had subconsciously placed a ward around the bed, as it was untouched, Danica's sleep shirt still on top of her pillow.

I turned away from the bed, and blocked out the wreckage of the rest of the room. Bael and Evie both parted as I stalked through the doorway and toward the bar.

"Tell us," Evie demanded.

My hand shook as I poured a scotch. "Lucifer stole her memories. But it wasn't a simple forgetting spell, because he's replaced those memories with others. He must have worked with the black witch. It would have required unimaginable power—likely borrowed from the underworld itself. She… she was wearing a dress. She didn't even know she was a witch. Didn't recognize me. Threatened to work with Gloria to have me blocked from her dreams."

"How? How did Lucifer do it?"

"He would have used Gloria, his power, and water from the Lethe."

Evie's face was ashen when I turned.

"The Lethe?" she asked.

"The River of Forgetfulness."

Bael frowned. "I thought Hades refused to get involved."

"He did," I growled. "If he provided the water, he *owes* me. Even if one of his subjects disobeyed him, he'll still be in my debt. Send a message to him tomorrow."

"What kind of message?"

"I want Cerberus."

The expression on Bael's face was a cross between a wince and a laugh. "Hades loves that beast. He'll never give him to you."

"Temporarily. Cerberus fights with us against Lucifer, or I make Hades pay when I take back my throne. Make it clear that water from his fucking river was used on *my* bondmate."

Just the thought made me want to rage through the underworld.

Evie had been quiet, but she slowly raised her head, tears in her eyes.

"If Danica doesn't know who you are, Kyla could have been slaughtered, and Danica would have no idea."

I nodded. "She thinks my mark is a birthmark. Couldn't recognize me. *Me.* "

We will have words about that, little witch.

"Could *I* dreamwalk to her?"

I shook my head. "This is a skill between mates. Others can dreamwalk, but it requires a specific set of powers."

Evie nodded, then sat on the sofa, her head in her hands. "It was bad enough knowing she was there, likely terrified, in danger. But knowing he's wiped her memories?" she lifted her head. "She won't even know to fight. To look for escape. We have to fix this, Samael."

Bael poured himself a drink. "It's temporary," he said.

I glanced at him, and he raised his glass to his mouth. "You really think Lucifer can keep *Danica* living in a dreamworld, unaware that she's a witch? The amount of power he must be using to keep her complacent is stunning. The question is, why?"

Cold unfurled in my stomach, slowly making its way to my limbs. "My spies have said they're unsure why he's keeping her alive. He's instructed his people not to kill her, although she's being watched carefully. He needs her for something. And if she doesn't get her memories back, she'll be at his mercy."

Danica

I dressed silently, took a deep breath, and pushed open the door to my rooms. This wing was quiet, everyone already asleep. I slipped out of my room and down the hall.

There were guards on the floor below me, and I passed them silently as I headed toward the throne room. They ignored me for the most part, although I had no doubt that news of my escapades would reach grandfather's ears.

The dream had left me shaken. I couldn't understand the tactics our enemies were taking, or why. Entering someone's dreams was a specific skill set. My grandfather used his dreamwalkers to spy on his enemies. The silver-eyed demon could have harmed me if he'd wanted to. And yet he hadn't.

I needed to figure out his angle. What was the strange demon hoping to achieve by sowing confusion and doubt in my mind? I shook the thought off. Either way, he'd been unsuccessful.

So why is he still at the center of your every thought?

I scowled, unable to help myself as I stepped into the throne room. Like much of the palace, the walls were made of obsidian stone, while the black marble of the floor gleamed like glass. My grandfather's throne was covered in black jewels, which seemed to suck up all the light in the room before reflecting it back until it almost hurt to look at it.

Above the throne, gold letters were carved into the black wall, stark against the obsidian.

As I watched, the gold shifted until the words

do ut des appeared. Something itched at my brain, but the words immediately shifted to demonish as a guard stepped into the throne room from a door on the opposite side. I nodded to him and backed out, traipsing toward the servant's quarters.

It was quiet here, too, most people in bed. The occasional lesser demon snarled at me, and I barely resisted the urge to bare my teeth back. A princess did not glower at her subjects.

I took the side exit and headed east along the palace wall. The door with the X waited, and I attempted nonchalance as I glanced around me. I may not be able to see anyone watching me, but I'd be naïve to assume grandfather wasn't having his guards keep an eye on me.

My hand automatically reached down to my side as if I was carrying a dagger. I frowned. Then I leaned close to the sharp obsidian rock of the wall and ran my hand down the stone.

Blood welled, and before I could talk myself out of it, I pressed my hand against the door. Grandfather's blood flowed in my veins. But whether or not the door would allow me entrance…

It swung open, and I took a deep breath, stepping inside as the door closed behind me.

The stairway was so dim, it was difficult to see. There was one torch at the bottom of the stairs, and I picked up the hem of my robe, keeping my gaze on my feet. If I fell down these stairs, I'd never hear the end of it.

Blowing out a breath, I raised my head as I reached the bottom of the stairs. Cells stretched out before me, with a walkway on both my left and right sides, leading to yet more cells. From the moans, mutters, and screams I could hear in the distance, the dungeon must stretch the entire footprint of the palace.

Déjà vu hit me once more. Along with a deep-seated feeling of terror. I rolled my shoulders and stepped forward.

"Mercy," a creature hissed as I walked past his cage. He had the eyes of a snake, his body covered in dark green scales. He leapt against his bars, and I jumped.

Another prisoner gave a low laugh from across the corridor. I ignored him, even as I picked up my pace.

I walked for what seemed like hours, growing increasingly despondent. Whatever I was hoping to find, it wasn't here.

I needed to tell my grandfather about my… issues. If he sent me to Heretix and I failed him, his faith in me could be dealt a fatal blow.

"Danica?"

I turned. No other prisoner had dared speak my name. This man was… human?

"Oh God, you've come. Kyla's a few cells down. Do you have the keys?"

I frowned at him. Then I turned to keep walking. He slammed his hand against the cell, and I glanced back at him, my gaze finding the thick metal ring around his wrist.

"It keeps us from our powers," the man said. "You're our only hope. There are others down here. Other mages. If you can get us free—"

"Why would I free my grandfather's prisoners?"

And why did this man speak to me with such

familiarity?

He gaped at me. "Are you... kidding?"

This wasn't helping. I'd come down here to *fix* whatever was wrong with my brain.

"Danica, it's me. Keigan."

"I don't know anyone by that name. If you think to confuse me into letting you free, you should know there are guards on every exit," I lied. "Besides, I don't have the keys."

His mouth fell open further. Then he cast me a look of such disappointment, my stomach churned. "Is this your tactic? Play nice with the underking and perhaps he will let you live?"

It was my turn to gape at him. "Let me live? My grandfather *loves* me."

He rested his head against the bars. "So that's how he did it. He took your memories. He took *you*."

I shook my head and kept walking, ignoring him as he called my name. But disquiet filled me. Whatever game the stranger with the silver eyes was playing, he'd somehow managed to find others willing to play it with him.

Something slammed against the bars on my left and I jumped. A wolf, so white it almost glowed. The wolf also wore a metal ring, although unlike the human, it encircled its neck. I had a moment of sorrow for the creature, but pushed it away. If it was in my grandfather's prison, it had likely attempted to harm us in some way.

The wolf slammed against the bars again, baring sharp teeth. I jolted back at its fury, and it let out a low growl. In spite of myself, I froze, staring.

Something about the wolf made me want to claw at my chest. She—and I wasn't sure how, but I *knew* the wolf was female—stared back at me. She chuffed, clearly displeased with whatever she saw, and I swallowed around the lump in my throat.

This wild creature had judged me and found me wanting.

Her gaze stayed on my face as she slowly lowered her head. At first I thought she was bowing, but a clinking sounded as she nudged something with her nose.

I peered down at it. "A ring?" My voice echoed, and the man—Keigan—let out an elated laugh.

"She has the ring. Tricky wolf. Take it, Danica."

It looked old, valuable. The wolf stared at me, waiting for me to pick it up, and I shook my head. "I can't take bribes."

A low rumble sounded, so quiet that at first I didn't realize what it was. She was growling again. Her lips pulled back from her teeth in obvious warning.

I shouldn't take it. My grandfather would be disappointed. He'd likely send guards any moment to escort me back to bed. But perhaps this was why my instincts had been urging me to come down here.

Keigan's voice sounded over the moans of whatever creature was in the cell next to the wolf. "Take the ring, Danica. Put it in your mouth."

I certainly would not. There was crazy, and then there was *crazy.* But the wolf was watching me expectantly, and I was obviously at least a little crazy, because I crouched and picked the ring up, sliding it into my pocket.

The wolf angled her head, as if she'd also been

expecting me to put it in my mouth. But I'd been raised better than that. If the ring was spelled, it could easily kill me, and I'd have no one to blame but myself.

She growled warningly at me again and I rolled my eyes.

"Danica."

I turned. Pischiel stood at the end of the cell. Prisoners began screaming, hurling abuse in a variety of languages, slamming body parts into their cages. He ignored them all, his gaze on me as he strolled toward me. His expression was carefully neutral, but his eyes... his eyes told me he was furious.

"What are you doing here?"

"I just... I couldn't sleep–"

"So you thought you'd wander through the dungeon? This is not a good way to ensure you stay alive, Danica."

I frowned at him. "The prisoners are all caged."

He clamped his mouth shut, taking my arm. I pulled back, gesturing toward the wolf, who was snarling at Pischiel. She slammed her body into the cage once more, and I jolted.

"Why does grandfather have a wolf down here?"

He studied my face. "That's a werewolf."

I frowned. Then I turned my attention back to the wolf. Of course. It made sense now. She was much larger than any of the wolves I'd seen in the wild.

"I assumed werewolves were a myth."

He smiled at me, his fury forgotten. "No. But they're incredibly dangerous. Especially to you. Now, let me escort you back to your rooms. And if I were you, I would consider thinking of a good excuse for your grandfather when he asks you about this in the morning."

The human in the cell was silent as we passed, but I couldn't help but glance over my shoulder at him. He watched me out of dark brown eyes, his expression carefully neutral.

There were several other doors close to the stairs. "Where does that door lead?" I pointed at one that seemed to be built *into* the staircase, which meant another set of stairs had to be hidden beneath it.

"Storage," Pischiel said, and I snorted.

"Just tell me I'm not allowed to know," I said. "Don't lie to me."

He gave me an assessing look and then shrugged, guiding me toward the stairs once more. A roar sounded from behind one of the other doors, and I froze.

"At least tell me what's behind that door." My voice trembled slightly, and Pischiel took pity on me.

"Lucifer's hellhounds. Don't worry, princess, they're kept locked away until he needs to use them."

Hellhounds. For the life of me, I had no idea what they looked like, although I must have seen them at some point. My mind provided an image of a slobbering beast with leathery skin and huge teeth.

I pushed the image away and allowed Pischiel to escort me back to my rooms. At the door, he held onto my arm for a moment longer.

"You know, I could put in a good word for you with your grandfather," he said.

I raised my eyebrow. "And why wouldn't you? We are, after all, friends."

"Friends? You know I want more than that, Danica."

I studied his face. So familiar, and yet occasionally, it felt like I was staring at a stranger.

A stranger who didn't really want me, but was pretending to for some reason. I knew what a man looked like when he was longing for the woman in front of him. I'd seen that expression in my dream, when silver eyes had burned into me.

"And what would convince you to talk to my grandfather?"

"A kiss. Kiss me, princess, and I'll tell your grandfather you were sleepwalking. Or perhaps *I* was the one to rouse your curiosity about the dungeon, and you took our conversation as a dare."

I angled my head. Pischiel was a powerful ally to have on my side.

"Just a kiss?"

Something like surprise flittered across his face. He'd expected me to say no. He nodded, his hand rising to cup my cheek. I had a sudden flash of silver eyes holding my chin captive as the demon glowered down at me, and I pushed it away.

"I'm… inexperienced," I murmured, a blush rising to my cheeks.

Pischiel grinned. "I believe you know more about kissing than you think you do." With that, he lowered his head. But he waited for me to take the next step. I rose to my tiptoes and placed one hand against his chest to help me balance. Then I pressed my lips against his.

Wrong. This is wrong.

Several things happened at once. My earrings began to burn my earlobes. My birthmark tingled, and something like sorrow welled in my chest.

Instinctively, I knew I couldn't let Pischiel see any of it. I deepened our kiss, attempting to ignore the lump in my throat. If not for my body's reaction, for the earrings—which I would definitely be removing from my ears—and the birthmark which had never tingled as far as I could remember, I would have enjoyed our kiss.

Pischiel's lips were firm, his hand warm on my cheek.

Knowledge shot through me. There in my mind and then gone in a flash. I leaned back and punched Pischiel in the mouth.

He gaped at me, leaning over and cursing. I stumbled into the wall. But my body wanted to leap at him, wanted to smash my fist into his face once more.

What was wrong with me?

Pischiel slowly raised his head, wiping at his split lip. "I'd thought I could play along, could work with my king on this, but even now, you think of another. Don't you?"

"I don't know what you're talking about."

He gave me a knowing look and wiped at his mouth some more. "Get to bed, princess. Something tells me your grandfather won't believe me when I tell him you were sleepwalking."

CHAPTER FOUR

Danica

Grandfather invited me to his office the next morning. I wasn't stupid enough to believe the invitation was because he wanted to chat about my love life—although he did *so* enjoy attempting to convince me to give Pischiel a chance. No, he'd been informed about my nighttime wandering.

Nerves twisted my stomach as Yusilin helped me dress in a soft gray gown.

"This looks lovely on you," she murmured.

I glanced down without much interest. The bodice gleamed with gray jewels, which matched the material, ensuring the dress was understated until the light caught it in the right place.

I cleared my throat. "Thank you." I wasn't sure why I was so nervous. If grandfather decided not to send me as his ambassador, I would be disappointed, but I would have other chances to prove myself.

"Is this your tactic? Play nice with the underking and perhaps he will let you live?" The man who'd said his name was Keigan had seemed

shocked that I didn't recognize him. He'd said grandfather had *taken* my memories. But that made no sense. I knew, down to my bones, that if I told grandfather I was having issues with my memories, he would be disappointed. He'd likely send me back to his healers.

Perhaps that's what I needed to do. Maybe the healers could help me.

"Danica?"

I turned. It had taken Yusilin a few days to get used to calling me Danica, but now it felt almost like we were... friends.

"I'm sorry, what did you say?"

"I said you are ready."

"Thank you."

My slippers slapped against the stone as I walked toward grandfather's office. My heart pounded in my chest until it felt almost like I couldn't breathe. By the time I was walking down the corridor, small black dots had filled the edges of my vision, and I was gasping. I ducked into the closest room and closed the door. Distantly, I noticed it was a sitting room, but I was already bending over in an attempt to catch my breath.

Had Yusilin tied my dress too tight?

No. This was... fear.

And it shamed me.

My grandfather had never hurt me. I had to be honest with him. I would need to tell him what was happening. There was a chance one of his enemies had managed to bespell me, and that was why I was having these issues.

I stumbled to the window and stared down at the gardens below me. A demon I'd only recently met glanced up at me. Garadiel. His expression was thoughtful as he placed his hands on his hips, legs spread. He looked at me as if he was weighing my worth. Obviously, he didn't like what he saw, because he shook his head and turned, striding away.

My breath slowed as I watched more of the demons coming and going. Daimonion stalked across the grounds, toward the palace entrance, and fury plunged into my chest, twisting as if it could rip something free. A group of his men walked with the assassin—demons who were sent to do less important or risky tasks for my grandfather.

Namiros was one of the worst. Each time he saw me, he gave me a sharp little smile that made something cold coil in my stomach. But Odax and Paymon were almost as bad, constantly feuding with each other to impress both Daimonion and my grandfather. Odax liked to terrify the maids, while Paymon enjoyed sharpening his knives and leering at anyone who'd recently annoyed him.

Namiros glanced up at the window, his dead gaze unerringly finding my own. His smile made me shiver, and I turned away from the window.

I knew we needed the assassins to keep us safe from our enemies, but I loathed all of them.

At least I was calmer now. Time to face my grandfather.

As usual, he sat behind his desk. Tension was carved into the faint lines beside his eyes, and he raised his head, gesturing for me to sit.

I sat. He made me wait for what had to be at least ten or twenty minutes while he finished up his paperwork.

I studied his face. It wasn't like my grandfather to

make his point with these kinds of power moves. Or was it? I reached up and rubbed at my temple. Grandfather sat back in his chair and watched me.

"Is there something wrong with your head?"

"No. Listen, grandfather–"

"No, *you* listen."

I flinched, and grandfather sighed, pinching the bridge of his nose. "I apologize for my tone."

"You seem… stressed."

"I am attempting to keep us from losing everything to our enemies. And you are not helping matters with late night excursions down to my dungeon. What, exactly, were you thinking?"

"I was thinking about the opportunity to be your ambassador, and I thought I should educate myself about what it actually means to rule. I realized I'd never been down to the dungeon before."

He didn't look convinced. "So you chose to go in the middle of the night, alone?"

"I uh, I couldn't sleep," I glanced down, my cheeks heating. "I met with Pischiel, and he escorted me back to my room."

"Yes. He mentioned."

I scowled, and grandfather's lips twitched. "I already knew of your trip to the bowels of this castle. Did you think my guards wouldn't notify me? They see and report *everything*."

That sounded a lot like a threat, and something twisted in my gut. Something that wanted me to throw back my head and *scream*.

"I'm sorry," I said. "I should have asked you to

escort me."

"Yes, you should have. Did you see what you needed to?"

His eyes were intent on my face, and I kept my tone light. "Honestly, I don't know what I was thinking going down there. It was cold, and damp, and miserable. From now on, I'll stick to the gardens."

"Good choice. You need to remember to keep yourself safe. Our enemies grow ever bolder. They would take this palace if they could. They would kill all of us. And it wouldn't be a quick death. No, they would make it last. That silver-eyed bastard would torture every one of us."

I felt the blood drain from my face. And grandfather tensed. He'd noticed.

"What is it, Danica?"

"Nothing."

"Do not," he said silkily, "lie to me."

I swallowed. "It's just… silver eyes."

He leaned forward, and I suddenly felt like prey. I shook it off. This was my *grandfather*, after all.

"I had a strange dream," I said lightly, getting to my feet. "That's all."

"Sit. Down."

I froze, but complied, shaken by his tone. We sat in silence for a few moments, and grandfather studied me as if looking for any hint of weakness.

"Grandfather–"

"I'm continually astounded by the lengths our enemies will go to in order to hurt us," he said softly.

"You're scaring me."

The bone bracelet encircling my wrist seemed to throb against my skin as a knock sounded on the door. Grandfather waved his hand, and the door opened.

"You called?" Gloria stepped into the room. Her eyes met mine, and my earrings burned my earlobes until it felt like they had been dunked in acid. I wanted to rip them from my ears, but grandfather was still watching me carefully.

"We have an issue," Grandfather said.

I imagined my hands around Gloria's throat. I would squeeze until she turned purple. Until the light faded from her eyes.

I glanced back at my grandfather, and he smiled at me, running one finger over the hilt of the jeweled letter opener on his desk. "Feeling... murderous, granddaughter?"

I swallowed. "I'm not sure what you mean."

He ignored that, turning to Gloria. "You gave me your word."

I enjoyed watching the blood drain from her face. I didn't know why, but it pleased me to see the terror on the witch's face.

"She must be stronger than anticipated."

"Bolster your spell, witch. Or die screaming."

I shot to my feet. "Grandfather–"

He ignored me. Gloria walked in my direction. She was just as frightened as I was. I could see it in her eyes. She reached into her bag and pulled out several stones, along with a blood-candle, which she lit. Then she pulled out a jar of some kind of liquid, which glowed like captured moonlight.

Her gaze fixated on the metal encircling my wrist.

I'd never seen it before. Had never noticed it before right this moment. It looked eerily similar to the bracelets grandfather's prisoners wore.

How come I'd never noticed it? Why was I wearing it?

Gloria gestured toward the bracelet, murmuring an incantation.

"What are you doing?" I demanded, but my voice was shaking.

Both of them ignored me. Grandfather studied me as if I was a bug.

And it hit me.

They'd taken my memories. My power. My *life*. And they were going to do it again.

My earrings burned. Gloria chanted. Grandfather watched me.

I snarled, swiped the letter opener off the desk, and lunged at Gloria.

Her eyes went wide, and Grandfather lifted his hand. Agony swept through my body and dropped me to my knees.

I screamed and screamed.

Samael

No matter how I tried, I couldn't reach Danica in her dreams. I attempted to create the connection again and again throughout the night, and then again during the day, since time passed twice as fast for her. But something blocked me. Had Lucifer hurt her? Was he hurting her even now? I could feel her, faintly at the end of our bond, so I knew she was alive. But I couldn't contact her.

I paced in the guest room I'd moved into. Danica would be... displeased to see what had become of our room. The ghost of a smile trembled around my mouth as I pictured her reaction. I was sure she would have much to say about the fact that my power had instinctively protected the bed. Her smart mouth had been just one of the things that had made me reluctantly fascinated with her when we first met.

Something latched onto my ankle.

I glanced down. Lia had been stalking me, hiding beneath the bed so she could lunge out at me. My mouth trembled. I leaned down to pet her, and she swiped out at my hand. Her claws were tucked away, and I allowed her to bat at my arm for a few minutes.

"Yes. I miss her too."

Someone cleared their throat. I turned to find Vas in the doorway.

"What is it?"

"The... gnome is here."

I frowned.

"Gary," Vas clarified.

I opened my mouth to tell him to leave. I wasn't interested in company. But Danica's face flashed across my mind. Her friend. The gnome was her friend.

I sighed. "Let him in."

I made my way to the living room and Vas returned a few minutes later with the gnome, who looked as exhausted as I felt. His gray skin was sallow, and his hair stood up as if he'd been continually running his hands through it.

He nodded at me. "I see you're coping about as well as Danica did when you were out of commission."

I shrugged, stalking toward the bar. "Drink?"

"Wouldn't mind a vodka."

I poured, marveling at the fact that I was serving a lesser fae. The man I'd been just months ago would have never believed I would have ties to so many creatures I'd previously ignored. All of those ties came from my little witch.

I handed him his drink and gestured to the sitting area. "The difference is that Danica was at least out *doing* something. I'm relegated to calling in old favors and new alliances."

"Difficult place to be. Is it true that you can't go to the underworld?"

"I'll lose all power the moment I step through a portal. That doesn't mean I can't go."

The gnome studied me over his drink. "You think she'll be pleased if she discovers you've thrown yourself away?"

"I'm hoping it won't come to that. But if Lucifer demands my life in exchange for her freedom, the deal is done."

"She'll never forgive you. Would she even survive your death?"

"It's difficult to know. Some bondmates pass immediately. Others… linger. Danica is a survivor."

"Let's keep that plan up our sleeve for now."

In spite of the subject, I smiled. "Why did you come

here?"

"Danica would want me to make sure you're not contemplating anything stupid. Since you already are, she'd want me to attempt to talk you out of it."

I raised one eyebrow, and he shrugged. "If it comes down to you or her, I choose her. No offense."

"None taken."

Gary sighed, leaning back with his drink. "I also came to tell you that there are more people willing to go to war than you might expect."

"What do you mean?"

"I'm more popular than you'd think, given how little interaction I have with most of my people. The gnomes of Durham will join you. The seelie king may be a piece of shit, but Aubrey has already indicated he's ready to war the moment you say the word, and he has many of his own people who are loyal to him."

It wasn't often that I was speechless.

Gary sent me a sympathetic look. "Danica is the kind of person who inspires loyalty." He got to his feet. "Thanks for the drink. I need to get back to the boys."

"You likely shouldn't join this battle. You have younglings to protect."

He grinned at me, his sharp teeth flashing in the light. "I've named you and Danica as godparents."

I stared at him, speechless. His grin widened. "Yeah. She had the same reaction. Guess you better keep me alive." He strolled out, as if he hadn't just blindsided me.

I was a *demon*. What would I do with gnome younglings?

I shook that off. The gnome was just like Danica—

finding amusement in my disconcertment. I didn't have time to imagine life as a foster parent to Cil and Zip.

But Gary would find it difficult to risk his life when he was surrounded by some of my best warriors. I made a mental note to order Ag to ensure the gnome was well-protected during this war.

A roar sounded, and I pinched the bridge of my nose. I shouldn't be able to hear *anything* up here, but the griffin didn't exactly conform to the laws of logic. The creature was *displeased* at having both Danica and Kyla gone.

The wolves hadn't left. It seemed as if Nathaniel had half of his pack here, all of them staying on the guest floors. Everywhere I looked, wolves lounged, ate everything they could get their hands on, and planned vengeance against the demon who had dared take one of their own.

Never could I have imagined playing host to the pack, although—after they'd hosted *my* people while I was slowly dying—it was more than fair. Another alliance Danica had created.

Lilith stepped into the room. "It's starting to smell like dog down there."

I sighed. "What is it, Lilith?"

"Firstly, Bael wants to keep the butler. He says he'll put up with the scent of dog if it means he can have more of his cookies."

I pinched the bridge of my nose. Tobias was *Nathaniel's* manservant. A submissive wolf with a core of steel when it came to ensuring his people got enough rest and sleep. However, he didn't discriminate with his fussing. After ensuring his people were settled, he'd turned his attention on my demons, declaring they needed just as much care as the wolves.

I sighed again, well aware that Bael wasn't joking. But I would worry about a potential war with the wolves over their butler later.

Lilith smiled at me, but the smile disappeared when she glanced down at the papers in her hand.

"We have a reply from Elathan."

I tensed. "And?"

"He declines to be involved in your war. But you can trust that he will treat any of your remaining people fairly once you fall to Lucifer, and Elathan takes your territory."

My skin tightened. "Elathan has always been a short-sighted, power-hungry sycophant."

"Our spies say he is shoring up his defenses across California in case we come calling. He knows very well that we could *make* his people join ours."

"It would spread our resources too thin. And compelling people to fight just means you risk being stabbed in the back. We will see what he has to say when I take back my throne."

While I'd hoped the demon would see reason and join us, I hadn't truly believed it would happen. Still, his people could have made a difference on the battlefield.

"Anything else?"

"Odax has been seen attempting to sneak into our territory. We've been watching him to see what he does. Our sentries are waiting for your orders."

"Kill him," I ordered. "And return his body to Lucifer's territory." I smiled. "Make it public."

Lilith nodded, and I leaned back in my chair as she

walked out.

Odax was responsible for thousands of deaths. And yet he'd become sloppy over the years—as proven by the fact that my people had seen him sneaking around in my territory. His death would be no true loss to Lucifer, but it would enrage him just the same.

My hands fisted at the thought of an enraged Lucifer near my little witch. But I could practically hear her voice in my ear, hear her urging me to trust her. If there was one thing I knew about my witchling, it was that she was stronger than anyone suspected.

Still, my heart ached, and for the first time, I wished I was a werewolf. Wished I could howl my loss and sorrow to the world.

CHAPTER FIVE

Danica

"Your royal highness?"

I jolted in my seat, meeting Yusilin's gaze in the mirror. "Please call me Danica."

She chewed on her lower lip, her eyes sliding away from mine. "Of course… Danica."

I frowned. "Is something wrong?"

Yusilin shook her head, but she still refused to meet my eyes. She turned to collect the jewels I would wear to the ball tonight, and I watched her.

Truthfully, I didn't want to go to the ball. My head ached, and I felt weak, exhausted. But grandfather had insisted, and the last thing I wanted to do was to let him down.

Yusilin brought a case to me, holding it open.

"They're beautiful."

The jewels were pure, unrelieved black, matching the gown I wore. But they sparkled so intently, I almost felt the need to shield my eyes.

Yusilin fastened the necklace around my throat, and the heavy gems fell almost to the low cut of my gown. She gestured for me to hold up my hand.

"You should probably remove that bracelet," she whispered. "You know how your grandfather hates it."

I studied the white bone. It wasn't pretty, would likely look ridiculous with my dress. But…

"No. I'm not removing it."

Yusilin tutted, but she didn't seem surprised. I watched her as I offered my other wrist, but she stiffened, shaking her head.

I glanced down at my bare arm, but she was already fastening the black jewels next to the bone bracelet.

"They look perfect," she said.

"Thank you for your help." I glanced back in the mirror. Yusilin had curled my hair, pulling half of it up off my face where it was held in place with a diadem. It glittered with the same black jewels, which she'd slipped into various places in my hair as well. She'd also darkened my eyes and swept color across my cheekbones. Other than a coat of gloss, she'd left my lips bare.

I turned to slip my feet into the matching heels Yusilin had insisted I wear, while she began to gather up the dress I'd changed out of, carrying it toward the basket of laundry which one of the other maids was waiting to collect.

"Straight down to the laundress," Yusilin told her. "She'll want to wear the midnight blue gown tomorrow."

The maid placed the basket on her hip, but one of my heavy dresses hung over the side, unbalancing it slightly. Something fell from the dress, clanking to the floor as I glowered down at my heels.

My gown was long enough that I'd be ditching those heels at the first opportunity.

"Your royal highness?" the maid had stepped up next to me, and she held out a gold ring. "This fell from one of your pockets."

Yusilin looked shocked. "I should have checked your pockets. I apologize."

Was she *trembling?* I'd never done anything to make her fear me... had I?

"No damage done," I told her with a smile, slipping the ring onto my finger to demonstrate that little fact. It didn't go with my black jewels at all, but Yusilin smiled.

"You're ready. Best not keep your grandfather waiting." She opened the door to reveal Pischiel, looking handsome in bronze formalwear. His eyes darkened as he ran his gaze over my body. "You look beautiful. As always."

I studied his face. "Is everything okay?"

He shrugged, but like Yusilin, he couldn't seem to meet my eyes. "Fine. Let's go before our entrance is later than fashionable."

I watched him some more as we walked down the stairs and toward the ballroom.

"You seem... guilty about something."

Pischiel went still. "What would I have to be guilty about?"

I sighed. "Nothing. Ignore me. Yusilin was acting a little strange..." We were approaching the ballroom, and I took a deep breath as the guards on the doors flung them open. Heads turned, and I fought to keep my voice neutral as Pischiel escorted me toward the dais where my grandfather sat on his throne. The back had been carved out, leaving room for his wings, and the entirety of the throne was dotted with the same black jewels that decorated my throat and wrist. The throne was a priceless artifact and incredible display of wealth.

Hera sat next to that throne on a smaller ornate chair. The concubine smiled slyly at me, and I forced myself to smile back.

"Danica," Lucifer smiled at me. "You look lovely."

You look like you should die screaming.

I pushed my intrusive thoughts away and smiled. "Thank you, grandfather."

He seemed to be in an excellent mood, beaming at me as the music started up again.

Something flashed as Hera tucked her hair behind one ear. My breaths came faster. My fingertips tingled. Pischiel turned toward me, and his face tightened.

I jumped at Hera. My foot caught in my dress and only strong arms around my waist stopped me from face planting. Grandfather laughed as the music stopped playing.

"My granddaughter is showcasing that fiery temper."

Pischiel slowly released me, and I stared at Hera, slowly sliding one finger along my throat. Pischiel grabbed my hand and pulled it away from my neck, squeezing until I growled at him.

"Please, princess. Allow me to have your first dance," he gritted out.

"We'll continue this later," I smiled at the concubine, and the blood slowly drained from her face. Grandfather watched me closely.

"Do not disrupt my evening," he warned me, waving a hand at Pischiel, who led me onto the dance floor.

"What. Was. That?"

I stayed silent. Truthfully, I didn't know. All I knew was that bracelet did not belong on Hera's scrawny wrist.

"I'm sorry. I don't know what came over me. Something weird is going on..." I glanced at grandfather, who was watching us intently. I took a deep breath. Time for a change of subject.

"He wants us to date," I murmured.

Pischiel shook his head. "He wants more than that."

I peered up at him and blushed at the thought, my earlier fury draining away, until I could no longer understand just why I'd been so upset about Hera's bracelet.

Pischiel looked slightly sick. "Don't look at me that way."

"What way?"

"Like I'm a good man." He expertly turned me, navigating us around another couple who'd come close, their gazes fastened on us.

"You *are* a good man."

The song ended, and Pischiel bowed. "I need a drink."

I watched him leave, pretending he didn't just ditch me on the dance floor. Several female courtiers approached, begging me to sit with them, and I nodded. I recognized many of them by face, if not by name, and I followed them to a grouping of chairs. There, I studied Pischiel as he leaned against the black wall, raising his glass to his mouth as if it were a lifeline.

Demons laughed and danced and flirted. I watched, present but removed, as the women around me twittered, gossiping about people I didn't know. They seemed content to be seen sitting next to me, and I tuned them out as I surveyed both Pischiel and my grandfather.

My grandfather was, quite simply, beautiful. High, sharp cheekbones gave him an almost feral look, and his eyes—so like mine—seemed to glitter like jewels. But they were usually cold, like the gaze of a reptile, as he sat on his throne and moved his chess pieces around.

The bone bracelet around my wrist began to itch and throb, and I glanced down at it.

A face swam through my mind. Old and sly, with laughter in her eyes.

Her face disappeared and was immediately followed by an incredibly beautiful black woman who made me think of warmth and comfort, food and knowledge.

A woman with curly blonde hair and blue-green eyes was next, and seeing her made me feel like I was dying.

There was another woman too, smiling at me from behind a bar, working harder than any of the courtiers gossiping next to me could even contemplate.

I was going insane.

"Your royal highness?"

I jolted in my seat, and the woman next to me widened her eyes. Her wing brushed my arm as I turned, and I had a sudden vision of wings spread out on cool sheets, my hand stroking each feather.

Some mistake of genetics had ensured I'd never have my own wings. Perhaps that was why I was so obsessed with them.

I cleared my throat. "Yes?"

"What do you think?"

I had no idea what they'd been talking about, and I couldn't care less. "I think I need to go talk to Pischiel. Excuse me."

They got to their feet as I did, bowing their heads. I strode toward the demon, who was still leaning against the wall. He didn't spot me until I was within touching distance, his gaze fastened to the liquid in his glass as if it held all the secrets of the underworld.

"Princess?"

"I don't feel well," I murmured. "Will you escort me back to my rooms?" It would be a good opportunity to question him.

He glanced toward the dais, and I followed his gaze. Grandfather was watching us, interest flickering in his eyes.

"If you know what's good for you, you will stay," Pischiel murmured, his voice so low I almost couldn't hear his words.

"What's good for me?" Something itched in my mind, the feeling that I'd lost something dear.

"Danica. Danica. Danica."

That low voice in my mind wasn't mine. I tensed, and Pischiel studied my face. The corner of his mouth twitched, but his eyes hardened as he gulped at the remainder of his drink.

"I think your grandfather would prefer for you to stay. You want to be named his *ambassador*, don't you?"

Fury burned in my stomach. "Is that what this is about? The reason you abandoned me on the dance floor? You're feeling threatened because I might be named ambassador?"

He laughed, and it was so bitter I almost flinched.

"Forget it," I snapped, turning to stalk away.

A strong hand caught mine and swept me onto the dance floor. Given how much I'd watched him drink, I was surprised by how coordinated Pischiel was.

"You don't seem pleased to be dancing with me."

He stroked my hair back from my face. "Maybe because it's all a lie. I thought I'd be content with it, but it turns out a man like me can feel guilt and regret after all."

Was he slurring his words? He was obviously incapacitated, and if my grandfather realized just how much he'd drunk, he would be... *displeased*. The thought made my heart pound in my chest, and I tightened my hold on Pischiel's hand.

"You need to get your shit together," I hissed.

His eyes widened, and he froze. I clamped my hand over my mouth. I had no idea where that had come from.

"Well, there's another hint of the real Danica. Take my advice, princess, you need to stop allowing your grandfather to see it."

"I don't know what you're talking about."

"I know you don't. And if you don't keep the real Danica hidden, you'll only hasten your doom."

"You're drunk."

He laughed bitterly. "If only."

Whispers sounded, and I turned my head as courtiers cleared a path for my grandfather. He sauntered toward us, handsome and regal in his cloak and crown.

"Be very careful," Pischiel warned, his hands sliding away from me. He bowed to Lucifer and took several steps back.

"I find I miss our dancing." Grandfather's voice was full of good humor. I smiled up at him as he took me in his arms, and the music started once more.

"So do I."

"Do you?" grandfather's eyes were intent. As if he could see straight into my soul. I resisted the urge to pull my earrings out of my ears as they irritated my lobes again. Grandfather didn't appreciate it when I fidgeted in front of him.

"Of course," I smiled brightly. "I remember how you used to let me stand on your feet while you danced around the ballroom. You're the reason I love to dance."

His eyes—the color so like mine—crinkled at the corners as he lifted his hand to twirl me. I caught sight of Pischiel, once again leaning against the wall, his face pale.

Courtiers twirled and laughed as the dance picked up tempo. I knew the steps, but I still found I had to concentrate—especially in my heels. Grandfather had insisted on black marble for the floor, which made it slippery. Grandfather and I both matched the decor—both of us in the darkest black—while the rest of the court wore dark jewel tones, this season's fashion.

I'd been to another ball once. I hadn't danced, but the ballroom had been the opposite of grandfather's in every way. There was a balcony…

I frowned and grandfather's grip tightened on me. "Something wrong?"

"No," I forced a grin. "Just thinking of some court gossip I was told earlier."

The ballroom doors slammed open. Gasps echoed

throughout the room as a body was dragged into the room. Grandfather's face turned a dull red, then purple, as he went eerily still. Then his voice carried over the hush of the room.

"The dancing is over," he declared. "Leave. Now."

No one argued. Grandfather turned from me and stalked toward the body, passing Pischiel on his way. "If you're still sober enough to remember how to find my granddaughter's rooms, escort her there."

Pischiel flinched, but his jaw hardened as he nodded, taking my arm. I couldn't help but glance over my shoulder at the body, which was almost unrecognizable. My stomach churned at the sight of it. Nothing now but meat.

"Who is it?" I asked in a low voice.

Pischiel pulled me toward the door, and courtiers cleared a path, bowing and curtseying as we passed.

"Odax," he ground out.

One of Daimonion's assassin friends.

"Who killed him?"

"Either Samael or one of his men."

My head pounded suddenly, and Pischiel increased our pace, almost dragging me with him as we reached the stairs.

"Samael?" I knew that name. It burrowed deep into my chest, where it grew claws, ripping into me.

"No one you need to worry about, princess. And if you know what's good for you, you'll never say that name within your grandfather's earshot."

Samael

"Our spies say the body was found. The idiots dragged it into the ballroom, disturbing Lucifer's fun. He killed them all," Asmodeus smiled.

"He grew overconfident."

The last time Odax had traveled through the portal, he'd hoped to take one of my sentries unaware. That demon was young, untested, and female—all things that made her prey for the assassin. But she'd fought him off long enough to get out a mental call for help.

In the end, I'd let the demoness kill the assassin. I would have enjoyed it too much.

Asmodeus glanced at me. "There will be repercussions."

I nodded. Lucifer wouldn't let this stand. No, he would order Daimonion to kill someone close to us. And Daimonion would dispatch one of his other men in retaliation, unwilling to face me in my own territory where I had my powers. He wouldn't target one of my demons. No, he couldn't risk losing another of his men. But he'd go for someone else. Someone guaranteed to get a reaction.

Perhaps Evie.

Or maybe someone more easily targeted. Someone who was easier to approach–who wasn't in this tower for most of the day.

Hannah or Selina maybe. Or Gary.

I ground my teeth. All of them would need guards over the coming days, which would spread our resources thin. But there was little choice.

"Ag has dispatched bodyguards," Asmodeus said, and I glanced up. "It seemed like the smart move."

"Yes." I rubbed at my brow. "Anything else to report?"

"Lucifer has been attempting to sway Nacheran."

I let out a low growl. The region Nacheran ruled was large enough to be a threat to Lucifer if he decided to turn his allegiance elsewhere. His people were highly trained and lethal when armed. And I'd been attempting to negotiate with him for decades.

"We need to offer him something. Tell him he can have more land when I take the throne."

Asmodeus nodded, and I got to my feet. "Is that all?"

"For now." His gaze scanned my face. It was almost noon, and Asmodeus knew what I would do now. I'd attempt to find Danica in her dreams, as I did each hour.

"Keep me updated," I said, stalking to the balcony, where I launched myself into the air and up to my penthouse.

I lay down in the guest room, forcing my mind to go blank as I closed my eyes.

And this time… I found her.

Elation and hope warred within me, no matter how much I warned myself away from both.

"Danica?"

She turned, and I fought the urge to take her into my arms, to slam my mouth down on hers. To just… hold her. She was wearing a black gown, along with some of the jewels that had been passed down to my family. It hurt me to see them. Not because she was wearing them, but because I could imagine my mother gifting them to her.

"You've never looked more beautiful."

The words were out of my mouth before I could stop them, and my little witch blushed charmingly. My stomach sank. *My* Danica would have swept her gaze over my body, made a lewd comment, and stalked toward me, her mind on sex.

"Uh, thank you." She frowned, glancing around. "How did I get here? Am I in your dreams? Or are you in mine?"

"I am visiting your dreams."

Fear flashed across her face, and I held up my hands. Obviously, she'd been warned of dream visitors. Lucifer would do anything he could to make sure I couldn't talk to my bondmate. Couldn't remind her of what we shared.

"I mean you no harm."

"Then why are you here?"

"I am a... friend. A friend you have forgotten."

"Why would I forget my friends?"

I gave her a steady look. "I have a feeling you've forgotten many things recently. You may also have some memories which don't make sense."

She tucked a loose piece of hair behind her ear. "Perhaps."

I would make her trust me if it killed me.

"There's a chance I can help you with some of those memories. Would you like that?"

The wariness in her eyes killed me. But my brave little witch stared steadily at me while she considered it.

Finally, she angled her head in a way that told me she was not at all convinced, but she would at least listen. "What is your name?"

I had no doubt Lucifer and his people had poisoned her against me. "I believe I'll keep that to myself for now."

She narrowed her eyes at me, and the expression was so familiar on her face, it was all I could do not to fall to my knees in front of her. To beg her to remember me.

That would simply frighten her.

I didn't know how to behave with this version of my little witch. The version Lucifer had created. Oh, he would have enjoyed turning my warrioress into this meek shade of herself.

But he wouldn't enjoy what happened when she finally remembered who she was.

"Tell me then," she eyed me. At least she was curious.

I smiled. But my hands were shaking with the effort it took not to touch her. "Well, witchling, the first thing you should know is that our love? It is the stuff of *legends*."

CHAPTER SIX

Danica

I stared at the demon who wanted me to believe we were in love. He stepped closer, and his hand shook slightly as he raised it to my face. He closed his eyes as his hand cupped my cheek, and then they opened once more, blazing with fury and… determination.

I *had* seen that expression before. I knew I had.

"Will you sit with me?" He dropped his hand and gestured to two armchairs that had appeared out of nowhere, even as the mist continued to envelop us.

I nodded and curled up in the chair, gesturing for him to talk.

His silver eyes watched me as if it was impossible for him to look away, as if he would never want to look at anything else ever again. Whoever had come up with this tactic was *good*. I'd always wanted someone to look at me that way.

"Our story is unconventional," he finally said, and the hint of a smile played around his mouth. I suddenly wanted to see what he would look like if he gave into that smile. Would his eyes crinkle around the corners? Did he have a dimple?

"Unconventional how?"

"You stole something from me. I didn't know it was you at first. When we met, it was because you had come into my territory uninvited."

"That doesn't sound like me."

"Believe me, it is. You have a tendency to do what you want and deal with the consequences later. It was one of the things that first attracted me to you. I couldn't understand how a human with so much to lose could be so determined to find her answers that she would risk my wrath."

"Your wrath?"

His eyes glittered as he swept his gaze over my body. "Few would dare to sneak into my tower. Even fewer would risk interrogating a demon in territory I had declared neutral."

I cast him a disappointed look. "Now I know you're telling me an untruth. I would never—"

Those silver eyes burned into me. "This is *my* story time, witchling."

"Why do you call me that? I'm not a witch."

"You're wrong about that too, but we'll get to that later. For now, it's time I remind you of how handsome you found me. How you wanted nothing more than to roll me beneath you and ride me like a—"

My cheeks burned. "Now I know you're lying."

I wasn't pure, but I was inexperienced. Grandfather was a traditionalist, and he'd risk no bastards eventually having any claim to his throne.

He sent me a look so heated, my heart fluttered. "Not lying, little witch. Unfortunately for both of us, you were terrified, and I was enraged. A demon was killed in my territory, and I decided you were to blame."

"That doesn't—"

"Sound like you. I know. Someone had been killing my demons, and I tasked you with discovering who."

"Why would I do that?"

"The other option was death."

"You threatened to kill me? And you want me to believe we were… lovers?"

Was that a wince? The demon cleared his throat, looking almost… awkward. "I didn't know what you would become to me, of course. Although, subconsciously, I must have known you were mine. Because I bonded you to me in a way I shouldn't have. And yes, little witch. We *are* lovers."

"If this is the case, why don't I remember?"

A muscle ticked in his jaw. "Your memories were taken."

That was even more difficult to believe. The demon slowly got to his feet, his wings extended, and déjà vu swept over me. I tensed, and he let out a low curse, but seemed to come to some decision as he stalked toward me.

I curled up in the chair. This was my dream, but I'd let down my guard. If he wanted to hurt me…

"Get that look off your face."

I trembled as I gazed up at him.

"I don't know what you mean."

"You never need to fear *me*. You are perhaps the only

creature in all the realms who is safe from my wrath."

I opened my mouth, but he was suddenly kneeling in front of me, his hand fisted in my hair. His expression was hard, but his eyes were… tormented.

"*Remember* me, Danica. Remember *us*. Please. I can't do this without you."

His voice was pure agony, and something twisted deep in my chest. I raised my own hand without meaning to, cupping his cheek as he had mine.

He seemed to come to some decision, because his mouth was suddenly caressing my neck. I tensed, but he kissed me so gently, with such tenderness, my eyes burned.

He moved to my lips, and I opened for him, shuddering, and his mouth teased mine, achingly slow, as if we had all the time in the worlds. And then our kiss deepened, his tongue sliding into my mouth, and the déjà vu struck again. I couldn't help but kiss him back, my mouth conforming to his, my hands rising to clench in his hair.

I felt as if I'd kissed him hundreds of times before. It was this kiss–more than any story he could tell me–that made me want to believe him. If only so I could feel his mouth on mine some more.

He dragged his mouth away and pressed it to the corner of my lips, then kissed his way up my cheek. His whole body shuddered, and he buried his face in my hair.

"*Remember, little witch.*"

Danica

I woke, hopelessly aroused.

And the memory slammed into me.

I stood, frozen, unable to move. There was a body on the ground below me, and I was straining, doing everything I could to break the ward. If I could just move the knife...

Blood dripped from my nose, and the ward seemed to 'pop' as it broke. Adrenaline made my muscles tremble, and my vision narrowed as I twisted toward the door.

A high demon blocked my only exit. A high demon who burned with power and fury.

Despite my terror, my gaze couldn't help but sweep over him, noting every inch of his hard body, from his blue-black hair to his blazing silver eyes and down along the hard plane of his chest.

I'd had that chest pressed against me. I'd slammed my hands into it in fury, clutched at his shirt in need, pressed my head to his heart, just to hear it beat.

I knew it, deep in my bones.

"Well, this is interesting." I flinched at the promise *of death in his voice. His gaze shifted to the demon on the floor, his extremities already ash. The older demons were like that when they died, as if their body belonged only to the underworld, and when they were done using it, the underworld snatched it back.*

"I didn't kill him," I blurted out, and Samael shifted *his gaze back to me, scanning me from head to toe. His gaze lingered on my face, and I wiped at the blood smeared above my lip.*

"You broke my ward," he mused. *I didn't know how he could make such inane words sound like a death threat, but my hand tightened on my knife. At the very least, I could go out fighting.*

"It wasn't easy," I admitted. *"Listen, I think I have some explaining to do. This isn't what it looks like."*

Had I really been that nonchalant?

"You didn't come into my territory and threaten one of my patrons with bodily harm, even though violence is forbidden without my permission? That patron wasn't killed by someone who managed to escape my ward while you were trapped in it?"

I blinked. "Fine. Turns out it's exactly what it looks like." I attempted a nonchalant shrug. Samael ignored me and turned his head as another demon approached.

"Get Sitri," he ordered, and the demon faded away. Just a few seconds later, another demon appeared.

Where Samael was beautiful, this demon was almost pretty. His dark hair fell over his face, hiding his eyes, which were a pale purple—almost lavender. Those eyes seemed lost, even as he focused on my face, his lips forming in a pout that told me clearly, without words, that I was in deep shit.

"Invitation," Samael ordered, and I tensed. *"Please,"* he murmured, *"disobey me. I haven't gotten my hands dirty for weeks."*

My heart pounded so hard it felt as if it would jump out of my chest. The silver-eyed savage wanted me to believe we'd gone from *this* to lovers?

The flashback had faded while I dealt with my confusion. But I focused on it once more, unable to look away.

"Your first choice? Both you and the traitor die. This Steve dies harder, begging for death for daring to cross me."

He would have done it too. I could see it on his face. I'd let this man kiss me?

My voice sounded high and thready. "And the second choice?"

"You work for me."

"In what capacity?"

His gaze dropped to the demon on the floor. "This isn't the first death in the past few weeks, although it's a different method. Something is hunting demons, and your reputation precedes you. You'll be my personal bounty hunter."

"For how long?"

He tilted his head in that alien way that told me, more clearly than words, that he was not—and would never be—anything close to human. Both demons stared at me like I was a particularly dense brand of stupid and I ground my teeth. Demon vows were—

"Forever," Samael said, pure male satisfaction dripping from the word.

"I'll make you a deal."

My hands shook in real time, and I curled them into my covers. I'd dared to attempt to bargain with this man? I pushed the flashback—or memory—away, throwing the covers off myself as I got to my feet. But the memory wouldn't be denied.

The demon pulled me close, until I was just inches from him. He smelled like burning wood in a winter cabin—the comforting smell at odds with who he actually was. Demons had an affinity with fire—something I wouldn't forget.

Samael turned my arm over with a hum. "Usually, I use the inside of the arm. But for you, I like the idea of my mark being a little more... visible."

The pain was sharp, his hand a blur as he cut a long line down my forearm. I gasped, instinctively attempting to pull my hand away, and he tightened his hold, shaking his head. His thumb danced across my inner wrist.

Samael leaned close. "You smell familiar, little witch."

"Yeah, I get that a lot. Guess I've just got a generic scent to me."

Samael gave me a slow smile that was all twisted sheets and hot, sweaty bodies. "There's nothing generic about you."

"I'm just a basic witch," I mumbled.

He inhaled my scent again. "There's nothing basic about you, either."

He pressed his arm to mine, and I was engulfed in fire.

It ripped through me, and I fell to my knees, my arm still in the demon's hand. His eyes burned into mine, his expression hard as tears dripped down my cheeks. I gritted my teeth and forced myself to stand, glowering at him.

The demon's eyes glowed. "I'm going to enjoy this," he said. He removed his hand, and I breathed around the urge to puke.

Gold twined up my left forearm in an intricate design.

It danced in the dim light like it was alive. On anyone else, the shimmering color would be beautiful. On me it marked me as Samael's. My hands itched with the urge to grab the knife and slice it off.

"It would reappear on your scarred flesh," Samael said softly, warning dripping over every word.

I stumbled to the bathing room and made it to the sink before I lost my stomach. My body shuddered, sweat cooling on my skin, and I stared at the birthmark on my wrist.

Not a birthmark at all.

My mind was a confused mess, but it also seemed... clearer somehow.

I *did* believe that I'd bargained with the demon, and the *birthmark* my grandfather so loathed was a representation of that bond.

Which meant grandfather was lying to me.

And I was going to find out why.

I rinsed the sink, then stalked to my closet, pulled out the first dress I found, and wrestled it onto my body. I didn't bother tying it properly. I had no idea where I was going, but I was driven to do *something*.

A young girl laughed with me as our heads pressed against each other—hers a wealth of blond curls, mine dark and straight. The light was dimmed, our flashlights lighting up some kind of tent.

"Shhhh," the girl laughed. "The monster's coming,"

A woman stuck her head into that tent, a tray of food in her hands.

"Monster, huh? Would a monster feed you? Or would it eat *you?"*

She placed the tray on the ground and crawled into the tent, tickling us both until we squealed.

Then we were both beneath the bed covers, a little older, whispering secrets—most of them about boys. We pinky swore to never tell, and one day...

One day she was torn from my arms, and I was packed away, sent somewhere new.

Then there was training. A craggy-faced man with a continual scowl. Knives and guns and poison. Hand-to-hand combat and running—always running.

There was the blonde girl again, but she had grown into a beautiful woman. Her expression was bitter, her eyes hurt as she shut her door in my face.

I wanted to curl up and cry.

But one day, we were talking once more, this time in some kind of tavern surrounded by all kinds of different creatures. She smiled at me, and it was like we were children again, both of us up to no good.

There was a word for this relationship. A word I hadn't let myself think. I mouthed the word to myself.

Sister.

And another word came. A word that made my throat ache, made my hands fist.

Evie.

I had a sister.

My face was wet, and I brushed the tears away. Something rubbed against my face as I wiped at my eyes–something that felt like cool metal. But when I pulled my hand away, there was nothing there. On my other hand, my ring glinted in the light, the gold warm and familiar.

They'd kept me from my sister. My grandfather had

never mentioned her, and I *knew*, down to my bones, that if I dared speak her name, I would risk his wrath.

I shakily got to my feet, fury roaring through my body, making me hot with a mixture of rage and grief. The ring seemed to taunt me, and the next memory unraveled like a slow understanding.

"The ring removes enchantments. That much, Edward was sure of. According to the poem, it also contains a spell of invisibility when you put it in your mouth. That's how Angelica escaped the sea monster. And now we know that its resistance to enchantment means it's a key part of the Spell of Three."

Those were *my* words. That was *my* voice in my head. I didn't know who I'd been speaking to, but I didn't give myself a chance to back out, riding my rage through to its inevitable conclusion.

I pulled the ring off my finger and placed it in my mouth.

CHAPTER SEVEN

Danica

I instantly disappeared.

I inhaled so sharply, I almost choked on the ring. Spitting it out into my palm, I shuddered, visible once more. Before I could talk myself out of my next move, I shoved it back into my mouth and cracked open my door.

Then I made my way through the palace, striding to the servants' quarters and out the door that led to the dungeon.

I instinctively knew what to do next, and I didn't question it as I slid my palm down the stone of the wall next to the door, drawing blood. Then I slipped inside, peering into the darkness as I made my way down the stairs. A wolf had given me the ring. I remembered that much. And she'd been here, locked away in the darkness.

I didn't go straight to the wolf. First, I had to search for my sister. When I attempted to bring her face into focus, my head ached with a pain so encompassing, I wanted to vomit again. But I *knew* she existed.

I wasn't crazy.

There were hundreds of strange creatures in these cells. None could see me, but some froze at the sound of my footsteps on stone. Others lifted their noses into the air, scenting me as I passed their cells. Still others ignored me entirely.

I peered into each cell, looking for blonde curly hair. My heart slammed in my chest as I searched for her, but there was no one familiar in this row of cells.

Until I made my way to the last cell on the right.

The creature was sickly pale, her skin likely starved of sunlight. Her dark hair was long and tangled around her waist, and she peered in my direction, one black eye peeking out from between hanks of that hair. Her lips were so red they looked as if she'd recently painted on a coat of dark lipstick and left it to stain.

She smiled at me.

"Come closer, witch."

I glanced around, but she was speaking to me.

"Yessss, I can see you. I have powers that creatures such as yourself can only guess at."

I took a single step closer and removed the ring from my mouth. "I'm not a witch," I whispered, careful to keep my voice low.

She laughed at that. "Perhaps we can make a bargain, you and I."

I was interested despite myself. Something about her seemed familiar.

"What kind of bargain?"

"I hold one of your memories."

I scowled. "Of course you do." The only person who didn't seem to have my memories was me.

"If you're going to be rude, witch, I will not allow you to enjoy story time."

Something about the way she sat back in her cage, as if she had all the time in the world, made me fight back a smile.

"How do you have one of my memories?"

"There are seven of us. Myself, and six of my sisters. All of them taste freedom, except for me. We may be impervious to torture, but we can still be caged."

"I'm sorry."

She ignored that. "My sister bargained with you recently."

"What kind of bargain?"

"She gave you some information you desperately needed, in exchange for one of your most precious memories. A memory of *love*." She sneered.

Obviously, she wasn't a fan of romance.

"Your sister has one of my memories?"

"Yes. And now, so do I."

"How?"

"We share all things. All of us have been harmed irrevocably by the males who should have protected us. So all of us enjoy the fruits of our labor."

"Mmhmm. And I suppose you want to share this memory freely with me out of the goodness of your heart."

She laughed. "I will share this memory with you in exchange for one thing."

"What?"

"Freedom."

"I don't have the keys."

"Oh, but I believe you will. And when you do, I want

to feel the sun on my face. I want to taste fresh air once more."

I didn't understand. She sighed. "War will come to this place. And when it does, you will set me free."

I couldn't imagine having the opportunity to do that, but I nodded. "*If* I ever have the chance to free prisoners from this dungeon, I will open your cell."

She studied my face. "Done. Now come closer and take your memory."

I trembled, and she tutted at me. "One must face their past with courage, witch."

"Even if they don't know what their past holds?"

"Especially then. What use is courage if not used to face the unknown?"

I leaned closer to the bars, and she took my head between her hands.

And there was the demon with the silver eyes. Again. And I was frowning at him. Pissed off by how much I needed him. I was almost shouting, my voice passionate, tinged with desperation.

"You infuriate me, challenge me, annoy the shit out of me. You're bossy and controlling, and dealing with your ego is no fucking picnic, let me tell you."

He raised one eyebrow, and I threw up my hands, turning away to pace.

"Just a few months ago, if someone had told me I'd fall in love with you, I would've told them to get their head checked," I muttered.

"I'm not sure if that's complimentary."

I ignored that. "And now… I miss you when you're not around. I had to actively fight with myself not to come to this tower every damn day."

"Danica—"

"I want to fall asleep next to you, and fight with you, and fuck you, and complain to my friends when you're being your usual, overly possessive self. I want to be yours. But only if you're mine, too."

Strong hands gripped my shoulders, turning me, and Samael's mouth crashed down on mine. He buried his hand in my hair and the world faded away as I lost myself in the feel of him surrounding me. My demon. Mine.

"Is that a yes?" I mumbled against his mouth.

"Say it again," he ordered, and I rolled my eyes. Bossy demon.

"I love you."

He let out a groan and then he was lifting me in his arms, stalking through the doorway, into his penthouse, and through to his bedroom, where he slowly laid me down on his bed. He handled me so gently, it was as if he thought I was suddenly breakable.

"This doesn't mean you can tell me what to do all the time."

"Quiet." He nibbled on my lower lip.

"And I'm not going to give up my career for you."

He laughed. "Of course not." He pulled back long enough to strip off his clothes and my mouth went dry. I forced myself to raise my gaze to his face in an attempt to get my point across.

"I'm serious, Samael."

"I know." He let out a frustrated groan as he pulled my shirt and tank-top over my head. "So many clothes in my way." His gaze got stuck on my breasts and the next

groan that left him was a different sound entirely.

"I want you, little witch. Not a woman who will do everything I say without question. Although that might be an interesting experience for a few days."

I narrowed my eyes at him, and he laughed, nuzzling my breasts. He unhooked my bra with deft movements, and a dark possessiveness slid into his eyes.

"I've had centuries of women doing as I said," he told me. "None of them could hold my attention for more than a few weeks. You? You will be mine forever."

I must be crazy, because the idea of being with the demon forever no longer scared the crap out of me. Well, only a little.

My earlobes burned as if they'd been set on fire. The bone bracelet tightened around my wrist, until it cut off my circulation, and the gold mark covering my arm heated until it felt as if it would burn me alive.

It was as if that one memory cracked something open inside of me, and new memories poured into me. One after another, after another. Meeting Samael. Hating him. Falling in love with him. Saving his life.

Then there was Evie, Vas, Kyla and Meredith. Recognition gave me back Keigan, Selina, and Hannah. Bael and all the other demons came next. I tumbled through space and time and finally, I saw Samael again as I knew him now. My bondmate. My love.

I wanted to scream out my fury, and I shook with it, the rage so encompassing, I teetered on the edge of sanity.

The Dearg Due slowly backed away from me, a hint of fear flashing across her face.

"Control yourself, witch, or your power will burn

you alive. There's no outlet for it while you're wearing that monstrosity."

I followed her gaze to the metal encircling my wrist. Now that the spell was broken, I could see it. And I could feel my power, raging below the surface—far below my shields, where I couldn't access it.

Cellen did this. Lucifer had taken his sister, but the seelie hadn't seemed broken up about the fact that he was leaving us at Lucifer's mercy.

I would kill them all for this. I would burn this place to the ground and dance on the ashes, if that's what it took. Bile burned up my throat as more memories trickled in. Lucifer had *programmed* me with that spell. He'd turned me into an unrecognizable version of myself, and he'd enjoyed it.

Oh yes. His amusement had been constant as he watched me. He'd been having a grand time.

And Gloria?

I let out a laugh that made the Dearg Due flinch.

I would make them rue the day they decided to come for me, oh yes I would.

"You're bleeding, witch."

I swiped a hand under my nose, wiping at the blood. Then I turned, stalking toward my friends.

Kyla snarled as I approached.

"It's me. The real me."

It took her a moment, and my chest clenched as the wild rage didn't fade completely from her eyes. Lucifer was keeping her in wolf form, something that would eventually turn her feral. Panic clawed at me, and she showed me her teeth. Right. Werewolves enjoyed fear.

My emotions wouldn't help her keep control.

"I'm going to get you out of here. I swear."

The rage left her eyes, and she lifted a paw, shoving it between the bars. I wrapped my hands around it, and my eyes burned. "I'm sorry. I'm so sorry you got stuck down here because of me."

She snapped her teeth at me, and this time, she was all Kyla. I choked out a laugh.

"Okay." I pressed my head against the bars, and she did the same on her side. My tears dripped into her fur. "Okay."

I stayed there for a long moment, and my thoughts began to clear.

"Danica?" a voice hissed.

Keigan. I lifted my head.

Kyla let out a low growl, and I glanced at her. "Still not a fan, huh? One day, we're going to have to all sit down and have dinner or something."

She ignored that, lying back down and curling up, her tail covering her eyes. Conversation over. Yeah, the wolf definitely wasn't herself. And she was much thinner, too. Shit.

I made my way down to Keigan's cell. His eyes were wary as he watched me, and I crouched in front of his cell. "I'm back."

He closed his eyes for a long moment, and when he opened them, they were wet. "I was worried."

"Yeah." I dropped my voice until it was a whisper. "I'm going to have to pretend to be that empty-headed idiot, so if I can't get to you for a few nights, that's why. I can't risk Lucifer knowing what's up until I've figured out how to kill him."

He stared at me. "You seriously think you can kill him?"

"I think he made the mistake of letting me into his castle with rowan around my neck." I could still feel it there, as invisible as ever.

Keigan gave me a slow grin. Then the grin fell. "It might not kill him. He could be too powerful."

"I have to try. And I have to learn this palace like the back of my hand. I have to figure out the guards' shifts, and I need to find a way to get Samael's army in here."

"Samael is powerless in the underworld."

"I know." And the thought made nausea sweep through me. "But he'll never leave me here. Even if I get free, he'll never let this stand. We're going to war."

Danica

That night, when I fell back asleep, Samael was waiting for me, already sitting in one of the armchairs. Now that I was paying attention, I could see the signs of grief and exhaustion, and the way they'd ravaged his face.

He surveyed me, and I caught the flash of despair, quickly followed by determination.

He would have spent the rest of his life making me *me*. He would never allow me to live a half-life. He would do whatever it took.

Our eyes met, and I tumbled into love with him all over again.

I couldn't help myself. I leered at him.

"You know, you said we're lovers, but I'm not sure I believe you. Maybe I need to try before I buy."

He stared at me, slowly getting to his feet. A dull hope shone in his eyes.

I leapt at him. He caught me, his hands clutching my body as if he'd never let me go. He buried his face in my throat and trembled against me.

I held on, clutching at him. "I really scared the crap out of you, huh?"

He merely squeezed me tighter. It took him a long time before he could finally speak.

"I knew you'd come back to me."

"You sure you didn't like the other me better?"

Samael shook some more, but this time it was with suppressed laughter. "Well," he said, lifting his head, "you *were* cute, with all the blushing and trembling."

I poked my finger into his ribs. He leaned his head against mine, and then he was hauling me back toward the armchair, sitting down until I was straddling him, pressing kisses to his mouth.

My face was wet. So was Samael's. I lifted my head, staring into his eyes.

"I want you to know that even without the earrings, the bracelet, even our bond… I would've fought my way back to you."

"Oh, witchling, I never had any doubt. Although it killed something in me to see you look at me with fear in your eyes."

"Some part of me knew you weren't a true threat to me. Or the way they'd programmed me would've ensured

I would've run straight to Lucifer when you appeared in my dreams."

I rose up on my knees until I was leaning over him, my strong, determined bondmate.

Pure love shone down our bond, and I realized just what Lucifer had done by clamping that metal cuff around my wrist. Not being able to communicate with Samael was hell, and there were only so many hours I could sleep each night.

"Forget it for now," Samael murmured, fisting his hand in my hair and bringing my head closer to his. "And be with me."

He didn't have to ask twice. His lips caressed mine, and I opened my mouth for him. His other arm wrapped around my back, holding me in place for him. Still so pushy, this demon of mine.

But I wouldn't have him any other way.

His mouth left mine to press kisses down my neck, lingering on the places that made me shiver against him.

In the blink of an eye, I was naked. I jolted, and the movement made me rub against him.

He let out a hoarse laugh, his tongue circling one of my nipples. My hands found his hair, and I held him to me, tendrils of sensation spreading throughout my body. God, I'd missed this. Missed *him*.

One strong hand drifted down, caressing over my stomach muscles. Those muscles clenched when his clever hand found my wet center. A groan left his mouth, and he turned his attention to my other nipple, his fingers dancing along my slit. He found the spots that drove me wild, never lingering where I wanted him the most.

"You're still a tease," I groaned, and felt him smile against my breast.

"I live to drive you wild, little witch."

"Uh huh." Two could play at that game. I lifted my hips, wrapping my hand around him and feeling him throb. I held him to my entrance, slowly sliding down.

He hadn't expected the move, and his head fell back with a hiss.

"Gods, woman, the feel of you around me. You're so hot and wet and *mine*." He grasped my hips and thrust up into me, this angle allowing him to easily hit my g-spot while I ground down on him.

My mouth found his neck this time, and I felt the sudden urge to mark him. To prove that I was still alive. Still here. And he was still mine.

It wouldn't carry over to the real world, would be gone when he woke up, but I needed it anyway. I bit down and he let out a rough growl, his hand pressing my head closer, urging me on.

"More," he demanded, and I sucked and bit, never tearing his skin, but marking him in a way that made me feel feral.

Then he was lifting me, no longer content to let me take the lead. He pulled out of me, and I whimpered, making him let out a rough laugh.

Within a couple of seconds, my ass hit the chair, and he pushed my legs wide. The armchair seemed to melt around my body, until my legs were splayed open over the arms, and Samael was eye-level with the wet heat of me.

I let out an embarrassed groan and his eyes met mine. "Perhaps you can blush after all."

I wiggled, attempting to close my legs–at least a little–but Samael's hands clamped around my thighs.

"Uh-uh."

He looked wild, cheekbones flushed as he scanned my body, his eyes lit with pure possession. Then he lowered his head, and I let out a sound that would have mortified me if I wasn't lost in the feel of his tongue dancing along my clit.

One large finger pushed inside me, and he lapped at me like he couldn't get enough. Then he found my clit once more and sucked.

I exploded, pleasure tearing through me, making me writhe against him. Distantly, I was aware of Samael letting out a rough curse, and the armchair lowered itself until he could thrust into me, still on his knees while I remained splayed out before him.

It was filthy, erotic, and I couldn't get enough. Samael pounded into me, one large hand drifting up my body to wrap around my throat. He didn't apply any pressure, but the threat of it just plain did it for me.

He laughed, and I clamped down around him. And then he was cursing as I shuddered in his arms, my climax engulfing my entire body. Samael continued to thrust, riding me through my climax, until I was completely limp beneath him.

Then he stirred himself within me.

Still hard.

"I can't," I murmured. "Not again."

"That sounds like a challenge."

If I didn't know him, I'd think he was unaffected. His expression was hard, unyielding. But his eyes burned with a mixture of desperation and tenderness.

He slid his hand down to my clit and thrust once more, and I tensed around him.

"There you go." His tone was smug, but I could see the tension in his shoulders. He was barely holding on. He set up a steady rhythm and pounded into me, his fingers caressing my clit.

A fire began to burn in my belly, the warmth spreading out through my limbs to my fingers and toes. I took a deep breath, and my climax hit, dimming the edges of my vision.

Samael growled, buried his head in my neck, and followed me over.

We lay like that for a long time. The chair shifted beneath us, becoming a wide sofa, and I relaxed in Samael's arms, soaking up the feel of his body against mine.

His arms tightened around me. "I hate that you're there. That I can't protect you."

"What I don't understand is… why Lucifer bothered with the games. Why does he want my power? Why not just kill me and get it over with?"

"I'm unsure. He's the king of the underworld, and the underworld allows him to borrow power when necessary. While you may be powerful, you haven't grown into that power. It's a drop in the bucket compared to Lucifer's." Samael frowned. "Logically, he should have killed you immediately."

"Maybe he just loves his new granddaughter so much, he wants to keep me around."

Samael's chest shook beneath me as we both cracked

up. I almost purred as he began stroking my hair.

"It may be good optics for you to be seen by his side, particularly since his people will know you are mine. But he could likely achieve almost the same by simply killing you. I don't know his motivations, little witch, but you need to be careful."

His finger brushed the shell of my ear and I shivered. "Kyla is in the underworld," he murmured.

"Yeah, in the cells. With Keigan."

"You can never allow Lucifer to know how much you care for them. He will cut them into pieces in front of you, until you agree to do whatever he wants."

I wanted to scream in frustrated rage. "I need to get Kyla and Keigan out."

"If you do, Lucifer will know." His hand took my wrist, thumb caressing right above my ugly metal accessory.

"Kyla's dying, Samael. She's turning feral."

"I know. Nathaniel can feel it. He is… unsteady."

"I won't let her die."

"I know. Just give us a chance to get to you, little witch. Let me put the pieces in place to remove Lucifer as a threat. For good."

I nodded, but my mind provided the sight of Lucifer's expression while he watched me, certain that he had me well in hand. I wouldn't do anything stupid, but I wouldn't just wait for Samael like a princess stuck in a tower, either.

Lucifer wouldn't know what had hit him by the time I was done in the underworld.

"I know you're not going to be content simply

waiting for me," Samael seemed to read my mind. He stroked one finger down my throat, then lower. "If you get the chance, attempt to convince Garadiel to see our side. We have been trying to sway him for years now, with no success. Perhaps you will have more luck."

"Lucifer has hellhounds, Samael. I don't know how many, but he's keeping them in the dungeons."

I'd nearly been killed by a hellhound soon after I met Samael. I remembered now, throwing myself over Ag's body in an attempt to shield him.

"I know. Lucifer has always been fond of collecting the underworld's most dangerous creatures and keeping them chained up and ready for when he needs them."

My eyes were growing heavy, the need for true sleep overtaking me. "Vulnerability," I mumbled. "Neck."

"Yes, little witch. The hellhounds have a vulnerable spot at the back of their neck." Samael's voice was tender. "Sleep."

"Don't leave me."

"I'll never leave you."

CHAPTER EIGHT

Danica

T he next morning, I got up early, before Yusilin arrived to wake me. I needed to have my game face on. She'd seemed ashamed after Gloria refreshed her little spell, unable to meet my eyes. But she'd also suggested I remove my bone bracelet.

Yusilin hadn't tried all that hard to convince me to take it off–it had seemed more like she was going through the motions. But I still couldn't trust her.

When Lucifer and Gloria had taken my memories, they'd also taken my weapons. They'd left my jewelry though, and it was ironic, in a way, since I had a pretty good feeling that both the protection spell woven into my earrings and the bracelet Hannah had given me had helped me regain my memories. No one in this realm had liked the bone bracelet, and it wouldn't surprise me if Hannah had ensured I was the only one who could remove it.

But they hadn't known about Angelica's ring and its ability to fight enchantment. Kyla was a sneaky wolf indeed.

A small part of me wondered what had happened to Cellen, not to mention his sister. I pushed that thought away. Whatever had happened to them hadn't been good. I didn't know Cellen's sister, but the seelie who'd dumped me on Lucifer's doorstep deserved everything he'd gotten.

My hand automatically slid down to where my Mark II should have been waiting in its sheath. I wanted my weapons back. I had no doubt that Lucifer would merely sneer if I attempted to shoot or stab him, but I had more than enough enemies in this place, and I was sick of feeling like I was walking around naked.

Besides, I had retribution of my own to mete out.

"Danica?"

I smiled as Yusilin walked in and her eyes widened. "You're already up. Difficulty sleeping?"

"No, actually, I slept like a baby. I just woke a little early. I think I want to wear the purple today. It's so pretty."

She nodded. "Of course."

I dressed, spoke of unimportant things, and ate breakfast. Then I opened my door.

Pischiel.

Fuck.

I smiled at him. "This is a nice surprise."

"I thought I'd convince you to take a walk with me."

"Sounds lovely."

I kept the vapid smile on my face as he offered me his arm. And I paid attention to every guard on each floor, memorizing our route down to the gardens.

Only Lucifer's most trusted demons were given

access to the palace itself, and there were hundreds of guards patrolling the sprawling grounds and beyond the palace.

Daimonion stalked past us with two of his men, their boots slapping on the stone walkway. I lowered my gaze before he could see exactly how much I loathed him. Vas had made me swear not to kill him. And since Daimonion had ensured Vas had grown up without his parents, I wouldn't steal Vas's vengeance from him.

"You're quiet."

"Merely thinking. It's a beautiful day."

"It is." Pischiel studied my face. "But not as beautiful as you."

Try that on someone else, you piece of shit.

I watched him watch me and attempted to call up a blush, but it wasn't happening. To Pischiel's credit, the words were rote, and I had a pretty good feeling he was about as interested in me sexually as I was in him.

Which was fucking zero percent.

I forced a shy smile. "Thank you."

"Your grandfather wishes for us to have lunch together. He told me he is ready to officially announce me as his heir, but he wants you by my side. What is your plan, Danica?"

Had his eyes turned shrewd, or was I reading too much into this little situation?

I picked up my gown so I wouldn't trip down the stairs, my mind racing.

"Do you need to know my answer now? Something tells me grandfather won't be stepping aside any time soon."

His gaze narrowed at that, and I beamed at him. "After all, he seems to truly enjoy ruling."

"He does. But no one can rule forever."

Isn't that the fucking truth.

"I can't give you an answer yet, Pischiel." I would play with him as he'd played with me. "I just… I feel like I don't truly *know* you."

A muscle twitched in his cheek, and I held back my smile.

"Then I will have to ensure you get to know me." His smile was sharp, and I simpered up at him.

"Pischiel," a deep voice said. We both turned. One of Lucifer's most trusted guards was standing at attention, clearly waiting to tell Pischiel something important. I wished I could eavesdrop, but it would be far too obvious here in the downstairs hall, which was beginning to empty out as people made their way to breakfast or to complete their tasks for the day.

"I'll see you later," I said.

Pischiel nodded and strolled away with the guard.

I turned and froze. Gloria stood at the other end of the hall. My vision dimmed until all I could see was her face. All I could hear were her footsteps on the stone floor.

It would be so easy to kill her here. To make her pay for her many betrayals. I didn't need weapons. I needed four seconds—five maybe—and I could snap her neck like a twig.

My hands shook with the effort to keep my cool, but I managed to smile at her, my expression placid. Then I turned and opened the closest door, stepping into the empty room. Black witches fed on negative emotions. If I got too close, she'd be able to suck up all of my loathing. Not only would she get a power boost, but she'd know damn well that her little spell hadn't stuck.

I planted my hands on my hips and examined the room without much interest. Some kind of sitting room, although it had obviously been shut up for a long time, since the chairs were covered in dust. I waited until I was sure Gloria had moved on, and then I cracked open the door, slipping out of the room.

I had things to do before lunch. Important things. I kept my expression serene as I passed the guards on the next set of stairs and moseyed down to the lower level. This was another entrance to the servants' quarters, although it was on the other side of the palace. And the door leading to this part of the garden didn't seem to be as heavily guarded.

I opened the door and kept my steps slow, stopping to literally sniff the flowers. Out of the corner of my eye, I spotted Garadiel.

Excellent.

He spoke to two of the other guards, clearly giving them orders, and they nodded. One of them, a guy with blonde hair in long coils, scowled, clearly unhappy, but he whirled and began stalking toward the palace gates.

The other guard nodded at Garadiel and followed at a more sedate pace. Garadiel turned, spotted me watching him, and tensed.

"Can I help you, your royal highness?"

"Actually, you can."

We studied each other for a long moment. He wasn't stupid. The flash of realization in his eyes told me he knew.

"Do not attempt to pull me into your games, princess."

"This isn't a game. It will be war."

He hissed out a breath, his wings rustling as if he'd like to flare them. But he had far too much control for that. His pale green eyes narrowed instead.

"My loyalties lie with my king."

"Good. Samael will be glad to hear that."

Had his mouth just twitched? No, his expression was stone.

"Do you know how long I've been in this role, your royal highness?"

"Please, call me Danica."

He continued as if I hadn't spoken. "Over a century of your time. During that time, he has survived fifty-four assassination attempts by those who do not live in the underworld. Do you want to guess how many citizens of the underworld have attempted to remove your grandfather from his throne?"

"I'm assuming plenty."

"No. No one would even attempt such a thing, because even the whisper of rebellion is squashed so brutally that people speak of it in hushed voices. I have a sister. She has children. I won't risk them."

"Are you hearing yourself? You're loyal to a man who holds that loyalty by threatening the people you love most."

He shrugged. "And where has Samael been for all this time? Hiding. Enjoying your world. If it comes to a choice between my king and the one who is powerless in this world? I choose my king. Excuse me, your royal highness, I need to get back to work."

I blew out a breath as he turned and walked away. That went well.

"What were you speaking to Garadiel about?"

I barely suppressed my jolt. Instead, I pasted on my smile and turned, finding Pischiel watching me.

"Are you following me?"

Surprise flashed across his face, and I cursed myself. Empty-headed Danica wouldn't have asked that.

"No," he murmured, his eyes on mine. "My meeting ended early, and I thought I'd get some fresh air before lunch."

"I had the same thought," I said brightly, forcing myself to step toward him and link my arm through his. "I was asking Garadiel about those plants near the gate. They look so… vicious."

His gaze followed mine to the thick vines which crept up the stone wall in the distance. The wall encircled the palace grounds, and almost every inch seemed to be covered in long, snake-line vines. Each vine was studded with thorns the size of my middle finger, and dotted between the thorns were large black flowers that looked similar to lilies.

"They *are* vicious," Pischiel murmured. "In fact, they're one of our best modes of defense against any other paranormals who would hope to take the palace."

I frowned at him. "In what way?"

"While demons could fly over the wall, any paranormals who attempted to enter on foot would be skewered by the garthia plants."

"Couldn't most paranormals just kill the plants?"

He smiled. "They're much, much hardier than you'd imagine. They've been fed the blood of every underking in existence."

Mental note, figure out what to do about the garthia plant. The unseelie would fight beside us, and unlike the demons, they couldn't just fly over the wall. It wouldn't help if they ended up stuck behind the gates.

Pischiel was studying my face again. I turned us so we were facing the palace. "It must be time for lunch. I'm starved."

Samael

My office door slammed open, and Vas stalked inside.

I took a slow, deep breath.

Don't kill him. He is young.

I lifted my head. "I suggest you—"

"Daimonion went after Meredith," he cut me off, and I surveyed his face. Vassago was known as the most laid-back of my demons, the most "human." And yet, anyone who saw him now would never describe him either way.

"Meredith," I mused. A muscle ticked in Vassago's jaw, and I watched it with interest. "The witch who owns—"

"The bar of the same name."

I steepled my hands on my desk. "Is she dead?"

"No. Daimonion sent one of his men, and he couldn't

get the job done." Was that pride in Vassago's voice?

"I was expecting Daimonion to strike at one of the people on the outskirts. Perhaps Hannah or Selina. But he couldn't resist the opportunity to play with you at the same time."

"This is not a *game*."

I raised one eyebrow. Vas cursed and stalked to the window, staring down at the city.

I forced myself to tamp down my impatience. "I apologize. I was unaware you had... feelings for this witch."

He shook his head. "It's okay. I know you're just getting into his head. And my feelings are... complicated. Mere wants nothing to do with me."

I smiled for the first time in what felt like days. "I wouldn't know what that is like."

A laugh rumbled from his throat, and he shoved his hand through his hair, turning to look at me. "I want to bring her to the tower."

"You believe she'll come?"

Vas's expression hardened. "She'll come willingly, or I'll drag her."

This was interesting, indeed. I'd never seen him so... tense.

"Let me give you a word of warning. Do nothing that will make your female hate you. Even temporarily."

He frowned. "She's not my female. The suggestion would make her sneer. But she's not safe right now. I'm going to go bring her back here. I'll give her a room near mine."

I nodded. Vas stalked out, and I flew down to the

conference room, finished with my calls for the day. I never would have thought that warring with Lucifer would require so many *conversations* with those who may join us.

The sheer willpower it took to hold myself back, to *not* think about Danica alone in the underworld, so I could function, could plan our strategy… it was exhausting.

I opened the balcony door, making eye contact with Nathaniel.

The werewolf Alpha was holding it together better than I was, although I could see the concerned expressions amongst his pack. I absently studied the way his pack interacted, noting which of his people were the most dominant. I didn't *think* I would war with the Alpha in the future, but both of us were long-lived. It made sense to be prepared.

There were four dominants whom Nathaniel relied on during this time: Hunter, Ryker, Xander, and Naomi. I hadn't yet determined the rank of each in the pack, and I had a feeling this was a strategy the pack employed when surrounded by strangers. The dominants were busy ensuring the pack had their needs met so the Alpha could devote his time to Kyla.

I angled my head in reluctant approval as Nathaniel deployed Hunter and Naomi back to their territory, and they immediately jumped into action.

The Alpha met my eyes. "Strategizing, demon?"

I gave him an icy smile. "No more than you are, wolf."

The close contact between my people and his was now leading to tension and spats. And yet I'd caught a few of my demon females giving his wolves interested looks.

The gods help us all.

Nathaniel bared his own teeth at me in a feral smile. Evelyn chose that moment to walk in, her eyes hard.

"Please tell me you're not both swinging your dicks around."

Evie was already turning away, sticking a photo on one of the whiteboards. But I caught the flicker of the wolf in the Alpha's eyes and shook my head. Poor bastard.

At least his future mate is here with him, and not in the hands of his enemies.

Fury burned low in my gut, and my tone was harsh. "What do we have?"

Danica

I spent the next two days exploring the palace and the grounds. I knew now why Lucifer had kept me in my rooms when he was 'entertaining'. This place… it was hellish.

On the outside, the palace looked as shiningly beautiful as it must have been when Samael's grandfather ruled. When his mother had birthed two babies here, watched them play in the gardens and run through that throne room.

But the more I crept around, invisible, the more I saw beneath that false front.

The dungeons weren't the worst place in this palace. No, the people there were mostly ignored, left to rot.

There were other rooms, other dark holes where people who were considered a threat to Lucifer's rule were kept.

And the sounds that leaked from behind those doors...

It took everything in me to keep walking. To not hunt down a weapon and kill whoever was causing people to make those horrifying noises.

I could take out a few of them before I was noticed... but then...

No. As much as I wanted to make these evil assholes pay, the cake wasn't worth the bake. Even if that cake would taste fucking delicious. I needed to bide my time and wait.

Still, I could barely meet my own eyes in the mirror each morning.

Skulking around at night had its advantages. The guards were more lax, focused on sneaking down to seduce the maids, drinking, and gambling.

My most important job was to speak to the guards Samael's spies believed might join with us. It wasn't easy. Everything I said to the guards had to have a double meaning, as I slowly felt out who could potentially be convinced to join us. I struggled to eat. The stress of watching every word—of communicating that I spoke for Samael, without ever saying anything that could be directly repeated to Lucifer—made my stomach continually churn.

And always, always, I watched Lucifer. I learned his moods, his habits, and the people he most often kept around him. I watched him when he didn't notice me, and I made a note of everything that seemed relevant.

Each night, when I was done wandering the palace, I snuck down to the dungeon. I brought both Keigan and Kyla extra food, although my friend no longer seemed to recognize me. She would usually let out a low growl, snap up the food, and then turn her back on me.

After visiting the dungeon, I'd meet Samael in my dreams and pass on everything I'd learned. Then we'd touch each other with a desperation I'd never felt before. Both of us knew what would likely happen if Lucifer caught me. If he knew that while the cuff around my wrist may prevent me from communicating with Samael during the day, the night was ours.

I was well aware that waiting was one of the most difficult things Samael had ever done. If he could, he'd march into this palace tomorrow. But while Samael the man wanted to do just that, Samael the ruler was experienced, patient, and smart. We needed our allies. We needed a pocket realm to hold our armies. And we needed the dragons.

On the fourth day, Yusilin was braiding my hair when my door slammed open. My eyes met Pischiel's, and he studied me like he'd never seen me before.

"Out," he ordered.

Yusilin's eyes widened, but she didn't argue, merely squeezed my shoulder and backed away. When she'd closed the door, I got to my feet as Pischiel stalked toward me.

"Danica Amana," he breathed, his eyes hard. "It's nice to finally meet you."

I gave him a slow smile, even as my pulse thudded like a drum, my hand tightening around the back of the chair.

"I'd say the same to you, but I'd be lying."

"How are your escape plans going?" I stiffened, and he scoffed. "You seriously think I haven't noticed? You're about as subtle as a sword to the gut."

"So what, you decided to watch me and see what happened?"

"I thought I'd take my entertainment where I could find it." His smile was cruel. "But you erred, princess. You tipped off the wrong demon, and you're merely lucky he came to me and not Lucifer himself about your little mission."

Shit. Who had I miscalculated with? I swallowed and surveyed every inch of Pischiel's face, hoping for some hint about what I had to work with. There were no hints. One didn't end up in Lucifer's upper echelon unless they had a damn good poker face.

"And I suppose you're here to bargain for your silence."

"Maybe."

I gave him a slow smile. He'd get his throat slit if he fucked with me, that's what he'd get.

Pischiel took a step closer to me, his expression dangerous. "What, exactly, are you hoping for here? You think you'll turn your grandfather's own people against him?"

I shrugged. "It's none of your business what I'm hoping for. You lied to me," I hissed. "You told me you'd tell Lucifer I was sleepwalking that night." And then I'd ended up with my memories wiped. *Again.*

He let out an incredulous sound halfway between a

groan and a laugh. "I did. I told Lucifer exactly that. And everything might have been fine if you hadn't mentioned the man with the *silver* eyes."

"Forgive the fuck out of me for being a little confused after my brain was turned to mush."

Pischiel took another step closer. His arms lashed out, his hands clamping onto my upper arms as he shook me. "Your only chance of making it through this is to convince your grandfather that he succeeded in turning you. Convince him you love *me*. He'll be happy to keep you under his thumb, to rub it in Samael's face that you're going to rule with his second."

I gaped at him. "You seriously think I'd do that?"

"I think you have few choices, *princess*. Do you think I enjoy this? I'm trying to keep you alive."

I glowered at him, but kept my mouth shut. He studied my face and then smiled. "You believe Samael will make it down here and rescue you."

I jerked, but he didn't let me go. "Did he not tell you he's completely powerless down here? You'd sentence your mate to certain death instead of keeping him safe?"

"Keeping him safe by one day ruling as Lucifer's puppet with *you*?" I was pretty sure Samael would rather die.

Pischiel's expression hardened, and his hands tightened on my shoulders. I was done with this.

"Let me go."

He shook his head. "I'm trying to save your life."

I punched him in the throat. He wasn't expecting it and he gaped at me, struggling to catch his breath. I followed up with a knee to the groin and he folded, his hands releasing me as he wheezed.

"Touch me again without permission, and I'll kill you."

"Ah, princess. You've just proven why Samael will stop at nothing to get to you."

"Then you're really going to love it when I gut you like a fish."

His eyes sparked. Then they lit with humor. "I'd almost like to see what would happen if you went up against Lucifer."

"What will it cost for your silence?"

He studied me. "If I said I wanted you to fuck me? What would you say to that, *your royal highness*? Would you lie on your back for me in an attempt to give Samael more time for whatever he's planning?"

My stomach swam at the thought. I took a deep breath, and he cursed, turning away.

"I apologize. I would never demand such a thing."

I remained silent, and he sighed, running his hand through his hair. "I was Samael's friend once."

I blinked. Of all the things I'd expected him to say, that certainly hadn't been it. "You must have been young."

He nodded. "I was a small boy. We were both just boys. We... played together."

His hands fisted, and his voice was hoarse as he turned to face me once more. "I could barely hold my practice sword. Samael's father gave me tips when I was finally big enough to swing it. His mother... she was so beautiful. And Alette?" he let out a rough laugh, his gaze steady on my face. "She followed us everywhere. She was pure innocence." He swallowed, and it was grief that creased the muscles next to his eyes. "My parents were part of the rebellion. They allowed Lucifer's people into the palace. They'd made sure to negotiate for places in his new court. My father was Samael's grandfather's second."

I froze. "Niyax."

"Of course, Samael would have told you." He dropped his gaze to the floor. "I was watching, you know. My father had insisted on it. He was convinced that I was soft, that I'd need to understand just how bloody war could be. He ordered me to stand in this room. At this window. So I could see him kill our *enemies*." He shook his head. "And you know what I saw?"

My lips were numb. "Your father killed his parents. His grandfather. Ordered Alette killed. The baby."

"Yes. And then Samael killed them all."

"You blame him for that?"

"No. But I find myself glad that he doesn't have that power anymore. That he can't wield it in the underworld. It takes centuries before a demon is powerful enough to use demon fire. Samael was the only exception. That power was the sole reason he survived, and if he could kill that many powerful demons as a child, I can't even imagine what he could do if that power returned.

"You believe Samael would simply kill Lucifer and be done?" Pischiel scoffed at me like I was a stupid child. "No. He'd kill anyone even remotely related to the rebellion that took his family from him. I can't blame him. I'd do the same thing."

I shook my head. "Samael's not like that."

The look he gave me was pitying. "You obviously

don't know him as well as you think you do."

"I know every inch of him. And I can tell you he wouldn't kill someone who was an innocent child that night. I wouldn't have fallen in love with a man who would do something like that. But Samael would certainly kill someone who threatened my life as an adult."

He gave me a faint smile. "And there you go. You truly believe you can convince the demon Lucifer named as his heir to turn on him?"

I shrugged, but every muscle in my body was tense as I watched him. "Do you even want the throne, Pischiel?"

One dark eyebrow rose as he angled his head. "Would you like me to tell you I'd give it all up for you, Danica? I'd be lying. You have no idea of the kind of things I've done to stay alive. To work my way up to a position of power."

"To honor your father's legacy?"

He stiffened. "Careful, witch."

"And there's the real Pischiel. About time we cut the shit."

His expression turned sulky, but I had a pretty good feeling he was playing with me. "And we're back to negotiations."

"How about this? Don't do anything to actively restrict my movements, don't tell Lucifer I have my memories back, and I'll convince Samael to spare your life."

He shook his head as if disappointed in me. "You truly believe it. You believe your lover can take Lucifer's throne."

"I know he can." Because we'd do it together. Pischiel

was silent and I shrugged. "Lucifer's a Machiavellian, overpowered demon with a penchant for turning his enemies to ash and an obsession with revenge. I have a little experience with a man just like that, and I know who I'm betting on. Do we have a deal?"

He studied my face. "Lucifer will find out. You're underestimating how loyal his people are to him. He has spies everywhere."

"I know. I just need a little time before he finds out."

"Fine. If Samael fails, perhaps I'll even be able to convince Lucifer to spare your life in return."

I shook my head at that. "He goes down, I go down with him."

A muscle ticked in Pischiel's jaw, but he nodded.

I took a deep breath, stalking toward the window. "How do I get Kyla and Keigan out of the dungeons?"

"You don't. Lucifer is the only one with the keys to the cells. He keeps them in his bedroom. Even if you freed your friends, you'd never get the cuffs off them. Your mage friend would have no powers, and the werewolf still wouldn't be able to shift. They'd be hunted and brought back before they made it to the palace gates."

I chewed on my lower lip. I couldn't just do nothing. There had to be some way…

"Watch for the maid," Pischiel muttered. "She's—"

"A spy. I know. I knew when she attempted to convince me to remove my bracelet." And yet I had my suspicions…

He smiled at that. "Whoever gave you that ugly thing is a force to be reckoned with. Gloria couldn't remove it. I couldn't remove it. And when Lucifer tried? It burned his hand."

I gaped at him, and his smile widened. For a moment, it was as if we were on the same team.

I shook that off. "You tried to make me remove it when I didn't have my memories."

Pischiel's shrug was elegant. "I follow orders, Danica. But now you're back. Whatever you do, don't take that ugly thing off."

He nodded at me and stalked out. I gazed down at where Samael's family's bodies had been displayed. Where his tiny sister had been murdered. I had to believe that everything we'd done so far had been for a reason. That we'd finally kill Lucifer and take his throne. I refused to believe anything different.

CHAPTER NINE

Samael

I stood in the conference room, surrounded by my people. This was the third briefing of the day, and I tamped down my impatience. Even I could see the toll this was taking on both the demons and the wolves as we prepared for war.

Meredith sat next to Vas, although she ignored him as if he were invisible. Vas, to his credit, didn't seem to mind. He'd insisted on the witch staying at the tower, and she, in turn, had insisted on attending every meeting. So far, she ran errands, got coffee, and chimed in with her thoughts when the discussion turned to strategy.

Steve pushed his chair away from the table and stood. As usual, his clothes were rumpled, although now it looked as if he had been sleeping in them for a week. He took his glasses off as I waited and wiped them on his shirt. Then he sighed, huffed a breath on them, and cleaned them once more.

He'd always been one of the few humans I could tolerate for longer than a handful of seconds, but today he was trying even *my* patience.

"Speak," I growled.

"We are monitoring almost every portal to the underworld. Each has a camera located nearby, so we can keep track of their comings and goings."

"I'm aware."

Steve slid his glasses on once more and Bael glanced at me, likely reading the impatience on my face. I would regret it if I killed this human, and more importantly, my little witch might never forgive me.

"Some of Lucifer's demons are crossing for just a few minutes at each time, staying close to the portal."

"Why are they crossing? What are they doing?" Bael asked.

Steve smiled. "There's no Wi-Fi in the underworld."

"So?"

"So each time they step through the portal, they use a laptop or phone."

Mammon angled his head. "Lucifer hasn't bonded to any demons in this realm, but that doesn't mean they're not sympathetic to his goals. While many in this country would consider Samael to be their true king, the world is much bigger than the United States. There are demons close to many portals across the globe."

Evie frowned. "So Lucifer needs a way to contact them. To rally them and prepare them for war. Why doesn't he use a black witch like we did with Hannah?"

"Communicating through realms is extremely difficult. Your witch allowed us to speak to three of our spies." Mammon said. "Lucifer will be attempting to convince thousands of demons to fight for him. In this, he's decided he may as well use human technology. One mass email or text at a time, and he can keep them updated, can send his propaganda."

Vas nodded. "Lucifer isn't stupid. He'll know Samael wants Danica back, and he has his own spies informing him that we're gathering our armies. So he's attempting to bolster his own. I bet he's promised them money, power, and territory in exchange for their loyalty."

"I may be able to help," Meredith said. Next to her, Vas went very still.

Steve frowned. "How?"

Vas clamped his hand around her arm. "Be careful, Mere."

Meredith looked at Vassago's phone. It immediately signaled a text.

He glanced at it. "You suck," he read and scowled. "Real mature."

Steve stared at her. "You just did that without a spell. You're a tech witch," Steve said, as if she'd revealed she was secretly a demigod.

Meredith nodded and Steve practically rubbed his hands together. Something clenched in my chest. If Danica were here, she would be glancing at me, her eyes laughing. Then she'd likely speak mind-to-mind, making some smart comment about a nerdy boner.

Meredith cleared her throat and then leveled Steve with a hard stare. "I'm going to need you to keep that quiet." She glanced around the room. "All of you."

Everyone nodded. Steve pushed his glasses back up his nose and gave her a dark frown, obviously offended. "I wouldn't work for Samael if I didn't know how to keep my mouth shut. Besides… if anyone found out…"

Vas tensed. "Explain."

"Well," Steve said. "Imagine you had someone who could hack into any network with magic. Then imagine how valuable they'd be to various criminal organizations around the world. They wouldn't all be terrorists—there are plenty of political regimes that consider us to be enemies too. The United States, I mean. Even a few of our allies would likely love to have access to every scrap of data we have."

Meredith looked like she wanted to sink into the floor. Vas looked like he was barely restraining himself from throwing her over his shoulder and stalking out of the room. After the numerous times he'd teased me and Danica, my little witch would have been extraordinarily entertained by this little interaction.

My voice was harsh as I pushed the thought away. "You want to disrupt their communications."

"Yeah," Steve said. "They're trying to organize supporters from this realm. If we can hack their system from afar, we can send a message of our own and then delete and block all contacts." He glanced at Meredith. "Is that something you could do?"

"Yes."

I ran it through in my head. Never had I imagined a war with Lucifer would include using human technology to disrupt his plans. My hands itched to pick up a sword and finally fight. But if I hadn't expected such a tactic, neither had Lucifer. Our army would already be hugely outnumbered. Anything we could do to prevent more from joining his side would help. And perhaps that message could convince some of them to fight under my banner instead.

"Make it happen," I ordered, turning to stalk toward the balcony. I wasn't going to enjoy my next meeting, but I knew enough about Gemma to be sure she would be offended if I sent one of my people to have this discussion with her.

I launched into the sky and made my way to Trinity Park.

The witch let me in, turning her back on me as she used her cane to hobble toward an armchair, where she sat and watched me out of narrowed eyes. "This is an unexpected visit," she said.

"Unexpected? You're aware of where Danica is."

She nodded. "Rumors of her capture reached even us. I'd like to say I was surprised, but few things surprise me about that girl. I always knew she'd meet a bad end."

I watched her. Whatever she saw on my face made her stiffen.

"If you've come here to ask for help with your little war, you've wasted your time. What interest is it of ours if Lucifer wipes you all out? Perhaps it will be an opportunity for the rest of us to finally demolish that monstrosity you call a tower after all these years."

"You know, I've always found it interesting—the insular nature of witches. How you cling to covens, most of you terrified by the idea of living your own lives, and yet you're quick to turn on each other whenever the chance arises."

"If this is about Evie—"

I slowly shook my head. "How powerful would the witches be if your covens were to actually unite?"

She frowned. "What business is that of yours?"

"I merely find it interesting that no witch in history has managed to unite all of the covens in a single city. While the High Coven rules over all of you, your individual covens are far less powerful than they could be. What a waste of potential. A witch who could achieve such a collaboration would make history. Perhaps even inspire a larger alliance across states, maybe even countries."

She leaned back, folding her hands in her lap. "You believe I don't know what you're doing?"

I smiled. "One doesn't need to be a seer to see your death, witch. I can smell it on you."

To her credit, she merely raised one eyebrow. "What of it?"

"Your coven can't keep you alive?"

She ran one wrinkled hand over the arm of her chair. "I do not wish for any further life-extending magic."

A choice I would never understand. The witch angled her head as if reading my mind. "Where is the meaning in living for eternity?"

"You exaggerate, witch. You haven't even lived for a century yet. Although," I mused, taking in her wrinkled skin, hunched form, and deep scowl, "I am walking perfection. I can understand why *you* would prefer not to continue in your current condition."

It would take centuries before the first rays of time began to touch Danica's face. Before the skin around her eyes began to gently wrinkle. I found myself looking forward to pressing kisses to every one.

Beady eyes narrowed once more. "Did you come here solely to point out the shortness of my lifespan?"

"No. I came to give you a chance to be part of history.

Rally the Durham covens beneath your flag and help us take back my throne."

She gave a rough chortle. "You truly believe we care about demon infighting?"

"What do you think Lucifer will do once he has Danica's power and he can leave the underworld? Do you think he'll be content to stay in his own realm? Or do you think he will try to take my tower and turn this city into his own personal hellscape? Do you believe he will allow your covens to enjoy their freedom?" I gave her a cold smile. "Lucifer enjoys black witches for what they can do for him. Even the occasional gray witch may survive. But *white* witches?" I tutted as I shook my head. "He won't even think twice about killing you all. Will that be your legacy to your coven, witch?"

Gemma slowly got to her feet. "You created the mess—you and the rest of those hellspawn. And you expect us to help you clean it up? Get out of my house."

"Do not ask for our help when his people come for yours," I purred. "I will make it clear to every single demon I call my own. Even if I fall, no demons are to help the white witches. Your decision will have consequences, and never shall your people be protected by my own."

I turned and walked toward the door, keeping my steps measured.

I warned them, little witch. As you asked me to.

Another elderly witch sat near the door. In her hands, she held a photo of Caroline—the witch who had been responsible for the murders of the coven just months ago. She seemed lost in thought as she stroked the photo, but she glanced up as I approached.

"The city will burn," Gail croaked out.

"Yes." I opened the door and strode out into the sun.

Danica

The next night, I crept down to the dungeons once more. Keigan's eyes widened as I appeared in front of him, wiping my ring on my shirt before slipping it back onto my finger.

"How is she?" I asked.

Keigan shook his head, taking the bread and cheese I slipped between his bars. "She howls. All night. Sometimes she slams her body into the bars. I think she's gone, Danica."

I refused to believe it. I opened my mouth, and Keigan's eyes widened as he focused on something behind me. He fell away from the bars, landing on his ass as he scrambled toward the back wall of his cell.

I turned, striking out with my fist, but it was too late.

"Treachery," Lucifer hissed in my ear.

My lungs locked up, my knees went weak, and the world spun drunkenly around me.

Lucifer's hand twisted in my hair, pulling until my eyes burned. I dug my nails into his hand in an effort to make him release me. He ignored me, pushing me to my knees.

"How long have you had your memories, granddaughter? How long have you played me for a fool?"

I stayed silent, unable to speak as terror clawed into

me, my vision dimming at the edges. He could kill me right now. I wouldn't be surprised if he did.

Lucifer twisted his hand further.

"Not talking? I can *make* you talk. Since you seem to enjoy attempting to make me look like a fool, I believe I'd even enjoy it."

In spite of my terror, I had to be smart. Lucifer respected strength, even when it pissed him off.

"That doesn't surprise me."

"How did you sneak down here, while you are being watched by some of my most loyal, powerful people?"

"None of your business."

"I gave you everything," he said conversationally, ignoring me. "I made you princess of the underworld, and yet you still insisted on spending your time with the rabble. Would you prefer a cell down here next to them, granddaughter?"

"No." As much as I wanted to be with Kyla and Keigan, I knew I couldn't help them if I was locked up beside them.

Lucifer was silent for a long moment. Then he crouched beside me, his cold gaze on Keigan. His hand remained buried in my hair.

"I've had this mage watched for a long, long time," he purred. "And do you know what I learned?"

"Let go of me."

He shook his hand in my hair, and my eyes watered at the pain.

"Focus when I'm speaking to you. What do you think I learned, granddaughter?"

I clamped my mouth shut.

He gave a low laugh. That laugh sounded a lot like my death. "Not planning to cooperate? You get that from your father."

I went still, but Lucifer was still talking. "Why don't you tell her, mage?"

Keigan stayed silent.

Lucifer wrapped his other hand around my throat. "Speak, or I'll hurt her. I can always have her healed later. If it pleases me to do so."

Keigan's eyes met mine. He looked like he was already mourning our relationship. "I—" he glanced up at Lucifer. "Please."

What the hell could be bad enough that Keigan would beg *Lucifer* for mercy?

"Do you *want* to watch her bleed?"

Keigan swallowed. Then he looked back at me, his expression guarded. "I was twenty-five years old when a man I considered one of my closest friends told me he had a dream for the future. For… humanity."

Oh god. I had a pretty good feeling I didn't want to hear about that dream. Keigan's hands clutched the bars between us and with a shuddery breath, he met my eyes.

"You have to understand, at first I thought we had the same dreams. A better world. A chance for humans to share in this magical DNA. To figure out where this DNA came from, and if it could be replicated, so that humans could be born with similar powers. It was an opportunity to even the playing field. To allow our species to take the next step forward."

My lips went numb. "You were part of the lab. The lab where my mom was held prisoner. Where Evie was born."

He nodded, dropping his gaze. "It was called HFE. Humans for Equality. It wasn't until your mother escaped that I learned the truth. The women never understood what they were signing up for when they agreed to the experiments. Some of them were stolen off the street. Some, like your mother, were lured close so they could be kidnapped. Then I learned just how valuable those babies were."

Lucifer's hand had loosened slightly in my hair, but it tightened once more as I clutched at the bars myself. "You had to have suspected."

He shook his head. "I thought we were doing the right thing. When I realized I was wrong, I left HFE. I joined the Mage Council instead, certain that the council was the only way to truly stand for humans. HFE let me leave. But only if I continued to gather information for them."

"You mean spy for them. You were passing on everything Albert did."

He nodded, finally meeting my gaze once more. "Then I learned of your mother's death. I thought she'd escaped, you see. I didn't know why she'd come back to Durham. But HFE… they told me I had to kill anyone who could lead to their discovery. Otherwise, they would release information that proved I'd been part of the kidnapping and murder of both humans and paranormals…"

And he'd be hunted by *every faction.*

His voice trailed off, and Lucifer leaned closer. Just that simple move was pure threat. Keigan glanced up at him and the remaining color drained from his face.

"At first, there was nothing to be done. HFE had covered their tracks. At least, until you stole the Dagger of Truth and found a lead. By then I'd gotten to know you. I knew your sister had been born in that lab. And even knowing that you could be my ruin, I couldn't kill you. You were getting too close when you questioned the lesser demon, and especially once you prepared to question Vercan. Both of them had to die. But I could never shoot you."

Somehow I'd forgotten that before Keigan was a Discipulus Mage, he'd done his time on the streets as well. And he was known for his skill with a crossbow.

I'd continually wondered why I hadn't been killed while the only leads I'd ever had were shot with rowan. It had made no sense not to kill me when I was getting close.

Unless you were someone I trusted, and you had a guilty enough conscience that you wanted to keep me alive.

"You told me you needed to stay in the council to drive out the sickness within it. You were willing to let Samael *die* so you could 'do some good.' Was any of it the truth?"

"Yes. It's… complicated, Dani. Just as I became your friend, I also wanted to make the council better."

"Don't call me Dani."

I wanted to scream, cry, and vomit, all at the same time. Keigan must've seen it on my face, because he closed his eyes briefly, forcing them open when Lucifer removed his hand from my hair and stepped back.

I fell onto my ass, gazing past him to where Garadiel

stood.

"See?" Lucifer's smile was sharp. "This is the human you have risked my displeasure for."

I ignored that, and Lucifer tutted. "Look at me while I'm talking to you, granddaughter."

I ignored him some more. Looked like I still had some defiance left after all. Lucifer laughed, but the rage was obvious beneath it. Then he was pulling me to my feet and shoving me at Garadiel.

"Follow."

I didn't look at Keigan again. With no other choice, I followed Lucifer through the castle, noting the way the guards stood at attention. Word had gotten around that the boss was up. There would be no drinking, gambling, or whoring tonight.

I had a pretty good feeling Lucifer knew every single thing that went on in his palace. If he allowed the guards such liberties, it was because it benefited him in some way.

Lucifer led us through the throne room and my gaze slid to the wall above his throne. The gold letters shifted and blurred.

Lucifer continued walking toward the narrow door to the left of his throne. I'd wondered where the door led, and I shivered at the thought of what could be behind it. At my back, Garadiel was a threatening presence. There would be no escape.

Lucifer opened the door. Garadiel poked me in the back, and I threw him a dirty look. With a deep, steadying breath, I followed Lucifer inside.

CHAPTER TEN

Danica

I don't know what I'd expected, but this wasn't it. Behind me, Garadiel went still, but Lucifer didn't seem to notice as he stalked across the empty room and to the glass case which displayed the scroll.

"Come, granddaughter," Lucifer said. "Come and meet your fate."

It was always drama with this guy.

Garadiel poked me in the back again, and I managed to restrain myself from snarling at him. Lucifer obviously wanted to put on a show, so I followed him over to the glass case, leaning over it.

"It's in demonish. I can't read it."

"Your lack of education is an insult."

Blah blah blah.

Lucifer turned back to the scroll and read.

"The Nephilim Prophecy."

That's what this was about? I'd already read the prophecy, but Lucifer obviously wanted to do his song and dance, so who was I to stop him?

"When the Morning Star goes to war with the Nephilim of his bloodline, only one shall survive,"

Lucifer intoned.

But then he kept reading.

"On the night of a hundred thousand stars, the Morning Star will drink of its bloodline, until even kings will bow to greatness."

I went very still. Lucifer's eyes had taken on a crazed light as he turned back to me.

"We're not at war, granddaughter. You're in my home, and will bond with my heir. You'll be loyal to *me*, and I will reward that loyalty by not killing the mongrel in my dungeons. By not sending my people to slaughter your sister."

I met his eyes. He now looked almost bored. "You have two choices. You will either submit and give me your powers on the night of one hundred thousand stars, and take Pischiel as your bondmate, or I will take your power by force and slaughter you directly after."

"Why even give me a choice?"

"My people have been pleased to have their princess back where they can see her. They enjoy that you were taken from Samael and look forward to seeing you bond with the demon I have chosen as my heir. There are bets on when you will have the ceremony, which color dress you will wear, even the sex of your first child." Lucifer looked hopelessly amused at the thought.

It was good PR. That was what it came down to. Lucifer didn't care one way or another whether I lived, but if I did happen to stick around, he'd keep me powerless, prance me around in uncomfortable dresses, and ensure Pischiel was keeping an eye on me at every turn.

"Wow, you must be really desperate at this point,

huh?"

Lucifer went still, his expression warning me not to continue. "What, exactly, do you mean by that?"

"Sounds like popular opinion is swaying toward Samael. Loyalty is hard to hold on to when you're a blood-crazed despot. So, you figure you can keep me around long enough to kill him and retain your tenuous grip on power."

"Tenuous?" He laughed, his hand lashing out to grab my wrist. He pulled me to my feet and dragged me back through the throne room, the guards jumping into action to open the balcony doors for him.

Fresh air hit my face, and within a moment, Lucifer had snatched me into his arms, his wings unfurling. We rose above the palace, and I held on for dear life, terror making my head spin. If he dropped me now, I'd be impaled by one of the pointed turrets.

Lucifer soared through the air, and I breathed through my mouth as my stomach swam. I was used to flying with Samael, but I trusted *him* not to suddenly drop me. Within a few minutes. we left the green fields surrounding the palace behind.

"Where are you taking me?"

Lucifer ignored that, clearly deep in thought. I had a feeling he was contemplating my death, anyway, weighing up whether it was worth keeping me around.

We flew over a town, then a few minutes later a larger city, the spires of the temples below us glowing in the sunrise. Demons flew through the air, using some kind of traffic system known only to them. All of them darted out of the way as Lucifer approached, and I dropped my gaze to the buildings below us. Narrow alleys, bustling streets, courtyards packed with vendors selling their wares.

And in the distance, to the west, emerald meadows stretched out until they met a chain of mountains, the peaks jutting high into the sky.

If the metal cuff around my wrist hadn't prevented me from talking to Samael, I would've told him just how beautiful his realm was.

Of course, Lucifer didn't head toward the meadows. Or toward the scent of salt in the air, which told me we were approaching an ocean.

No, he turned east, and the entrancing scenery below us... *changed.*

The grass turned yellow and dry. Then it disappeared completely, revealing nothing but mud and dust.

He continued to fly for another five minutes or so, and ugly wooden buildings appeared below us, caged by tall fences with barbed wire, guards stationed every twenty feet or so.

People shuffled along, one after the other, moving away from the entrance of the... mine. This was a mine. All of the people here wore metal around their wrists. Just like the prisoners who were currently rotting in Lucifer's dungeon. And most of them had nothing but stubs where their wings had once been.

Demon wings were made up of feathers, tendons, and muscles. Having them removed must be like losing an arm or a leg. Bile flooded my mouth.

It was dark, and from what I could see, most of the prisoners were walking toward the buildings where they must sleep. But ten or fifteen of them had been lined up near the entrance to the facility, all of them still had their wings.

There was no need to have anyone enter this mine and physically take whatever they were looking for. Some of Samael's more powerful demons likely had enough power to level this mountain, to cut it open and remove whatever they wanted without ever lifting a finger.

I bet that made it worse for the people trapped here. To know that each day they slaved was all for nothing. Their suffering was entirely pointless.

Well, Lucifer had a point he was making.

"I had this mine created soon after I took my throne," Lucifer spoke as if he was *proud*, and I wanted to throat-punch him. "Those who disobeyed, who chose not to kneel, who retained their allegiance to Samael, well," he said jovially, "death was too easy. One thing you'll learn in my court is that there are many things to fear more than death."

"These people aren't even real criminals?"

Lucifer's fingers dug painfully into my hip and shoulder where he held me. "Anyone who conspires against the underking is a criminal. You should keep that in mind next time you decide to disobey me."

Lucifer lowered us slightly until we were closer to the demons who were waiting by the entrance to the facility. All of them were shackled, and while some appeared scared, most of their faces were defiant. A handful of guards surrounded them, watching their every move.

"New arrivals," Lucifer chuckled. "Oh," he said conversationally, "we have a teaching moment. Watch, granddaughter. Watch and learn what happens when people defy me."

He fell silent as a demon was dragged out of the line. The demon's expression was tight, but he showed no fear as the guards pulled him toward a wooden block. He was then shoved over the block, several of the guards pulling his wings out from where he'd tucked them against his back. He fought them, kicking and headbutting, until one of the guards stabbed him in the stomach.

Not a killing blow, but it'd hurt him to heal, especially in this condition. I flinched, and Lucifer laughed. One of the guards raised his sword, holding it up in the air, playing to the crowd. I memorized his face.

"They grow back, you know," Lucifer said, as if we were gossiping over coffee, "and this little exercise has to be repeated. Often."

Bile crept up my throat, but I refused to allow Lucifer to see how this was affecting me. Below us, the guard sliced through the demon's first wing, and he screamed, raising his gaze as if imploring the gods for mercy.

These were people. People who had done nothing wrong.

My people.

For the first time, I had an inkling of understanding. I knew now why Samael continually seethed with a low-level fury, why he was so committed to his vengeance. These people were ours. Not to rule, not to pander to us, but for us to help. To free.

My hands shook, and fury speared into my gut. This place would be pure hell for creatures who were used to taking to the skies and spreading their wings.

Innocent people. People who hadn't done anything

except fight for what was right.

I rolled my shoulders. Lucifer thought bringing me here would make me afraid. Would make me bend to him. But what he'd really done was light a fire under my ass.

Below us, the demon's eyes met mine. His eyes narrowed, and then he was screaming once more as the guard's sword flashed through the air, cleaving through his second wing.

Lucifer turned, flying low and slow over the mine to ensure I saw every inch of the horror below us.

Sickness churned through my stomach. But I kept my expression carefully neutral. When someone wants to show you how twisted they are, the worst thing you can do is react.

Lucifer's grip tightened around me once more, his fingers digging in like talons. Grandfather was pissed because I hadn't given him enough of a reaction.

He'd get my reaction. Oh yes, he would. When he least expected it.

Because sometimes, in order to defeat a monster, you need to become one yourself.

Danica

Samael held me tight, wrapping me in his arms. I breathed in his scent, wishing more than anything that we could have just a few minutes together outside of our dreams.

"It was horrible," I admitted, the tears I hadn't let

Lucifer see dripping down my cheeks. "Thousands of them, Samael. And they're all people who opposed him in some way. People who were likely loyal to you."

He tensed. "And what has that loyalty gotten them? I've been in your realm while my people have been suffering."

"You needed the Black Books," I reminded him.

He shrugged, wiping the tears away from my face. "And now I have the books, but he has you, and my people continue to suffer." He cleared his throat. "My spies have never told me about this mine. Lucifer must be using his power to cloak it."

The look on his face tugged at my insides. This was the most disheartened I'd ever heard Samael sound. "When you take your throne back, you'll set them free," I murmured.

I rose up on tiptoes and buried my hand in his hair, encouraging him to lower his head so I could kiss him.

Heat curled in my stomach as his mouth caressed mine. Slowly. Gently. As if we had all the time in the world. I forced myself to pull away.

"We need to talk," I said.

He nodded, and we were suddenly sitting across from each other on the armchairs, a low coffee table between us. I smiled. Samael was attempting to keep his hands off me, at least long enough for us to talk strategy.

"I know why Lucifer is keeping me alive. Turns out there's more to the prophecy than I'd thought. I don't know why there was only a small part of it in that fae library."

I filled him in. Samael went incredibly still.

He hadn't known about it either.

"How come Lucifer has more of the prophecy?"

Maybe there was more to come. Worse things.

"Lucifer has long had access to the best seers in all the realms. I'm not surprised by it, but it adds a new level of danger for you."

He got to his feet and pulled me into his arms. Behind him, his armchair turned into a long couch, and I smiled. He was obviously done attempting to keep his hands to himself.

We lay down on the couch, and I shivered at the look on Samael's face.

"Can he do that? Take my power?"

"Yes. Such things are difficult to do and can only happen during certain periods of time."

"What is the night of a hundred thousand stars?"

"It's a celestial event. A meteor shower. It will begin several days before it peaks, until the sky seems to burn with meteors that look like falling stars. A hundred thousand of them."

I swallowed. "How do you know this?"

"When I was a small child, my grandfather told me stories about how he watched the stars when he was young. He said the sight stole the breath from his lungs."

Samael's voice turned cold. "I hadn't thought to keep track, but if my calculations are correct, the peak of the shower is nine days from now, give or take a few hours. Your time."

I was shaking, I realized, and Samael pulled me even closer, running his hand up and down my back. The thought of Lucifer sucking out my power, of making me his puppet... I'd prefer death.

"Danica?" Samael sat up, catching my chin in his hand. From the look on his face, he'd been attempting to get my attention for a while.

"We will be there before the meteor shower peaks. We will have the pocket realm, the dragons, and Finvarra's forces in place. Lucifer won't have a chance to take your power because he will be dead before that happens."

I shivered. "If the worst happens..."

"Do not think like that. I swear to you, I will never allow him to make you his puppet. No matter what happens, I will never stop fighting for you. I will turn to dust before I leave you alone with him."

I raised my hand to his cheek and smiled. "I know. I love you. Now why don't you tell me whatever it is you're holding back?"

Samael's lips curved. "I can get nothing past you, can I?" he sounded pleased, and I winked at him.

"Nope. So spit it out.

He sighed. "The pocket realm we are bargaining for is unlike the seelie library where you first read the prophecy," Samael said. "That realm had an exit portal built into it."

My fingers went numb. "The pocket realm Taraghlan is giving you doesn't?"

"No. Someone on the outside must say the incantation in order for it to open. The portal will only open for a few minutes at a time."

So someone couldn't say the incantation, open the portal, and then hand the artifact over to be smuggled deep into enemy territory.

I took a deep, steadying breath. My skin felt so tight it was as if I would burst out of it at any moment.

"What's the incantation?"

He didn't wince, but I knew he came close. "*Mors vincit omnia.*"

I went very still. 'Death always wins?' Someone has a sick sense of humor. "What happens if the artifact attached to the realm is destroyed while you're inside?"

Samael's silence told me everything I needed to know. They'd have no warning, no way to get out of the portal if the incantation wasn't spoken on the other side. They would be trapped for eternity. All of them.

"It's too dangerous."

Samael stroked one finger down my cheek. "We have to work with the limitations we have."

"Those limitations could get you killed," I hissed. My eyes burned with frustrated tears I refused to let loose. I knew my demon. He hadn't survived centuries of attempted assassinations because he was stupid. If I hadn't ended up in the underworld, he never would have considered such a dangerous plan.

"I don't like the direction of your thoughts," he told me, and I scowled at him.

"I know damn well you can't read my thoughts."

"But I can feel the emotions caused by those thoughts. Every single one of our people will know the incantation, little witch. All of them will know that if something goes wrong, their priority is to get to the artifact and create the portal."

"But you'll be behind enemy lines."

He smiled at me. "Do you believe that could stop

Bael? Mammon? Any of my people?"

I studied his face. Samael was the biggest control freak I knew. I never could have imagined he would allow himself to be smuggled close to the palace in a pocket realm. And I knew damn well if I wasn't the one trapped in the palace, he would never have allowed such a thing.

I opened my mouth to tell him just that, and he shook his head at me, clearly determining my train of thought.

"I won't ask my people to do something I won't do. That's not how I lead. All we can do is take as many precautions as possible."

CHAPTER ELEVEN

Danica

Another day of fuckery. Oh goodie.

I stifled a yawn, and my corset dug uncomfortably into my ribs. Now that Gloria's spell had broken, Lucifer had declared I was *allowed* at court. And by that, he meant my attendance was mandatory.

It was easy to see why. Here, his subjects flinched each time he stood, bowed so low it seemed their heads would hit the ground when they approached his throne, and spoke in hushed voices.

Although, that didn't stop them from gossiping as though their lives depended on it.

According to Pischiel, Lucifer had originally figured that allowing me at court would make it difficult for the spell to contain my memories. Now, since I already had them back, it was a special way for him to torment me.

And it tormented me alright.

I knew plenty of demons. I *liked* plenty of demons. That was something I'd never thought I'd admit to, but Samael's people were my friends. Most of them were truly *good* at their core. Sure, plenty of them had slightly different ideas about morality than most people—especially when it came to humans—but they didn't torture and kill needlessly.

The demons here? I couldn't tell if they were the product of the rotten core at the center of this realm, or if they had always been evil. Many of them were the demons who'd remained after the portals opened and the people loyal to Samael had fled. And that meant that many of them were likely part of the insurgency that had cost Samael his throne and his family their lives.

I forced myself to ignore them, to pretend like their eyes weren't continually on me. Lucifer had made it clear that if I didn't play along and pretend to be a willing part of his court, he'd have no need to keep me around after taking my power.

I glanced from the overdressed demons to the throne where my grandfather sat. My stomach roiled at the content look on his face, and I shifted my gaze to the wall behind him instead.

Above the throne, those gold letters moved once more, making my eyes blur. First came Latin, quickly followed by English, as if ensuring I couldn't misunderstand. I shook my head at myself. The words continually shifted into different languages—obviously part of the magic of the palace, ensuring everyone in attendance could read them.

I couldn't help but watch as the words *do ut des* appeared. They made me shudder, and thanks to the education Edward had ensured I got while training under him, I knew what they meant even before the words shifted to English. *I give so that you might give.*

The words spoke of sacrifice, although I was sure Lucifer had never given a single bead of sweat for his people.

Pischiel followed my gaze from where he stood next to me. "What is it?"

"How long have those words been here? Did Lucifer create the spell?"

He shook his head. "Oh no. They've been part of this palace since it was originally built, thousands of years ago. His majesty would remove them if he could. He doesn't like anyone's attention on anything but himself in this throne room."

Pischiel's mouth dropped open as if he was surprised by his own words and he glanced around, obviously worried someone might have heard.

I grinned at him, but the smile dropped from my face as I considered what that meant.

The idea wasn't a new concept to me—it had been part of Roman civil law during classical times. But it had also been used when humans were sacrificing each other to the gods, hoping that those gods would show benevolence in return.

"Do the words mean the same in demonish?" I whispered, and Pischiel shrugged.

"I can't read your languages. But in demonish, they speak of sacrifice in exchange for power."

Sounded pretty similar.

"Are you well? You've gone white."

I shook my head. "Lucifer isn't going to just take my

power and be content, is he?"

Pischiel shifted uncomfortably on his feet. "He has always said that with your power, he won't need to rely on his pact with the underworld. His lifeforce will likely still be tied to it, but he'd be able to leave. He feels… disgust for humans. When he learned your father had joined with your mother, and that a child would result, he almost destroyed this palace."

"Because of the prophecy."

He raised one eyebrow. "What prophecy?"

"You haven't heard? I guess it makes sense that Lucifer would keep that as quiet as possible." I lowered my voice until it was barely a whisper. "When the Morning Star goes to war with the Nephilim of his bloodline, only one shall survive."

Now it was Pischiel's turn to pale. "Ah. That explains much."

"It gets worse. 'On the night of a hundred thousand stars, the Morning Star will drink of its bloodline, until even kings will bow to its greatness.'"

Pischiel's eyes sharpened. "The night of a hundred thousand stars."

"Yeah. It's pretty obvious which one of us would survive if the two of us warred." I held up my wrist, and his gaze dropped to the metal cuff around it. "He's already taken my powers."

"But he wouldn't have wanted to risk any threat," he murmured. "And if he takes your powers for himself, he can use you while preventing that war. He could hold you here forever, threatening to kill you if Samael retaliates."

"Yeah."

Pischiel glanced toward my grandfather. A servant was kneeling by his throne, holding up a cup of wine for him. He ignored her, watching as his subjects paired up to dance. Lucifer occasionally decided to turn nights at court into impromptu balls, and the music was ridiculously jaunty.

His eyes slammed into mine, and I bowed my head, waiting until I could feel his gaze move on before I raised it again.

When I turned my attention back to Pischiel, he looked more shaken than I'd ever seen him.

"I need some air," I said softly.

He nodded. I was allowed nowhere without an escort, and Pischiel was usually that escort. I was becoming more attuned to him, hoping I could sway him to our side.

At the same time, I found it difficult to believe my grandfather would *ever* remove his ass from that black throne. Sure, he may need to name an heir, but he'd been alive for centuries, and since I was apparently the only hope to kill him, he'd likely be alive for centuries longer.

But Pischiel hadn't known about the slaves in the mine. Oh, he'd known the mines existed, but he'd imagined the work was done by magic, or perhaps by the lesser demons. His expression had hardened when I'd described what I'd seen, but he'd finally shaken his head. "And what do you expect your grandfather to do when he's challenged, Danica? Do you believe he should allow his enemies to wage war against our realm?"

I'd merely raised one eyebrow as he'd turned and stalked out. Pischiel didn't like being left out of the loop, and he'd learned his king hadn't exactly been telling him everything. Yet he'd still defended him.

Maybe there *wasn't* any hope for him.

"We can get some air on the balcony," Pischiel said. He took my hand and led me through the crowd, and my breath caught as something in my chest began to ache.

"What's wrong?" he asked as soon as we stepped outside.

"Nothing."

"Danica…"

"I miss my bondmate," I snapped, careful to keep my voice down.

Every balcony I saw made me remember fighting with Samael, pouring out my heart to him, and being wrapped in his arms as he rose into the sky.

Pischiel merely nodded and turned his gaze to the distance. I stepped up beside him and we both looked down, past the gardens and the stone wall of the palace, and further into the night.

"Tell me about this," I pointed to the metal around my wrist.

Pischiel eyed me. "What do you want to know?"

"How do I remove it?"

"You can't. Only a spell with the underking's blood can remove it, or just the blood of the underking himself."

"What if you cut off the hand?"

He raised one eyebrow. "You're not full demon, princess. I don't think your hand would grow back."

I rolled my eyes. "Of course it won't." I thought about it for a little longer, and then I smiled. "Lucifer's blood runs through my veins." It was why I could get into the dungeons.

Pischiel closed his eyes as if he didn't know what to do with me. "You're not the ruler of the underworld. You may have his blood, but you'd need Lucifer's blood *and* a black witch."

"I know where I can get a black witch."

"And why would she betray Lucifer?"

"She's not an idiot. She made the wrong call and now she knows which way the tide is turning. She'll have her own spies in my world, and she'll know just how many allies Samael has. I know Gloria, and she'll decide to play both sides."

"And what exactly are you going to offer her?"

I scowled. It sucked, but sometimes you had to make sacrifices to get shit done. Unbidden, the words from above the throne flashed through my mind once more. *I give so that you might give.* Well, I was going to give Gloria the chance to play both sides, as she so loved to do. And she was going to give me what *I* needed.

"Danica?"

"Immunity," I sighed. "I'm going to offer her immunity."

Pischiel just shook his head. "You take that cuff off, and Lucifer will immediately know. I won't let you throw your life away to prove a point."

I rolled my eyes at him. "It's not for me."

I turned my gaze down to the garden, counting off the guards and memorizing their current locations.

Pischiel shifted on his feet. "Each time I think I know what you're planning, you do something different. If you're not taking the cuff off yourself, what *are* you doing?"

I frowned. "Right now? I'm making a mental SWOT analysis."

"Swot?"

"Strengths, weaknesses, opportunities, and threats. Spoiler alert: I'm the threat."

He heaved a sigh. "You're going to end up dead."

"Aw," I said. "It's nice that you care."

He scowled. In spite of everything, we'd become something that—if it wasn't for the fact that he was Lucifer's protégé—could almost be considered *friends.*

"You end up dead, and I'll be losing my head directly after," he snapped, but there was no real heat in it. "You take too many stupid risks, and if you're not careful, your bondmate won't have anyone left to come for."

"Pull yourself together, Pischiel. I know what I'm doing." I hoped. I gave him a long look, still half-convinced he would sell me out. "Just remember: Snitches get stitches."

He rolled his eyes and I turned, walking back into the throne room, where I almost collided with Garadiel. I gritted my teeth, attempting to dodge around him, and he moved to the side, blocking me once more.

I scowled at him. "Can I fucking help you?"

"I would be honored if you would dance with me, your royal highness."

I opened my mouth to tell him exactly what I thought of him, but I could feel Lucifer's eyes on me.

"Sure," I ground out, taking his hand. "I'd *love* to."

"You have been causing problems," he murmured as soon as we began the dance. Thanks to Gloria's little mind-rape, I could still remember the steps as if I'd done it a hundred times before. Because in the life she'd created for me, I had.

"I may have to dance with you, but I don't talk to narcs."

"Narcs?"

"You told Lucifer I had my memories back, you piece of shit."

A muscle ticked in his jaw. The guy was built like a rock—larger even than Samael and Bael. The bigger they are, the harder they fall.

"I did not."

I snorted. "You expect me to believe that?"

"You're desperate, your royal highness. And while I'm sure you have many redeeming qualities, none of them are even distantly related to *subtlety*. I had three guards come to me and report that you seemed to be acting strangely. I advised all of them not to say anything. Someone else must have told his majesty that you were suddenly yourself. I was merely on duty that night."

I sniffed. "Fine." I leaned close as if I was murmuring something flirtatious in his ear. "Have you seen the light and decided to join us?"

"No. I asked you to dance because I have a message for you."

"A message from who?"

He ignored that. "Your father is alive."

"I'm aware."

He angled his head. "You don't care."

"My father left my mother to raise me. He told her just how much danger she was in, and then he left. I don't feel the need to chat to him about my hopes and dreams."

Even if he *had* been tortured when he returned to his father…

That muscle twitched again, this time further up in his cheek.

"If you speak to him… I will consider what you proposed."

"Why do you care if I talk to him? Where is he?"

He merely watched me, expression inscrutable.

I sighed. "If I speak with him, I want your vow that you will join us." I could take some father-daughter time if it meant we gained an ally as important as Garadiel.

He thought about it for a long moment. "If your father agrees that this is the correct course of action, I will join with you."

That was more than I'd been expecting. "Fine. Where is the son of a bitch who abandoned me when I was still a fetus?"

Garadiel's lips tightened and he leaned close, his face dark with barely suppressed rage. "In the same place he has been for three of your decades, *your royal highness*. Hidden away in darkness."

Danica

I slipped the ring into my mouth, my heart pounding as I pressed my ear against my door. Then I slowly inserted the key to my quarters into the lock. The 'snick' made me flinch, the sound so loud it felt like a gunshot in the quiet room.

If there was a guard in the hall, I was screwed. But I'd memorized their route. I should have fifteen seconds to get from here to the stairs. From there, I'd just need to be quiet.

I removed my slippers, unwilling to risk scuffing the stone. The floor was cool under my bare feet, and I hauled my dress up above my knees, ensuring I wouldn't do something stupid like trip on it.

My father was alive.

And he hadn't just abandoned me and never come to see me. He'd been taken out of the picture and shoved in a cell. I might have walked right past him while I was invisible and never known it. He may even have heard Lucifer threatening Keigan. May have seen me begging Kyla to remember that she wasn't just a wolf.

My skin turned clammy. I didn't know what I was hoping for. That he was an asshole who deserved to be locked up? Or that he was a good guy that *didn't*?

I cracked the door open, peering through the gap. A bead of sweat slowly rolled down the back of my neck and I barely breathed.

Go.

Moving faster now, I pulled the door open wider and slipped through, before closing it soundlessly behind me.

My pulse thudded, but I forced myself to take the first step. I needed to haul ass if I was going to get to the stairs before the next guard walked down this hallway.

A shudder shook my body at the thought. Lucifer wasn't playing around. He'd found the entire process of stealing my memories *amusing*, but it was clear he was no longer entertained. My death would likely keep him engaged for at least a few minutes.

Don't think about that.

I wished I could talk to Samael. But it was only in dreams that I could hear his voice. Could bask in the feel of him.

I crept down the hall, barely breathing as I aimed for the stairs.

The thud of footsteps on stone. From behind me.

I froze. If I moved, I took the chance that I would make a sound. If I didn't move, the guard would walk into me within the next thirty seconds.

My heart pounded so loudly I was half-convinced the guard could hear it. I trembled but forced myself to keep walking, gritting my teeth as the side of my gown brushed the wall. But the guard's footsteps continued on with the same even thud, and I finally reached the stairs, letting out an almost silent breath.

The next part was easier. There were fewer guards on this level, and none in the servants' quarters. The fresh air caressed my face as I stepped outside, and I inhaled the night breeze before striding toward the metal door.

This would be the trickiest part. I cut my hand and waited, trembling as I watched for the guards. I'd planned every second of my movements between my room and the dungeon, but if one of them left his post early or decided he needed to take a leak, he would for sure notice the door opening by itself. And I remembered exactly what had happened last time Lucifer had caught me in his dungeon.

But we needed Garadiel.

Breathe.

I sucked in a deep breath and paused, but there was

no movement. Craning my head, I took in the windows above me. No curtains twitched. No guards stood poised to raise the alarm.

Go.

I hauled the door open, stepped through, and closed it silently behind me. Then I leaned over with my hands on my knees and panted, my whole body shaking.

No. I didn't have time for a breakdown.

I straightened and walked down the stairs. The cells were as quiet as usual, the silence broken only by the moans and groans of the prisoners. I strode straight past Keigan, who was lying on his side, curled into a ball.

I refused to pity him.

Kyla lifted her head as I approached her cell. I pulled the napkin full of the leftover meat from dinner out of my pocket and slipped my hand between the bars, placing it on the ground of her cell.

She ignored me, immediately falling on the meat. She was thin now, so thin her coat had turned dull, and there was no sign of intelligence in her eyes.

Oh God.

My throat tightened as I squinted in the dim light. I had no doubt that Lucifer was having her watched. If I managed to get the cuff off from around her neck and she changed back, he'd kill her for sure.

But maybe I could have a fake cuff made, so she could change just long enough to remember she was human for a few minutes. Then she could change back, but not be forced to remain as a wolf.

She lifted her head and showed me her teeth.

"I miss you," I whispered. "I'm going to get you out

of here."

An almost soundless growl was my only reply. She couldn't see me, but she would recognize my scent. Except she no longer seemed to care who I was.

I forced myself to keep moving. And I peered into every cell I passed, stalking through the dungeon, making my way down each row.

I searched again. And again. Had Garadiel sent me down here to amuse himself? He hadn't been all that clear when he'd murmured instructions to me while we'd finished up our dance.

I turned toward the stairs. And froze.

A door was built into the side of those stairs. The door Pischiel had said was for storage. I hadn't paid much attention to it before, because I'd always approached the stairs from the left corridor.

I tried the handle. Locked. I pried open the wound in my palm, ignoring the sharp pain. Then I pressed it to the door.

It swung open.

I didn't hesitate. This would be just like Lucifer, to lock his own son away from the rest of the prisoners, in absolute solitude. People went crazy when they were completely removed from society. Would my father even be sane?

It was so dark, I could barely see the steps in front of me. I gave my eyes a few moments to adjust, then pulled my gown higher, using my other hand to balance against the wall as I made my way down the cracked steps.

I counted them as I walked. Two hundred of them, becoming narrower as the staircase wound to the right.

Finally, the staircase ended, and my feet hit stone so cold, I could feel it through my slippers. Shivers racked my body.

If I extended both arms, I could touch the stone walls on either side of the narrow hall. Down the end of the hall, a single torch of demon fire danced, the light weak but welcome.

Eighteen steps, and I was standing in front of the cell.

I removed the ring from my mouth and stared into my father's eyes.

CHAPTER THIRTEEN

Danica

I snuck down to see my father twice more, spending hours with him. I told him about my life, and he listened intently, laughing at my childhood antics. He'd often clasp my hand, his eyes burning as he seemed to memorize my every word.

Tonight, I told him about Evie, Kyla, and even Keigan, although my voice broke when I told him how Keigan was involved with my mom's death.

Agates was quiet for a long time. Finally, he looked up, toward the cell where Keigan was held. "He was the closest thing you had to a father as an adult. I can hate what he did, but still feel gratitude for the way he was there for you. People aren't merely black or white, Danica. Even my father was once both."

"That's hard to believe."

"He loved my mother more than anything once. But he loved power more."

I went still. My father, so attuned to my every

movement, noticed.

"What is it?"

"I just… what if the same thing happens to Samael?"

Agates was silent for a long time. Then he sighed. "My mother was many things, but she wasn't a fighter. When my father began to choose the dark path, she withdrew. When someone you love begins to change like that, you have to ignore the instinct to pull away if you want to help them. You have to fight for them, no matter how much it hurts. Something tells me you're not the type to withdraw when Samael does something that displeases you," Agates' lips twitched, and I let out a choked laugh.

"No. No, I'd never let him become obsessed with power. Even in my realm, if power was all he wanted, he could have taken it all. But instead… he took just enough to keep his people safe and allow him to search for what he needed to take back his throne." Relief made my hands shake. "Samael's not interested in power for the sake of it."

"That's what I thought."

I chewed on my lower lip. Being so helpless, seeing the people who had suffered under Lucifer's rule… I now knew I would do anything to keep the people I loved alive. Anything. For a moment, my mind froze. And then it replayed all the times I had lost control of my power. The time I blew the Mage Council facility, the time I almost killed a defenseless griffin. The time I coldly threatened Mariam with war if she didn't do what I wanted.

It wasn't Samael who would be at risk of becoming an evil overlord. It was me.

Well, this was a disturbing and unwelcome revelation.

"Danica?"

I pushed the thought away. Samael and I would just have to work together to make sure neither of us ever lost sight of who we were. That was a problem for another day. We all had to survive this day first.

I gazed at my father. "I can't wait for you to meet Samael. Can't wait to get you out of here."

Agates smiled, but his eyes stayed serious. "You're more than I could have hoped for, Danica. Your mother would be proud."

I tucked my knees into my chest. "She always told me to stay away from the demons. A few weeks ago, I drowned when I was visiting the merfolk. And I saw Mom. She was still so beautiful. She told me it was okay that I was with Samael. That I was supposed to meet him."

"I hope I'll get to see her myself one day." His eyes were suddenly filled with so much longing, I had to look away.

That reminded me. "I better get back," I murmured. Even with my ring, I didn't dare spend too long on my visits down here. All it would take was one guard to be suspicious and to check my room, and I'd be in deep shit.

"I'll return soon."

"Look after yourself, daughter."

"You too."

I made my way back up the stairs and to the door. I'd brought Kyla meat earlier, and she hadn't bothered eating it while I was there. Instead, she'd let out a low warning growl from where she was lying in the back of her cage.

I took a deep breath of the fresh night air and froze.

My instincts drove me closer to the gardens which

backed onto the palace wall.

And that was when I saw her.

Gloria was sneaking *in* to the palace. Which meant she had left without permission.

I could use this.

Stalking toward her, I glanced around, but there were no guards in the area. Likely why the black witch had chosen this entrance.

I couldn't let her learn about my ring, so I took it out of my mouth and slipped it into my pocket. Gloria was so intent on ducking out of view of the guard, posted ten feet away on the wall, that it took her a few moments to notice me.

She jolted. I smiled.

"Out of bed at this hour?"

Her eyes narrowed. "And who will you tell, half-blood? Do you think your grandfather would be pleased to learn you were sneaking around at the same time?"

Someone wrapped their arm around my waist. I jumped, cursing inwardly. I'd been so focused on Gloria, I hadn't noticed Pischiel creeping up behind us.

"My, my, this looks a lot like treason," he grinned at Gloria, but I could feel the tension in the arm clamping me to his side.

Gloria's face slowly began to drain of color. "Danica also happened to be where she shouldn't be," she began, and Pischiel chuckled.

"No, she wasn't."

As much as Pischiel annoyed me, I couldn't deny that he could occasionally come in handy. I didn't know what kind of game he was playing, but I needed Gloria for my plan. I hadn't expected to find something to hold over her so quickly.

"You'd lie to your king?" Gloria had the audacity to pretend to be shocked by this.

I rolled my eyes. "Who do you think Lucifer will believe? The black witch who already betrayed her allies once, or his heir?"

Now she looked sick. I was small enough to enjoy it.

"What is it that you want from me, Danica?"

Your blood on the ground in front of me.

"It's funny," I murmured. "I'd planned to offer you immunity for when Samael gets here. It would've made me sick, of course, but I would've offered it to get what I want. This is much better. You don't *deserve* to dodge Samael's retaliation. You're now my bitch," I informed her. "Soon, I'll need a few specific spells. You'll help me with those spells, and we'll keep this little late-night meeting to ourselves."

A branch cracked, and we all froze. Even Pischiel was tense. If we were caught, it certainly wouldn't look good for him to be found chatting with me and the black witch.

"Decide," I hissed.

Gloria's eyes darted. "I won't do anything that will risk Lucifer discovering any treachery."

"He won't find out."

She hesitated, and a bead of sweat rolled down the back of my neck.

"I still want immunity."

I laughed. "That's just too precious."

Her eyes burned as she glowered at me. "Fine," she

gritted out.

"Nice doing business with you."

Pischiel and I turned, heading toward the well-lit path leading through the palace grounds. I glanced at him as a muscle ticked in his jaw. "The Spell of Three. I'm assuming Gloria placed one on herself while she was spelling the mages."

"Yes. Lucifer believed it was prudent given she was betraying Samael."

I waited, and Pischiel finally heaved a sigh. "Lucifer made her remove it the moment she arrived in the underworld."

My grandfather was no dummy, and he wasn't going to risk a Spell of Three hitting him if he lost his temper. That was good news for me, because chances were, I was going to have to kill the black witch at some point.

"Thanks."

"Don't mention it."

I opened my mouth and his arm squeezed tighter around me. If a guard happened to spot us, it would look like we were two lovers out for a stroll.

"I mean it, Danica."

"I appreciate it, that's all."

A muscle ticked in his cheek. "I may hate that witch enough to enjoy watching her squirm, but that doesn't mean I enjoy betraying my king. What spells are you going to use from her, Danica? You wouldn't be stupid enough to try to take that cuff off your wrist, would you?"

"Never you mind."

His scowl deepened. Oh, he didn't like that. "What the hell are you doing away from your rooms? Are you trying to end up dead?"

I shrugged and he let out a bitter laugh. "Fine. Don't tell me. It's a good reminder of whose side I'm on."

Fury burned low in my belly. "You chose that side again and again," I hissed. "And for some stupid reason, you refuse to see the light."

We walked down the hall in the servant's quarters, snarling at each other, and he let out a low growl as we both stalked up the back stairs.

"Reason? How about centuries of loyalty, Danica?"

"Loyalty to a tyrant!"

He merely shook his head. "I was left alone in this palace, my only relation an enemy of Lucifer's and on the other side of the underworld. Do you know what would've happened to me if Lucifer hadn't taken me in?"

I was done listening to this. I pulled away from him as we arrived at my door.

"Yeah," I said sweetly, unable to stop myself. "You might've grown up with a moral compass."

Turning, I opened my door and shut it in his face.

Danica

"Pass the water," Pischiel muttered.

I ground my teeth and lifted the jug, handing it to him.

Lucifer had ordered us to breakfast, along with Daimonion and his crew of assassins, as if we were one big, happy family.

Those three words were the first words Pischiel had spoken to me all morning. Agates had asked me to get Pischiel onto our side. Instead, I'd completely alienated him.

Good work, Danica. What's your next trick?

Namiros leered at me from across the long, rectangular table, and I fought the urge to flip him off. Paymon's seat was conspicuously empty. I didn't miss watching him sharpen his knives, the constant bulge in his pants making it clear he was fantasizing about doing something that would make me throw up.

Rumor had it, Paymon had been sent to pick off one of Samael's people. And he hadn't returned.

I barely suppressed a grin as I glanced at the empty seat. Next to me, Pischiel tensed. I turned my head to find Lucifer watching both of us with an inscrutable expression that didn't bode well.

"Lover's spat?" he smiled at us, cold and humorless.

"Just a misunderstanding," I said sunnily.

Lucifer narrowed his eyes at me. Daimonion murmured something at that moment, stealing my grandfather's focus, and some of the tension melted from my muscles.

Pischiel continued to ignore me, but that was just fine. I'd take a new tactic. There was no way I could charm him into seeing the light, but perhaps I could shame him into it.

Yeah, because shaming people into decisions always works out well.

I quashed that little voice in my head and stuffed a forkful of eggs in my mouth. Along with a variety of foods from my realm, the table practically groaned beneath delicacies from both fae realms, and, of course, various regions of the underworld.

Lucifer got to his feet, wiping his mouth with his napkin. He surveyed me one last time and then dropped his napkin on the table. I kept my face blank as I stared back at him.

We both knew why he did this. Why he forced me to eat with my enemies. Another little power play from a despot who thrived on them.

As if reading my mind, he smiled. Then he said something in a low voice to Daimonion before turning to walk away.

Pischiel got to his feet, too.

"I want to talk to you," I muttered.

"Yeah? Well, maybe you can't have everything you want." Pivoting, he stalked off.

That went well. Perhaps I *shouldn't* have implied he was morally bankrupt.

Garadiel met my gaze from where he sat next to Lucifer. I kept my face carefully blank, but his quick nod told me he'd gotten my note.

I took a deep breath and forced myself to finish eating.

I had things to do today. Not only was it time to get what I needed from Gloria, but I needed to smuggle more food to Kyla, who had now lost so much weight she looked like a shadow of herself.

Panic cut into my chest, scalpel-sharp. But I slowly lowered my fork and got to my feet, keeping my expression bored as I turned and headed in the direction of my rooms.

Before breakfast, I'd talked to Yusilin, chatting about inconsequential shit and steering the conversation until she'd casually informed me that Gloria occupied one of the towers at the back of the palace. I needed to duck into an empty room and use the ring before I snuck up to her rooms.

I meandered up the stairs and found a supply closet. A quick in and out, and I was on my way, creeping up several more flights of stairs until I'd found the narrow staircase leading to Gloria's tower.

I climbed the stairs and removed the ring, careful to keep it hidden from Gloria. She'd warded her door, and I scowled, everything in me longing for my power. I slammed my hand against the door, and after a long moment, it slowly creaked open.

"I'd like to say I'm surprised to see you, but I knew it wouldn't take you long to come to me for your blackmail." She dropped the ward.

"Is that what we're calling it?" I sniffed in feigned disinterest and stalked past her, raking my eyes over the circular stone rooms. It was quiet up here, and the scent of old blood and incense made me want to hurl.

"I need two spells." To start with.

Gloria narrowed her eyes at me. "If Lucifer learns of this—"

"He won't. If you're worried about this, just think about how displeased he'll be to learn you've been sneaking out. And I'm sure Pischiel could add on a few more infractions."

"You'd lie?"

"Like a fucking rug. Get to work."

She firmed her lips but bustled around, collecting ingredients. I watched her like a hawk. Pischiel had told me what to expect for these spells, but the fact was, I had to trust Gloria enough to use them.

I gave her a long, slow smile. "Just so you know, if you betray me with this, I'll kill you."

She glowered at me. "You wouldn't risk Lucifer's wrath."

"Do you really think I can't make it look like an accident? I'll ensure I'm having a meal with Lucifer while you die, begging for mercy. And I know you're no longer covered by your own Spell of Three."

Her face was a mask of fury. But she believed me. I could see it in her eyes. And yet, there was a hint of respect in them, too. I should've known Gloria would respond best to savage threats.

She got to work. I paced back and forth, picking over every part of my plans. I trusted Samael to do what he needed to do, and my father was trusting me to do what *I* needed to do.

"It's done."

Liquid sloshed in the large metal container as she handed it to me. I placed it on the ground and took the next spell, an unassuming white paperweight which she'd hexed with a spell that made me nauseous to think about. I placed it in my pocket.

"This is the incantation for your death spell. Speak it only when you're ready." She handed me a piece of paper and I slipped that in next to the paperweight.

"There's something else."

Gloria eyed me over the stone table.

"You wish to help the wolf."

"Yes. Are there any spells that can help her hold on to her humanity?"

She shook her head, and my heart sank, but I forced my voice to remain threatening. "If I find out that there is a spell, and Kyla can't come back from this, you're dead."

Gloria scowled at me. "Wolves are resistant to magic. You know that."

"I need you to *do something*."

I whirled and stalked toward the window, staring down at the forest below me. Gloria enjoyed an excellent view from the back of the palace up here in her tower.

I was engulfed in my fury, *seething* with it. And I was likely giving Gloria a delicious meal. It was that thought that forced me to take a deep breath, rolling my shoulders as I studied the green landscape below me.

I could imagine Kyla racing through that forest. I had to do whatever it took to ensure she would be okay.

"There is one thing. Difficult, but... it could perhaps buy her time."

"I'll do it."

Gloria sighed as if I was an impatient child. I bared my teeth at her.

"You must connect her to her Alpha. Right now, being separated from him by both the portals and the cuff around her paw is making it more difficult for her to hold on to her humanity. Wolves are notoriously difficult to enspell, but if you place this charm in her cell, it will open her mind while she is sleeping." Amusement flickered in her eyes. "Not that you would know anything about dream walking."

"If you have something to say, then say it."

"You may think you have me over a barrel, Danica, but never forget that I *chose* to help you this morning. And I know plenty of things about your own activities that Lucifer would love to learn. If I go down, you go down with me."

"Noted."

She shook her head, turning away to collect more ingredients, chanting until I heard a low 'pop' as the charm was complete. She'd attached it to what looked like a chicken bone, and I wrinkled my nose as I slipped it in my pocket.

Then I took a deep breath as I glanced down at the ring on my finger.

"One more thing."

Gloria squinted at me. "Nothing else. I'm not your witch to command, Danica Amana."

"Not even for the chance of a clean slate with Samael once this is all over?"

She studied me. "Speak."

I filled her in. Gloria shook her head. I begged, cajoled, and turned to horrific threats that made me nauseous to even speak them. Finally, she agreed that it could be done. I handed her the ring in my pocket. And she did what I wanted.

I turned back to the window while she gathered more ingredients, putting together the spell. Then I frowned. The wind was picking up outside, and I'd spotted something between the branches, just close enough to the castle for me to see.

I craned my head, squinting as I waited for the

branches to shift once more.

The edge of a wooden building. And I had a good feeling I knew what it held.

Had I imagined the dull roar that the wind carried back toward me as the trees shifted?

"Turn toward me and take your spell," Gloria ordered wearily.

I took a deep breath, steadying myself as she bespelled me. Then I took my ring back. The knowledge in Gloria's eyes told me she knew what it was, and why my plan had a chance of working. But it couldn't be helped. Hopefully, her natural instinct to stay alive would prevent her from betraying me within the next few days.

Five minutes later, I was striding out of the tower. I placed the ring back in my mouth and made my way back down to my rooms, where I shoved the metal container of liquid behind a group of long, formal dresses in my closet. The death spell went in the pocket of a black winter dress in the back of my closet, the charm for Kyla in the opposite pocket.

I'd have to find a better hiding place later, before the maids went snooping.

But first, I needed to show my face. Needed to be seen walking around the gardens or something, so Lucifer's spies wouldn't report me missing. Already, I'd had a suspicious absence of at least an hour.

Making my way downstairs, I kept an eye out for Pischiel. He was nowhere to be seen. I scowled. How was I supposed to shame him into being a good person if he wasn't accessible?

I found Garadiel monitoring the gardens. He nodded

at me, and I nodded back, heading toward our meeting spot.

"Where are you going?" Namiros hissed.

Where the fuck had he come from? His tone was insolent, and I ignored him, striding toward the closest exit to the gardens.

Namiros didn't like that. I could feel him practically breathing down my neck as he stalked closer, and I ground my teeth in an effort to stay calm as I passed one of the sitting rooms.

Strong hands shoved me without warning, pushing me into the empty room.

I hadn't expected Namiros to get physical, and I stumbled as I tripped over the long hem of my dress. He slammed the door behind him. Then he was on me with a speed that demonstrated just why he was one of Daimonion's men.

His hands slammed into my chest and the backs of my thighs hit the arm of one of the sofas as I tripped backward.

Either Namiros was out of his damn mind, or he'd decided Lucifer wouldn't mind if he played with me.

Adrenaline skipped my brain and arrived straight at my knuckles. I rolled off the sofa, launched myself at him, and plowed my fist into his face.

He cursed, cupped his nose, and I took my chance.

Namiros was a demon assassin, and I was weaponless and wearing a restrictive dress. I ducked out from between him and the sofa, sprinting toward the door. My best bet was to run like hell and draw as much attention as I could.

A hand burrowed into my hair and hauled me back.

I yelped, kicking out, but he easily dodged it, pushing me back onto the sofa. Cold rage burst through me.

I. Was. Sick. Of. This. Shit.

I *hated* this place. *Loathed* that I was forced to play nice with assassins who were trying to kill my friends. *Despised* being cut off from my power and stripped of my weapons.

I lowered my head and leapt off the sofa, charging him. The element of surprise was all I had, and my head hit his solar plexus, the breath leaving his lungs in a *whoosh.*

My hand closed over the dagger on his side.

His hand closed over mine.

My other elbow came up, and he slapped me across the face.

It was an open-handed slap, designed to piss me off. It succeeded.

I snarled, my elbow flying straight into his gut.

And Lucifer opened the door.

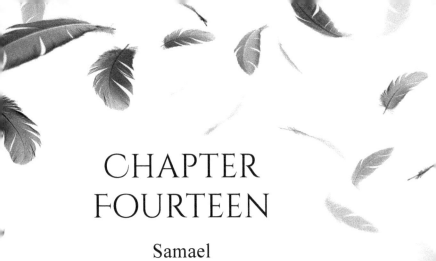

CHAPTER FOURTEEN

Samael

I walked into my bedroom, with some idea of taking Danica's sleep shirt and placing it on my own pillow in the guest room so I could breathe in the scent of her as I slept.

Pathetic. But necessary.

The griffin opened one eye and stared at me. He was large enough that he was sprawled across the entirety of the bed, although his nose was buried in Danica's sleep shirt, his head on her pillow.

I let out a low growl. "The pillow *and* the sleepshirt? As Danica would say, that is a dick move."

The griffin moved his nose away from the sleep shirt and gave me one regal nod. I leaned forward and snatched the sleep shirt, raising it to my nose.

"Smells like griffin," I snarled. My witchling's sweet scent was nowhere to be found. The griffin looked into my eyes, and I sighed.

"Keep it." I handed it back. Lia stalked into

the room, jumped onto the bed, and casually hissed at the griffin, who watched her curiously.

His tail moved, and the feline crouched, ready to leap.

"Don't eat the cat." I warned the griffin. "Danica would cry."

I left the room and made my way down to the conference room. It smelled of stale coffee and exhaustion. Everyone went working as I walked in, and my eyes met Nathaniel's. I raised one eyebrow as I passed the Alpha. "You look like shit."

He let out a low growl. "Ditto, demon."

Tobias stepped into the room, a large platter of sandwiches in his hand. "I think it's time for everyone to have a bite to eat," the butler said.

Nathaniel nodded at him. "Thank you." He picked up a sandwich and took a bite, and his wolves took that as a signal to help themselves.

Sitri's eyes widened. "This is delicious," he said, lifting the top piece of bread to contemplate the meat, cheese, and salad Tobias had put together. Bael took a bite as well, but instead of inspecting the contents of his sandwich, he was surveying Tobias. Nathaniel shot him a look, and Bael sent him a shit-eating grin straight back.

"I will not war with the wolves over their butler," I warned Bael.

He glanced at me. *"Of course not, boss. If I stole him, the wolves would never know."*

"You better be attempting to be amusing–"

Ag stepped into the room, and I instantly knew I wasn't going to like what he had to say.

"I have a message from Taraghlan," Ag announced.

The room turned silent. The pocket realm was due to be delivered today. If the seelie king was sending me a message instead of providing me with the pocket realm, something had gone wrong.

And his people were going to die.

"Speak." The word was more of a growl. Ag sent me one considering look that would have gotten anyone else killed.

"The bubaks knew Taraghlan's people were coming. They took the artifact and ran."

Cold rage spread its tendrils through every inch of my body. I had given the seelie king a chance to keep his word, a chance to choose the right side.

Our forces were due to be in the underworld days before the night of a hundred thousand stars. But this delay could mean my little witch was left to fend for herself.

No. I wouldn't allow that to happen.

"Ran. Where."

"We believe they headed to Alychia. One of the most dangerous regions of the seelie realm. Our spies believe the bubaks have been attempting to find a way to use the pocket realm to secretly breed so they can grow their people," Ag said. "All it would have taken was a single rumor that we wanted it."

The beast inside me, the one who had lost his mate, who had been ruthlessly collared by my determination to remain logical and in control...

It broke free.

I felt my wings extend. Heard Evie scream as one of them went through a wall. Saw Nathaniel leap toward her and cover her body with his.

Dimly, I was aware of Ag and Bael speaking in quiet voices, urging me to fight the need to slaughter anyone who kept me from my little witch.

They. Ran. From. Me.

My wings retracted with a snap as I strode out of the room and leapt off the balcony.

They put my bondmate further at risk. They *dared.*

My mind was filled with static as I flew toward the portal that led directly to the seelie realm. The edges of my vision narrowed until all I could see were the steps I would take to kill any who opposed me.

Taraghlan made a deal. It was up to him to take the artifact from his subjects.

And the fact that he hadn't been successful meant he was either incompetent, or was once again delaying and betraying me.

Neither would be tolerated.

A change in the wind made me glance over my shoulder. Ag. At my back, as always. His expression made it clear he was unimpressed by this move, and in spite of the situation, I had the strangest urge to laugh. I took a mental snapshot of his annoyed-yet-resolved expression to show Danica the next time she was asleep.

I was through the portal five minutes later, dodging the seelie guards five minutes after that.

Oh yes, they'd known I was coming. Behind me, Ag fought with a fury few realized he was capable of. Most people were used to seeing him rely on his strategic brain.

"You may wish to think this over," he called to me as we flew, dead fae littering the ground below us.

While I'd allowed Taraghlan to send his people, my spies had kept me updated. I knew exactly how to get to bubak territory. From there, I could reach Alychia by flight much faster than those desiccated scarecrows could by land.

Ag was still talking. I glanced over my shoulder at him. "There is no other choice. They chose to run. That means they chose bloodshed."

"If Taraghlan didn't betray you, slaughtering his subjects is a declaration of war."

"I won't kill all of them. Just any who attempt to keep that fucking artifact from me."

I was owed the artifact and the pocket realm it held. Taraghlan was the reason Danica was in the underworld in the first place. If he *hadn't* betrayed me, then he should have kept a closer eye on his people.

It took hours to fly toward the artifact, and I strained my wings, racing against time. Finally, in the distance, a sea of white came into view on the open plain below. I landed on a hill with Ag next to me, and we both took in the sight.

Here it was. The proof Taraghlan had circled around the truth. He may not be able to lie, but there were plenty of ways he could deceive when he needed to. One of his regiments was posted here, hundreds of them. And all of them blocked my way to the bubaks, who had likely already fled.

Any respect I'd had for Taraghlan as a ruler disappeared. He'd known I would come here, known I would slaughter any who prevented me from getting to my bondmate. And he'd chosen to throw his people away, obviously seeing them as nothing more than a distraction—a way to waste our time.

A muscle jerked in Ag's cheek. "We're going to need more of our people," he said. "We can't afford for both of us to be drained."

We stood in silence, watching the seelie go through their drills. Both of us knew what this meant. Killing the seelie and hunting the bubaks would take time.

Time Danica didn't have.

Danica

Lucifer's expression was darker than I had ever seen it.

He glanced at Namiros. The demon had backed away from me the moment the door opened, but it didn't change the fact that Lucifer had caught us literally at each other's throats.

Behind him, Pischiel stood in the doorway, his face ashen. From the look in his eyes, he fully expected to watch me die.

His hand wandered down toward the dagger at his side and I widened my eyes at him. If he attacked Lucifer, he'd die with me.

I swallowed, squaring my shoulders. Lucifer was still watching Namiros, clearly contemplating how much the demon was worth to him.

Namiros's expression was stone, but you'd have to be blind to miss the fear in his eyes.

"I need you," Lucifer finally said. "For now. But I don't need you to be able to fly."

He glanced at Namiros's wings, and they burst into flame. The smell of burning feathers hit first, followed by the acrid scent of burning flesh.

The demon ground his teeth, attempting to take it stoically. But unlike the slaves in Lucifer's mines, he obviously wasn't used to this kind of pain.

The screams started, and I shuddered, fighting not to slam my hands over my ears. Behind Lucifer, Pischiel sent me a warning look. I wanted to roll my eyes at him. It wasn't as if I could escape Lucifer's attention by being quiet. While my grandfather's eyes gleamed with interest as he watched Namiros's wings burn, I had no doubt he was aware of my every move.

The demon hit the ground, passing out. Disgust gleamed in Lucifer's eyes. "Weak," he said. Then he looked at me.

"Bring me the black witch," he said, and Pischiel turned, relaying Lucifer's orders.

We stood and stared at each other as we waited. I refused to give him the satisfaction of seeing my terror.

A hint of a smile curved his mouth. "Why do I have a feeling you wouldn't have screamed, granddaughter? It's a shame you don't have wings and I can't test out that little theory."

Ever since the first time I'd seen a demon, I'd longed for wings of my own. When I'd learned I was half demon, I'd been sad that I was missing whatever genes my father might have passed down.

This was the first time I was truly grateful that I

would never fly.

Gloria stepped into the room. Despite everything she'd done, a hint of pity twisted in my gut. She may be a traitorous black witch who'd betrayed us, but she looked like someone's grandma.

"Your majesty?" she croaked out. Her gaze flicked to me, and my heart pounded harder in my chest at the calculation in her eyes. My pity disappeared. Gloria was ready to try to save her own ass by telling Lucifer all about how she'd helped me.

"I tire of my granddaughter sneaking around. Take her memories once more. And make it hurt."

Oh shit.

There was no way I was getting past the door. But there was a window to my left. I could make it out within a few steps.

Lucifer must have made some kind of gesture, because a guard stepped past Pischiel, advancing on me.

I backtracked, but it was no use. Another guard entered the room, approaching from the left side of the room. Blocking any chance I'd had to use the window.

Strong hands clamped around my arm. My elbow shot into the guard's gut, and I was rewarded by a sharp inhale, but his hands merely tightened.

My eyes met Pischiel's. For the first time, I saw something that might've been sympathy within them.

It was too fucking late for that.

Gloria swallowed. "I will need time, your majesty. My powers… they are not infinite, and I reinforced the spell not long ago."

"And yet your reinforcement *failed.*" Lucifer's voice

was as warm as honey. Uh oh.

Gloria began to tremble. "The bond..." she murmured, "It provides too much protection. Maybe if I had more Lethe water... Or perhaps if I could sacrifice another child. Something young..."

I stiffened, and the guard squeezed my arm harder. Gloria must have seen her fate in Lucifer's eyes, because her expression turned ugly as she lifted her hand to point at me.

She was either about to curse me, or she was planning to tell Lucifer everything. And all my plans would be ruined.

My mind raced.

I could take the guard holding me. Stomp of my foot to his instep while my other hand slid down to his knife, tauntingly close to my right hand. Bury that knife in his gut and lunge toward Gloria.

Three steps.

I raised my right foot.

Then I froze.

Gloria was gasping. Blood slowly trickled down her neck and we all watched as the line spread across her throat, more blood pouring like a river from the wound.

I glanced at Lucifer. His eyes were shrewd as he watched Gloria die. He turned his head, and I shuddered as he examined me. There was no life in that gaze. He'd just slit her throat with a mere look. And he was considering slitting mine as well.

Gloria fell to the ground. Dead. Lucifer was still surveying me, and there was something alien behind his eyes. Kill me now, and he didn't have to worry about the prophecy. But then he'd miss out on my power and the leverage he currently had over Samael.

We both stared at each other. The room seemed to collectively hold its breath. Behind him, Pischiel had turned gray. I wanted to tell him to get his shit together— if Lucifer looked at him right now, he'd have no doubt that his heir was playing the kind of games Lucifer would have to kill him for.

I kept my face carefully blank as he stepped closer.

"You're incredibly lucky," he hissed, and the hair on the back of my neck stood up. "You're lucky I need you to attend the dinner for our guests tonight. And that they would notice if you were recently maimed." I shuddered at that, and he smiled. "You will laugh, and flirt, and make Nacheran believe that you will one day support Pischiel as he rules this realm. Or I will forget I need your power. And granddaughter?" he leaned forward, until his breath was hot on the side of my ear as he lowered his voice.

"I would never kill you quickly."

With that warning, he glanced at his guards. "My granddaughter is to remain in her room from now on. She may leave only when escorted, *after* I have given permission."

Lucifer turned and prowled out of the room.

CHAPTER FIFTEEN

Danica

I studied Nacheran as he ate at the other end of the table. The demon was quiet, his expression inscrutable as Hera talked inanely at him on his left. The concubine was wearing Samael's mom's bracelet again. *My* bracelet.

One more thing to do. I'd take it off her wrist even if it meant I had to cut off her hand.

"You've met my granddaughter?" Lucifer asked Nacheran, his voice almost jovial. It made bile claw its way up my throat.

Nacheran nodded, his eyes hard. "My information was that your granddaughter was bonded to Samael himself, Your Majesty."

"Incorrect," Lucifer said, the smile still on his face, although his eyes were filled with warning. "She was targeted by our enemies because they learned she was my family. Thankfully, our people were able to rescue her. Isn't that right, Danica?"

He'd ordered me to wear a dress with long sleeves, along with a pair of gloves. The gloves were hot and stuffy, but I didn't risk pissing him off tonight. He wanted to make sure Nacheran didn't spot the golden mark that told everyone I was already bonded.

I forced a grin, glancing at Lucifer as if he really was a sweet old grandpa. "Of course. And I've never been happier."

Nacheran didn't look convinced. I had to sell this, at least in the short term, or Lucifer may just lose his patience. I reached for Pischiel's hand and clasped it.

"You'll have to come to our bonding ceremony," I told Nacheran.

I was the only one who noticed the way Pischiel tensed in surprise, but he immediately grinned at Nacheran. "I've been considering taking a hunting trip before I'm a bonded man," he said. "I'll keep you updated."

Nacheran's eyes met mine. I smiled at him. He looked disconcerted. I'd sold it. My hand tightened around Pischiel's and I let go, reaching for my water goblet. Hopefully, no one noticed my hand shaking.

The meal seemed to take an eternity. Fourteen courses in total, one after another, and I beamed through all of them. By the time Lucifer got to his feet, waving his hand as he encouraged Nacheran's men to carry on without him, my head pounded with a vicious headache.

As soon as Lucifer left, I got to my feet.

"I think I'll turn in too." I dropped a kiss to Pischiel's forehead. "Goodnight, gentlemen."

For now.

As soon as I got back to my rooms, I dismissed the maids and grabbed the charm Gloria had given me for Kyla. There were more guards out tonight, and I tiptoed down to her cell, placing the charm between the bars in one corner, deep in the shadows.

She lifted her lip, showing sharp fangs, but didn't move from where she was lying.

"This should help," I whispered. "Open your mind to your Alpha, Kyla."

A growl ripped through her throat, and I turned, walking past Keigan's cell.

Our eyes met. He opened his mouth. I kept walking. My heart hurt even thinking about him, thinking about how he'd been part of that lab, how he'd worked for the people who'd killed my mom and then actively covered up her murder.

I returned to my room, took off the gloves, and paced, waiting for the meal to wind down. Finally, what had to be an hour later, I heard voices as a few of Nacheran's men made their way down the hall and past my door.

It was time.

I popped the ring in my mouth and cracked my door open, sliding out before anyone could notice. I followed the men down the hall, heart thudding. Nacheran rounded the corner behind me.

Fuck.

I plastered myself against the wall, watching him come closer. He came within touching distance and my mouth went dry. His nostrils flared, and he hesitated for a long moment. Finally, he kept moving.

I shadowed his steps. He opened the door to his own quarters, just a few doors down from my own. Lucifer had ensured he had one of the best guest rooms in the palace.

I followed him into the room, ducking under his arm.

He closed the door with a sigh.

"You may as well reveal yourself, your royal highness. I know you're here."

I spat out the ring. His eyes followed it with interest. "I've heard of that little trinket. I attempted to find it myself once."

"You wouldn't have found it. The seelie king had it."

"As much as I'd like to hear that story, I'm sure you're short on time."

I nodded. If we were found talking alone... my mouth went dry once more.

"I've heard rumors," I began slowly. "About your loyalties."

His gaze narrowed, expression turning disdainful.

"So your grandfather sent you in here to what? Sniff out where those loyalties lie? I'm surprised. Usually, Lucifer is much less obvious than this."

I took a deep breath, and then I rolled up my sleeve.

Nacheran's gaze dropped to my arm and then flicked back up to mine.

"You *are* bonded to Samael."

"Yes. My grandfather has quashed my powers with this cuff." I held up my other hand. "But that doesn't change anything. I speak for both Samael and my father, along with their people. Will you join us?"

He turned and paced to the windows, pulling the thick curtains closed. Then he gestured to the small sitting area near the fire. I sat on an antique sofa, and he stood in front of the unlit fire, hands on his hips as he regarded me.

"If Lucifer learns of this..."

"He won't."

"And Pischiel?"

"Pischiel knows where my loyalties lie," I said carefully. "He has done nothing to impede my plans. However, I won't mention that we have spoken."

He turned and paced. I let him think it through, attempting not to think about what would happen if we were discovered here. I kept my ring in the palm of my hand, ready to shove it in my mouth at any second.

"You're asking me to commit treason."

"Yes." There was no point sugar coating it. I was taking a risk even suggesting it to him, but Agates had assured me it was the right call.

"If your little plan fails, my people will be slaughtered. My land will be taken."

"Yes. But if it doesn't fail, your people will no longer live in fear."

"Everyone lives in fear. And there's little point exchanging the terror you know for one that could be worse."

It took me a moment, but then I understood. My mouth fell open. "You think Samael could be worse than *Lucifer?*"

He shook his head at me as if I was a young, naïve child. "I know that if my throne had been stolen, my family slaughtered, my palace invaded, and my people subjugated? My rage would be infinite. And then, after all that, if my bondmate had been taken?" The ghost of a smile curled his lips. "You're expecting logic where there may not be any left."

Desperation clawed at me, but I fought to keep my voice even. "What is it that you want?"

"If your plans fail, if Lucifer learns of the betrayal, and our collusion, I want what Samael has."

I frowned. "I'm not sure I'm following."

"An escape hatch for his people. I want territory in your realm."

I swallowed. Nacheran's eyes were grave. He wanted me to have more skin in the game. I blew out a breath.

"Samael rules most of the demons in our realm. His territory is… vast. There are other countries, continents. But you and your people would need to obey the laws of the land. No hunting humans. And you would need to answer to Samael."

My voice hitched on that last word, and this time, his smile was genuine. "You believe me unable to bow to your mate if my people were to flee to your realm."

I opened my mouth, and he shook his head at me. "If you fail, my people will die. We will play by your rules in order to have a safe haven. And if you somehow manage to take the throne back? All of us will bow to Samael's will."

I chewed on my lower lip. "So that's a yes?"

It felt unreal. All of this started because I had to make a deal with a demon. Now? The demons were making deals with me.

"Yes. We will go to war with you, your royal highness. I greatly hope you know what you're doing."

"Please call me Danica."

He shook his head, and I left it alone.

"Good doing business with you."

I made my way back to my room, where Pischiel was waiting. He glanced up as I opened my door, watching as I took the ring out of my mouth.

"You'll need to use the ring," he told me. "It's suspicious enough that I'm going for a late-night stroll near the stables. If anyone learns that you've been there…"

He shuddered, and I took a deep, steadying breath. "Maybe you shouldn't come."

A roll of his eyes and he was standing in front of me. The demon could move fast when he wanted. "We'll have to walk," he murmured. "It will draw less attention."

Danica

Half an hour later, I was gingerly picking my way through the forest, attempting not to make too much noise. From the annoyed look Pischiel shot in my direction, I wasn't being successful. I flipped him off, but it was less satisfying knowing he couldn't see it.

He wasn't being so icy to me tonight. I didn't fool myself into thinking he'd forgotten our argument, but we were both aware that this little jaunt was far more important.

"I haven't been here since I was young. Lucifer brought me to see the wyverns, but he warned me that they were bonded to him by blood. He's safe from their rage, but no one else is."

"Bonded how?"

"He feeds the females his blood while they're pregnant."

"Lovely."

Pischiel was more tense than I'd ever seen him as the building came into view.

"This can't be it." It looked like a large wooden shack. A shack the size of a football field, but a shack the same. There was no way those flimsy wooden walls could hold creatures who were rumored to be almost as deadly as their dragon cousins, even though they were much smaller.

"Just wait."

A sentry flew overhead, and we both froze. Pischiel seemed to melt into the forest around us, hidden by the shadows of the large oak next to him.

"Cool trick."

We waited for what felt like years, but was likely only a few minutes.

"Pischiel—"

"Shh. Wait."

He was right. A few minutes later, another sentry flew past, patrolling this area of the grounds.

"Come here," Pischiel hissed, and I grabbed onto his arm.

Since I was invisible, his hands fumbled, but he managed to lift me, staying low as he flew us just above the ground. Thanks to the way I'd grilled Vas as we flew, I knew how difficult it was to fly that low, especially while holding another person. By the time we landed a minute or so later, Pischiel was panting.

"I'm not that heavy," I muttered darkly around the ring in my mouth, and he choked out a laugh. We both ducked into the shadows of the building's entrance as another sentry flew past. Then Pischiel cracked open the door.

"No ward?"

He shook his head. "They need to be fed up to twelve times a day."

I stepped inside, my eyes adjusting to the dim light. And that's when I heard it.

Far, far below us. Screams, roars, and the sound of chains clanking on metal.

I was glad Pischiel couldn't see the way I'd begun to tremble. Then he held out his hand and my clammy palm met his.

The ghost of a smile crossed his face. "Frightened, princess?"

"Shut up and show me how to get down there."

The building was completely empty. Nothing but dust and muddy footprints on the floor, which proved that it wasn't an empty warehouse after all. Pischiel led me across the empty expanse and to a flimsy door.

The staircase was even more narrow than the one leading to the dungeon. If it was claustrophobic for me, it had to be hell for Pischiel, as his wings scraped the sides of the stone walls.

We traveled down, down, down, until I lost track of how long we'd been walking, and all I could focus on was putting one foot in front of the other and not falling into Pischiel as I navigated the narrow steps.

Finally, finally, we stopped at another door, and I removed the ring from my mouth. The sounds were louder now—so loud that Lucifer must have placed a suppression spell on the worst of the noise. Pischiel opened the door, and I gaped.

We stood on a platform, looking down at level upon level of caged wyverns. The cavern must have been at least a mile deep, and the wyverns all seemed to catch our scent at once, the roaring and screaming growing so loud it seemed to echo in my brain.

The wyverns' scales were dark. The light was so dim that I couldn't tell if they were entirely black, or if some were a midnight blue, others a dark green.

Unlike dragons, the wyverns only had two legs. But that wouldn't hold them back. When they took to the skies, they'd be sleek, fast, and deadly.

Thousands of them. There were thousands of wyverns in this place.

My heart thundered in my chest, and nausea swept over me, quick and all-encompassing. It took a few tries before I could speak, my mouth too dry to talk. "Can they communicate like the dragons?"

The blood had drained from Pischiel's face, and his eyes were bleak. He obviously hadn't expected this many either. "They're incredibly smart. Can take orders when they choose, or when they've been trained to. But if they can communicate, it's only with each other."

The wyverns closest to us tossed their heads. They strained, screaming out their rage and making their chains rattle. They couldn't stretch their wings, and being kept from the open sky had driven them into a killing rage.

Dread uncoiled from my gut and crept through my body. It froze each muscle, every nerve and sinew, until even my face was numb. Lucifer had enough wyverns to bring down thousands of our demons if they took to the skies. Enough wyverns to make us regret ever thinking we could win this war.

Enough wyverns to tear apart and *kill* everyone I loved.

And for the first time, I had no idea what to do.

CHAPTER SIXTEEN

Danica

I slept for long enough that I met Samael in my dreams.

"Something's wrong." I said as soon as I saw his face.

His jaw tightened. "The seelie king is playing with us. He may not be directly allied with Lucifer, but he wants us out of the picture for when he wages his own war on Finvarra. The artifact was a trap, the location of it a way to waste our time. We will fight the seelie he has stationed in the area and then we will slaughter the bubaks and take the artifact. We *will* get the pocket realm, little witch. But it will take time."

The expression on his face… he looked like someone had ripped his guts out and dropped them on the ground in front of him.

"It's okay, Samael."

"You don't understand."

"I do." I swallowed, my hand shaking as I lifted it to his jaw. "There's a chance you won't make it before Lucifer takes my powers."

I could feel his self-hatred down the bond. Could feel how much it was killing him that instead of our war being waged days before Lucifer could take my power…

"How close will it be?"

"Close. And the demons who fight for the artifact won't be fresh for the battle against Lucifer."

"Goddamn it. How is Lucifer constantly five steps ahead of us?"

Samael pulled me into his arms. "We're chipping away at his defenses too, little witch. Your friend Meredith has made it incredibly difficult for Lucifer to bolster his forces with demons from our realm."

I smiled at that. "She's an asskicker. I always knew that about her. I spoke to Nacheran."

Samael raised one eyebrow and I filled him in.

He grinned. "Do you know how long I've been working on swaying him to our side? You never cease to amaze me, witchling."

"I *am* pretty fucking awesome." My smile fell. "There's something else you need to know. Lucifer has wyverns. Thousands of them."

I filled Samael in on what I'd seen, the conditions the poor beasts had been kept in, the rage that had poured from each and every one of them.

By the time I was finished, his expression was grim.

"There had been rumors that he kept a stable of wyverns, but never would I have expected he had thousands of them."

"We can't lead our people into certain death," I said, and Samael cupped my cheek in his huge hand. He was so warm against me. I turned my head and nuzzled his palm.

"It's not quite that bad, little witch." He tucked my hair behind my ear, his eyes serious. "I don't want you to worry about this, Danica. You're doing enough where you are. Focus on anything you can do, any further alliances you can create to get out of the palace if it gets too close. If I'm not there in time."

I knew my demon. Knew how much it killed him to even think he wouldn't save me. Thankfully, I'd grown up saving myself.

I smiled at him. "It's going to be okay," I told him. "I'll see you in a few days. Right now, I need to go talk to my father."

I'd learned how to wake myself up from dreamwalking with Samael. It was a handy skill to have, but I wasn't looking forward to telling Agates that Lucifer had been quietly breeding thousands of wyverns all these years. Although he *would* be pleased to learn about our new alliance with Nacheran.

"Be careful," Samael brushed my hair back from my face, gently running his fingers down my cheek. "Look after my bondmate."

I winked at him. "Only if you look after mine."

I woke in my bed and immediately sat up, reaching for my robe. I would've given almost anything for a pair of comfortable pajamas, sweatpants, or even jeans.

The palace was silent as I popped the ring in my mouth and opened my door. But some long-buried instinct hissed a warning at me, and I froze, listening once more. But there were no footsteps, no voices, nothing.

I forced myself into action, my footsteps silent on the

stone floor. By the time I got down into the dungeon, my instincts were screaming at me.

I hesitated. Maybe I should come back tomorrow. But the thought of my father, alone in that cell...

I blew out a breath and began making my way down the two hundred stairs. At one point, I stumbled, my thighs jelly after all the stairs I'd climbed at the wyverns' stables.

The ring slipped dangerously close to my throat as I missed my footing, and I pulled it out of my mouth. If I swallowed it, I was in big trouble.

I trotted down the last few steps and breathed out a sigh of relief as I hit the ground.

My father's face was ashen. His mouth was open, neck straining, as he threw his head back and roared.

Roared silently.

Someone had created a silence ward. My gaze dropped to his hands, which had been shackled to the bars.

His eyes met mine. "Run," he said, and the world spun around me as the silence ward dropped.

"Oh," Lucifer said, and I began to shake. "It's far too late for that."

He appeared next to me, his power revealing him, along with Daimonion, several guards behind them. I kept my gaze on Lucifer.

He glanced at Daimonion, who leapt at me, clamped his arms around mine until I couldn't move. I could feel his pleasure as he watched this little scene play out.

"My son and my granddaughter, conspiring against me," Lucifer mused.

"We weren't conspiring," I snapped, my heart pounding so hard, I wondered how it was still in my chest.

"I just wanted to see him. To know him."

"If I'd wanted you to meet him, granddaughter, I would have invited him to court."

I swallowed. "Please—"

"Silence."

I was going to vomit.

"Danica."

My vision narrowed to my father's face. He refused to even look at Lucifer, his gaze on mine. "I'm so proud of you," he said.

Lucifer shifted next to me, and I glanced at him. I knew that expression. I choked out a breath. "Please, grandfather. I'll do *anything*."

"I had almost forgotten you were down here, Agates," Lucifer mused, ignoring me. "How… absentminded of me."

I shook my head, my breath sawing in and out of my lungs. There had to be some way to stop this. Some way to convince him.

"Danica," my father said again. He was looking at me with a mixture of pride and love and sadness. "You were the best thing that ever happened to me. And you were worth every second in this place."

A sob choked out of me, and my vision blurred. I blinked, desperate to see his face. To memorize every inch.

"Touching," Lucifer said, his voice bored.

I wanted to fold in two. To beg, to plead. But my father's gaze was steady on mine.

I'd thought I understood what torture was. Thought I'd seen it on earth, and then truly understood it when I was in Lucifer's court.

I hadn't had the first clue.

"I'd imagined you would learn your lesson within the first two decades, but you obviously have far too much of your mother's blood," Lucifer told Agates. "Goodbye, son."

"No," I screamed, my throat raw. My father's expression twisted as I bucked against Daimonion's hold, but I didn't have a chance against the assassin. "Dad, please," I gasped out, and Lucifer clicked his fingers.

Flames ripped up my father's body, engulfing his feet first. But his gaze was alight with pure love, his expression tender. He refused to show Lucifer an ounce of his pain, keeping his eyes on me the whole time. "Love you," he gasped out.

And then he was gone.

All sounds became a dull hum.

I couldn't feel my limbs.

My father clutching my hand, hope and wonder on his face as we had our first conversation.

His face when he talked about my mother, about how much he'd loved her.

The pride in his eyes when he looked at me.

Gone.

He was gone.

The sound of my heart pounding was all I could hear as numbness spread throughout my body.

The numbness broke, and I broke with it, screaming my rage.

Distantly, I was aware of Lucifer frowning at me, as if I was causing a scene. He stepped closer, and I ignored him, the entirety of my focus on the ashes in that cell. All that remained of my father's body.

I watched as if from a distance as I slammed my head back into Daimonion's face, shoved an elbow into his gut. His dagger was in my hand before I was aware of it, and I snarled as I thrust it into his stomach.

He grunted. Surprise lit up his face. But the dagger disappeared, stolen by Lucifer's power as he pulled me away.

"I hope you learned your lesson," he smiled down at me.

"I'm going to enjoy it," I said, my lips numb.

"You're going to enjoy what, granddaughter?"

I met his eyes. "I'm going to enjoy it when I kill you."

It was the first time I'd seen surprise in his eyes, although it was quickly followed by his usual bored amusement. But I'd caught the glimmer of disquiet.

His hand swung toward my face, and everything went black.

Samael

Bodies lay strewn on the ground. Lilith rampaged across the battlefield, and I let out a low growl as her hand lit up with demon fire.

"No powers," I let my voice carry over the grassy plain and watched as that power winked out, and she threw a knife instead, the seelie who'd attempted to cut her down, falling to his knees. He choked, blood pouring from his throat, and Lilith glanced at me over her shoulder and winked.

I sighed, swinging my sword and beheading a seelie who lunged at me. My power itched to break free, and I ruthlessly tamped it down. I needed to save every drop of it for our battle. We all did.

Even though I would be powerless when I first arrived in the underworld, I had no plans to stay that way.

Our wards, however, were necessary. I gave another seelie a sharp smile as he threw his power toward me, only for it to hit my ward. It dented that ward, and I absently shored that section up, striding toward the seelie, who paled.

His king had left him here to die. He'd known his people didn't stand a chance, but every minute we spent in this part of his realm was delaying us. While my people weren't actively using their powers to fight, shielding still took energy, still drained them.

Fury scorched my insides. Whatever the seelie saw on my face made him shudder, and he took a step back.

"We surrender," he yelled, and I angled my head.

"Weapons down," I ordered all demons in the vicinity.

A few of them kept fighting, because a few of the seelie hadn't heard their order.

Vas gutted a seelie who'd attempted to lunge at Bael's unprotected back, and Bael nodded his thanks, beheading another attacker with a swing of his sword.

"Surrender," the seelie screamed, his gaze on the seelie who'd just fallen to the ground, dead.

Slowly, the remaining seelie raised their arms.

"You know, white is a real poor choice for battle," Vas said conversationally as we watched the seelie drop their weapons, blood staining their light-weight white armor.

"Your king ordered you here as a sacrifice," my voice rang out. "To slow us down, even by a few hours."

Because even a few hours in this part of the seelie realm was days for my witchling. Dread knotted in my stomach at the thought.

Several of the seelie shifted on their feet, the realization hitting them. These were young soldiers, low on power and skill. Soldiers whom Taraghlan had decided were disposable, thanks to his new alliance with Lucifer.

The seelie king was obviously planning for Lucifer to kill us and then join him to slaughter Finvarra's people. He was going to be disappointed.

"On your knees," Ag ordered.

It didn't take long to strip them of their weapons. They were quiet, most of them resolved, ready to meet their deaths.

Vas stepped toward me, his expression hard. "We can't leave them tied up and defenseless here."

Lilith shot him an incredulous look. "Excuse me?"

"Taraghlan will probably kill them for their failure. If not for their failure, then because they know they were left to die. And information like that tends to spread through an army. Bad for morale."

"Not our problem," Lilith snapped.

Vas's expression darkened, his brow lowering in a way that told me he wasn't going to let this go. He turned his attention to me. "What would Danica do?"

Lilith let out a sound like an angry cat. "Danica isn't here, and the longer we spend in this place deliberating their worthless lives, the greater the chance she'll end up dead."

Vas ignored her, and Lilith's expression turned cold. I gave her a look that told her she wasn't allowed to kill Vas, and she stalked away.

All of us were fracturing at the edges.

Vas was waiting for my decision. I surveyed the group of seelie.

"Let them live. They'll get word back to Taraghlan's army." I enjoyed the thought of that army slowly losing morale when they learned their king had sacrificed some of his people.

The closest seelie, the one who had surrendered, met my eyes. "If we make it to the middleground or the human realm, do we have your word your people won't kill us?"

"Tell me where the bubaks went and I'll consider it."

I knew, but I wanted it confirmed, wanted to be sure they hadn't taken a different route.

The seelie pointed west. "Through the forest. They separated into groups to make it more difficult for you to find the one with the artifact. My *king,*" he spat the word, "has allowed them to hunt and eat any humans who find themselves lost and alone in this part of our realm."

"How will we know which group has the artifact?"

"They wear the clothes of their victims. The leader has a bright orange shirt with a black checkmark on it."

I frowned and Vas angled his head. "The Nike logo."

I nodded. "Keep to yourselves. Stay away from humans, spread the word about what happened here today, and be sure to mention my *mercy.*" I gave him a sharp smile.

A trickle of blood dripped down the side of his face

from a wound on his forehead as he nodded.

"If you make it to the middleground or the human realm, my people will not attack."

I glanced at the nine demons I'd brought with me. Mammon was wiping blood off his cheek, but none of them seemed injured enough that I'd need to order them to return to the tower.

"Let's go."

We took to the air as one, hurtling across the sky toward the forest. By the time Ag spotted the first group of bubaks, I was once again deep in a killing rage.

The creatures stood approximately seven feet tall, sprinting surprisingly fast, given their lurching gaits. Their skin was the color of rotting flesh, their heads the shape of pumpkins. One of them looked up as our shadows fell over them, two holes in its head where its eyes should have been.

Bael glanced at me. *"It's not the right group."*

"I don't care. Kill them all for daring to slow us down."

Bael and Mammon peeled off to kill the first group. Lilith and Vas took the second group, Azazyel and Romyel the third.

And then I spotted orange, lurching between the trees. Ag instinctively shifted to the right, targeting the bubak closest to the leader, while the rest of my demons spread out, ready to pick off the others.

Wrath burned through me, and I tucked my wings close to my body, arrowing down through a gap in the forest canopy.

Black blood splattered my face as I attacked.

CHAPTER
SEVENTEEN

Danica

I lay on the floor of my bathroom, eyes open as I stared at nothing. Pischiel had attempted to haul me up once, and I'd headbutted him, ordering him out of my room. I didn't want anything to do with the demon who Lucifer had raised in his image.

My shields remained, even in sleep. I didn't want to be comforted by Samael. Didn't deserve to find solace in his arms.

Of course I wanted my mate. Craved his arms. Wanted to lose myself in him and hear him vow that it would be okay. But I also wanted to be engulfed in my grief and guilt. *I deserved* this. Deserved to lie here wishing that Lucifer had killed me instead.

Decades. My father had spent decades in that cell. How he must have hoped, when he learned Samael was coming. How he must have dreamed of feeling the fresh air on his face, the sun on his cheeks.

How he hadn't cursed me with his last breath,

I would never know. Instead, he'd told me he was *proud*.

Impossible.

I could hear hushed voices from my bedroom. The maids were having a field day with my breakdown. The one time they'd attempted to convince me to at least get off the floor, I'd screamed obscenities at them.

Look at me now, Dad. Are you still proud?

Lucifer knew he'd broken me. I was certain of that much, because he was leaving me alone. Leaving me to count down to the moment he took my power. I had no doubt he was pleased by my inability to function.

I didn't even have it in me to get up out of pure spite.

The large window over the bath looked out at the gardens. The meteor shower had begun. Slowly at first, but over the last day and night, I'd watched more and more bursts of lights streaking across the sky. I'd never expected the countdown to my death to be so beautiful.

Today, though, a beam of sunlight streamed through that window, bathing the bathroom floor in its glow. I stretched out a hand, still too numb to truly feel the warmth.

Pischiel hadn't given up. He'd had food brought in to my bathroom multiple times, even when I'd ignored it. He'd teased, cajoled, and then ruthlessly mocked as he attempted to rouse me.

His latest plan? Garadiel.

I'd listened as he murmured to the other demon a few minutes ago, before sending him into the bathroom. Now, Garadiel stood over me, silent as he obviously attempted to decide which approach he would take.

I knew him. Would bet that his eyes were currently

hard, his mouth a thin line of disapproval.

"Did you ever think maybe Agates wanted to die?" he finally asked. "That maybe he simply needed to see you, get to know you, before he finally escaped the hell his own father had trapped him in for so many years?"

I ignored him. Flecks of dust danced in the beam of sunlight. I focused on the way they floated through the air.

"I know you're mourning. Grief... it can feel like it's strangling you sometimes. Can feel like each breath is cutting into your lungs like blades. But you don't have the luxury of giving into that grief right now."

I wanted to ask him how he knew what my grief felt like, who he'd lost, but the curiosity disappeared within a microsecond.

"Lucifer is pleased." Garadiel's voice floated with the dust over my head. "His spies told him how you can't even get off the bathroom floor." A long pause. "You have work to do. Things you swore to do with that ring on your finger. Agates was communicating with the rebels. With those of us who still have hope. Your father promised you would save us."

I went still.

The words were like a hand clamped around my windpipe. The more I tried to ignore them, the harder they squeezed.

Garadiel cursed and stalked toward the door. "He'd expect better from you, Danica."

Your father promised you would save us.

Why? Why had he made that promise? I was only good at getting the people I loved hurt, or worse.

Kyla was all wolf—would likely never come

back. My father was dead. *Dead.* Keigan… even after everything he'd done, my chest hurt at the thought of him wasting away in the darkness.

Your father promised you would save us.

I tasted salt from my tears and my whole body went hot. He'd had no right to promise anything to the people who'd already suffered for so many years. Those people were suffering right now, too. In mines, in dark rooms, in ballgowns and in rags. Throughout this realm, they suffered.

I mouthed the words silently to myself. "Your father promised."

Silence.

I owed him this. Owed him enough to try. Owed him everything.

So get. The fuck. Up.

Samael

I sneered as I flew over Hope Valley, my wings aching from flying such long distances in such a short period of time. We'd slaughtered every bubak in the seelie forest. Since they hunted humans, Vas was more than happy to make them hurt as they died.

I could practically smell the fae, could almost hear them contacting each other to whisper about the *demon* in their territory.

The seelie's mansion demonstrated slightly better taste than most in the neighborhood, although why anyone would choose to live in the suburbs of any realm was beyond me.

I landed, and the greenery crept toward me. I shot one of the vines a vicious look, and Aubrey opened the front door. The vine froze.

"Samael. What can I do for you?"

I gave him a slow smile I was sure didn't reach my eyes. "We both know you've been keeping up to date with every move your king makes."

His expression was inscrutable, and he glanced at the maid who walked past him, her gaze curious.

"I think you should come in."

Ivy curled threateningly toward me as I stepped inside his home. I snarled at it, catching Aubrey's lips twitch as he turned to walk up the stairs, also lined with poisonous vines.

Nothing here could kill me, but it could disable me. Something I didn't have time for. I kept a close eye on everything alive in the house, which was almost fucking everything.

Aubrey led me into his office and closed the door, watching as I narrowed my eyes at a red-petalled plant that arched toward me.

"Not poisonous. Just curious," he assured me. "You seem… tense."

We'd barely spoken, but it didn't take someone close to me to notice I was on edge. I'd never been one to take betrayal lightly. I soothed myself with the thought of turning Taraghlan into a pile of ash and took a seat in front of Aubrey's desk, arranging my wings over the low back of the chair.

I wasn't surprised when, instead of sitting behind his desk, he sat in the chair next to me.

"Something has happened to Danica," he murmured.

I stared steadily back at him.

I hadn't spoken to my little witch while she slept. Two of her nights had passed, and she'd blocked me from her subconscious. Sometimes I could feel her, grief-stricken and filled with rage.

But she hadn't come to me.

Something was very, very wrong.

My spies had reported that she hadn't been seen at court. Hadn't been seen walking the gardens. My mind played through all of the things Lucifer could have done to her. All the ways he could have hurt her.

And now, the flame of her—usually so strong it threatened to burn everything in sight—was barely a spark.

Because I'd failed. Because I was late. Because I *wasn't there*.

Was that why she was staying away? Why she didn't want to see me? No, I knew my witchling, and she refused to blame me. No matter how much I blamed myself.

But there was no limit to the suffering Lucifer could cause her in an attempt to make Danica fall in line.

A sharp, cold panic took up residence in my gut.

"She is a prisoner," was all I said. Aubrey raised one eyebrow, but didn't comment. "By now you know your king, the one you are so loyal to, has betrayed me. That betrayal was created to ensure my doom, the slaughter of all my people, and the brutal draining of Danica's powers before she is murdered."

I watched as the muscles around his eyes tightened. "I have heard about his recent dealings with Lucifer," he admitted. "I can only say that I am disappointed in his actions."

"You once gave Danica a blade," I changed the subject to keep him off-guard. He raised one eyebrow, and I gave him a smile much sharper than that blade. "Did you think I wouldn't find out?"

To his credit, the seelie didn't look cowed. He merely crossed one leg over the other and smiled at me.

"You're not here about my friendship with Danica. Why don't you tell me what you want, Samael?"

A reluctant respect almost made me smile. "Ah, Aubrey, if only *you* were king."

"As I told Danica, I'm loyal to my king." He almost winced as he said the words and I rolled my eyes.

"Your king will die for his betrayal," I promised. "If not by my hand, then by Finvarra's, with the full support of both the demons and the werewolves. It's your choice who steps into that role eventually, and frankly, the sad state of your court is none of my concern. But you have a chance right now. A chance to change the trajectory of this war and save Danica's life. You have a choice to make, *princeling.*"

Yes, he'd kept that information quiet, but Aubrey had enough power–and enough support–to eventually claim the throne. As of now, he had no plans to do such a thing. My spies had told me he enjoyed his life in this realm. Besides, civil war was never pretty.

Aubrey's expression darkened, and I caught movement out of the corner of my eye. One of his vines slipping toward me, crawling over his desk. I allowed my hand to glow with demon fire and the vine stopped moving.

"Your king negotiated with Danica while I was turning to dust after the Spell of Three. She made a deal with him, and in turn, he delayed her, choosing not to tell her she needed a witchbone in order to save my life. You'll remember this well, since you were the one who told her she needed it. Likely against your king's wishes."

"You're welcome for that, by the way," Aubrey gritted out.

"As the humans like to say, that was strike one," I said, ignoring him. "Betraying me and delaying my ability to find this artifact was strike two." I pulled the artifact from my pocket and placed it on his desk. The seelie stared at the unassuming candlestick holder like it was more poisonous than every plant in this house.

My smile widened. "Would you like to know what strike three was?"

Aubrey closed his eyes, but he nodded.

"Strike three was learning that Taraghlan wasn't just delaying me in the hope that I'd lose my bondmate and then my life. No, it turns out your traitor king made a deal with Lucifer himself."

The blood slowly drained from Aubrey's face, and he opened his eyes once more. "I assume you're planning to declare war."

I bared my teeth. "You assume correctly." I gestured at the artifact. "I'm sure by now you know what I need. Can it be done?"

He gazed at the pocket realm, which could hide

hundreds of thousands of soldiers at one time. Then he met my eyes, and his expression was resolved.

"Yes," he sighed. "It can be done."

"Good. Bael will bring you anything you need. I suggest you tell your people to wear something to differentiate them from any seelie who turn up on that battlefield. We wouldn't want to accidentally kill them."

Danica

That afternoon, I managed to get up, bathe, and shove some food in my mouth, although it was as tasteless as sawdust. The maids seemed pleased, and Pischiel slapped me on the shoulder, his hand shaking with obvious relief.

As soon as I'd choked down some food, I crawled into my bed. The moment I fell asleep, Samael's arms came around me. His eyes were haunted as he pulled me close to him, and I mentally cursed myself.

He'd thought I was in trouble. Blocking him out had been a shitty thing to do.

"What happened, little witch? Why couldn't I contact you?"

My throat ached as I attempted to pull air into my lungs. I'd been shoving down my grief so I could function, but now it rose up like a wave that would pull me under if I let it.

"Lucifer killed my father."

Samael gazed down at me, his eyes dark. "I'm so sorry, Danica. I should have spent more time looking into his disappearance."

My eyes burned, but I couldn't give into the tears. If I did, I didn't know if I'd be able to function again.

"I'm surprised you hadn't heard." I murmured as Samael pulled me closer, until I could lean my head against his chest.

"Lucifer will have sworn his people to silence on pain of death. By killing Agates, he risks making him a martyr."

"So let's spread the word. Send the news through the underworld and our realm. Maybe it'll help convince people, who would otherwise be on the fence, that they need to join us."

Samael slowly nodded. I blinked back tears as he shifted back, catching my chin in his hand as he looked into my eyes.

"You didn't come to me."

I took another deep, shuddering breath. A single tear escaped my eye, and he kissed it away.

"I knew you'd comfort me. I know it sounds stupid, but I don't *deserve* to feel better. It's my fault he's dead, Samael. Mine."

"Ah, witchling. Do you really think Agates would want you to punish yourself for Lucifer's actions?"

"If I hadn't been caught with him, he would still be alive. We could have freed him, Samael."

"He judged the risk worth it so he could see you. Don't forget that. He knew what could happen."

I studied his face. His expression was blank, but I could feel his hurt, deep beneath his shields. As he had likely felt mine, but I'd shut him out. My gut twisted at how badly I'd wounded him by not allowing him to comfort me.

"I'm sorry. I should've come to you. I could barely… function, Samael."

"I understand, little witch. This bond is still relatively new. We will have centuries together, centuries in which you will learn to trust me with everything."

His hand came up and stroked the side of my throat, the movement possessive. "But don't push me away again."

"I won't." I took a deep breath. "I have to wake up now, Samael. I need to go start some shit."

His eyes flashed. "You're supposed to be lying low."

I forced a grin. "Lying low was never my kind of thing."

"Danica!"

I opened my eyes and threw my legs over the side of my bed, getting to my feet and throwing on the closest dress.

I was lucky I'd convinced Gloria to cooperate before Lucifer killed her. And I was also thankful that witches' spells weren't tied to their lives. Gloria may be dead, but our little secret would still function. As long as she hadn't betrayed me one last time.

She'd had Lucifer's blood on hand, since it was used in the spells to clamp the metal rings around each slave's wrists. Obviously, the underking wasn't doing such a thing himself, so he'd had the spells sent to another black witch who lived near the mine.

That witch would die, too.

But first, I would be using the death spell. A spell so

brutal that it sickened me to use it. But I'd seen the horror of those mines. Not only would I free the slaves, but I'd use it as a rallying point for anyone considering switching their allegiance to Samael.

Is that all people are to you now? Tools to be used?

I pushed that thought away. We were at war. But my stomach twisted uneasily. I popped the ring in my mouth and retrieved the spells I'd moved to a closet in one of the dusty sitting rooms. Then I made my way through the palace.

Pischiel was waiting for me behind the palace, on the edge of the forest. I could hear the wyverns' muffled shrieks, and removed the ring long enough for Pischiel to silently grab me. I shoved it back into my mouth and he hauled me into the air, using the cover of darkness. If anyone looked, they'd just see a single demon flying somewhat weirdly through the air.

I hadn't wanted to have to rely on Pischiel to fly me to the mines. He'd sworn he could be trusted, but I was prepared, just in case he got any interesting ideas.

Pischiel was quiet as he flew us toward the mine. I'd given him directions, and now I gazed up at the night sky, watching the falling stars. They were already falling closer and closer together. Sweat broke out on the back of my neck, and I pushed away the knowledge of what those stars meant.

As soon as we were far enough away from the castle, I spat out the ring and Pischiel jolted, unprepared for me to suddenly become visible. I'd learned that speaking with the ring in my mouth made me come dangerously close to choking on it.

"Set me down close to the sleeping quarters," I told him.

"I'm going with you."

"The spell is calibrated to hit anyone who is on the ground and isn't wearing one of these fine pieces of jewelry." I held up my hand, and the metal glinted in the light of the moon. "While some part of me would enjoy watching Lucifer's heir burn, I need a ride back."

His lips tightened, as if he'd say something nasty, but he clamped down on the urge.

"Fine."

I handed him the container that held the second spell. It sloshed within the metal urn. "You hold on to this. Whatever you do, don't drop it." He snorted, which I guessed was fair, since his reflexes were likely a hundred times more honed than mine. "The guards will be warned if they see me with you. I'm putting the ring in my mouth now."

"Don't choke on it."

"Cute."

I slipped the ring off and popped it in my mouth as we approached the mine. Pischiel tensed again as I suddenly turned invisible. He'd used his power to disrupt his features, turning them murky, so no one would recognize him as Lucifer's heir.

The night was still. I shuddered, still shaken by the horror I'd seen on my last visit. But it was eerily quiet at this time of night, the prisoners locked away. Still, the guards were alert as they patrolled the mine and surrounding area.

The mine unraveled below us, spanning miles and

miles. The opening was a black hole, cut into the side of the mountain. It was pure blackness down there, and I fought to keep my shit together.

"Be careful." Pischiel dropped me a few feet from the ground and darted back into the air.

I took the ring out of my mouth, wiped it, and slipped it back onto my finger. One of the guards immediately appeared out of the dim light.

"What are you doing here?" he demanded. I recognized him. This was the guard who'd sliced off the prisoner's wings. The one who'd enjoyed it.

My breath dried up. Chills broke out down my arms. A bead of sweat dripped down my neck.

And I felt them. All of the eyes on me, from across the mine. Guards watched, waiting for their friend to strike me down. But prisoners watched too, likely peeking through cracks in the walls of their windowless sleeping quarters.

"This little gift is from Samael," I announced, my voice echoing across the mine. Then I reached into my pocket and threw the paperweight into the air, murmuring the incantation.

My heart leapt in my throat as the guard pulled his sword. Gloria had assured me that the cuff on my wrist wouldn't interfere with a pre-made spell, since it didn't require any of my own magic. But I didn't trust her entirely. I could feel Pischiel in the dark somewhere above me, ready to drop and haul me back into the sky.

The spell unfurled like a rose as the white paperweight hung in the air. Pink sparks fell from it, one by one. Then they shot into the sky like a firework.

That's when the screaming began.

Vomit crawled up my throat. And every guard in the mine erupted into fire.

They hadn't expected it. None of them had shielded themselves from what had looked like an unassuming spell. Now they were burning alive.

The scent of burning flesh filled the air. I leaned over and puked. Then I lifted my head and made myself watch until it was done.

The scent of charred meat filled my nose and I heaved once more, but I had nothing left in my stomach. Finally, I wiped my mouth and lifted my head.

"They're all dead," I said.

Pischiel dropped to the ground next to me, his expression sick as he took in the ashes floating on the slight breeze. He couldn't look at me, but he did something with his power that made my voice carry over the entire mine.

It took me a couple of tries before I could speak properly. "Please come out so I can help you lose the cuffs around your wrists."

They came then. The strong first, striding out of the sleeping quarters, disbelief on their faces as they took in the piles of ash where the guards had been. It was ironic, really. The only way Gloria had been powerful enough to wield such a spell was because Lucifer had been giving her an all-you-can-eat buffet of sacrifices and horror.

One of the prisoners leaned over and spat on the ashy remains of a guard. Others were helping those who were weaker, leading them from the wooden buildings. Several of them lifted their heads, taking in the stars falling above us.

Even in their sleeping quarters, the prisoners were trapped with no view of the sky. The only time they'd gotten to see it had been when they were walking to and from the mine entrance.

My grandfather was an expert when it came to torture.

I cleared my throat. "Anyone who has enough power needs to get to the closest portal. It will take you to the human realm. There will be guards on the portal, but they won't be expecting so many of you, so you can take them by surprise. If you have enough power, you'll need to help those who can't cross."

Samael wouldn't be expecting this many demons to show up in our realm, but I knew he'd help get them settled.

"Why are you doing this?" A voice asked. "What's in it for you?"

"I get to see the expression on my grandfather's face when he realizes you're gone. Maybe his eye will even twitch."

A few laughs broke out. Near the back of the crowd, someone coughed hoarsely. Typically, demons couldn't get sick. Perhaps being cut off from their powers for so long had weakened them. I shook my head, hoping they could make it to the portal. They had no wings, and it seemed as if many of them could barely stand.

The demon was still studying my face. I sighed.

"Because no one deserves to be a slave. And because I represent Agates and Samael. Not my grandfather."

"What do you want from us?" another demon spoke up. I recognized him. This was the demon who'd lost his wings. The one who'd looked at me, clutched in Lucifer's arms as the underking enjoyed the show.

"I want you to *live*."

Murmurs broke out at that. More demons were joining the crowd, and next to me, Pischiel was tense.

There were thousands of demons here, so we needed to hurry this along before Lucifer noticed us missing.

"This is going to take some time. The spell needs to touch all of the metal bracelets around your wrists. I need some volunteers."

I showed them how it worked, holding my breath as Pischiel opened the container. I dipped my finger into the liquid spell and pressed it to the metal cuff of the closest demoness. She gaped as the cuff fell off, and I blew out a deep breath.

"My power," she murmured, "it's weak, like the faintest breeze. But I can feel it again."

I grinned, and she threw her arms around me. "Thank you."

She pulled back, brow creasing as she shoved her shoulders back. "Form some lines, people, let's take back our freedom."

It took a long time. Someone came up with the bright idea to pour the spell into several empty buckets, and fifty or so of the other demons helped press the spell onto the metal cuffs. Finally, when everyone was free, the sick and weak were lifted onto the backs of those who could carry them, and they slowly began to trudge out of the mine.

I took a deep breath. "The closest portal—"

"We know where it is," the demon I'd watched lose his wings told me, lifting his face to the breeze. "Several of our people have attempted to escape over the years. For some, it is their last choice. The only option left to them."

I swallowed. Suicide. That's what he was talking about. "I don't know where the portal will take you—which part of my realm."

He smiled, his dusty hand coming up to cup my cheek. "We will be okay. Thank you."

"Do you mind if I ask… what's your name?"

"My name is Kazbiel. And you are Danica. Our savior."

I took a deep breath, my eyes hot. "I wouldn't go that far. It's nice to finally meet you, Kazbiel. And I'm sorry I didn't do anything when the guard cut off your wings."

He slowly shook his head. "I knew who held you in his arms, could tell from the sick smile on his face. But watching you gave me hope."

The prisoners had begun burning the mine. Some of them had found chemicals, which they lit on fire. Others were slowly getting their powers back. One of the stronger demons held up his hand, and the barracks exploded with demon fire.

Pischiel dropped in front of me. "Time to go."

I nodded and he lifted me off my feet. We shot into the sky as the mine burned.

I would never get to meet my grandmother. Lucifer didn't even have a painting of her in the palace. But in this moment, it felt like she was watching over me. And I knew she was proud.

Pischiel's voice was tight. "Are you happy now, Danica?"

"I'll be happy when Lucifer is burning too."

"You know, I never thought I'd say this, but if anyone can make sure the underking ends up dead, it's you."

"You're damn right." I studied his face as the palace came into view in the distance. I'd had him burn my cloak, which had been covered in blood and ash.

"Why did you do it, princess?"

"Don't call me that."

"Lucifer isn't stupid. He'll know. He may not be able to prove it, but he'll know it's no coincidence that his mine burned while you were in the underworld. He'll make you pay."

He was right. I swallowed around the lump in my throat. Truthfully, Lucifer terrified me on such a deep level that I lived in continual fight-or-flight mode, waiting for him to grow bored and end the so-called threat I presented.

Not for the first time, I cursed the stupid prophecy. But it was the sheer unpredictability of my grandfather that worried me the most. Now that I was allowed at court, I got to see that instability first-hand. Some days, he was jovial, laughing with his subjects. And yesterday he'd made me watch as he whipped a young slave so hard he'd fallen to the floor unconscious.

My grandfather had been livid that the slave had passed out, ordering the healers to rouse the young boy so he could whip him some more.

"Danica?"

I blinked, pushing Lucifer's brutality out of my mind. "Because… because if I die here, which isn't *unlikely*, I want to know I did something. Something more important than wandering around the palace in ridiculous dresses.

So before you go running to Lucifer—"

"I gave you my word."

I turned my head and showed him my teeth. "Excuse the hell out of me if I don't trust the word of the man Lucifer is grooming to replace him."

A muscle twitched in his jaw and I studied his face as I continued. "Your friend? The kitchen maid you like to flirt with when you think no one notices? What do you think would happen to her if you betrayed us?"

He looked at me like he'd never seen me before and something in my chest twisted. Then his eyes shone with a dull fury. "You're threatening my friend?"

"Of course not. Merely reminding you that I have people everywhere. And if you get any ideas about turning me in…"

His mouth twisted, but instead of dropping me, his arms clamped around me, squeezing tight.

"You cold bitch."

"Thank you."

"You want to kill Lucifer? From where I'm flying you're just like him."

He was lashing out, and he knew exactly where to strike. I kept my face carefully blank gazing down as the palace came into view.

"You sweet-talker."

I shoved the ring in my mouth as Pischiel approached the palace. His landing reminded me of Vas, with the way he tucked his wings in and dropped to the ground. The thought of my friend made me so homesick, my throat ached.

"Where have you been?"

I jumped. Pischiel's arms clamped around me once more, and we both turned to find Daimonion stalking toward us, several guards in his wake.

"I don't owe you any explanation of my coming and goings," Pischiel bit out. He pinched me, and I knew he was silently telling me to freeze.

I trembled in his arms. I may be invisible, but Daimonion was suspicious. I could tell.

Pischiel turned, letting out a sudden, loud laugh to cover my movements as I slowly turned to slide past him.

My heart slammed in my chest, as if it would jump out and flop onto the ground in front of me. I dared a single glance back over my shoulder, but Daimonion was still staring at Pischiel, who had his blank face on.

Fuck. I *really* didn't want to get Pischiel dead.

He's Lucifer 2.0, Danica. He was raised by him— trained by him. He would probably end up just as evil as him.

I tiptoed in the opposite direction and made my way back toward my meeting spot with Garadiel. We still had work to do.

CHAPTER EIGHTEEN

Samael

The breeze was light on my skin. To my right, a forest stood, spreading for miles. To my left, our armies were currently camped and preparing for battle. The pocket realm had more than enough space for us. If I didn't know I was currently tied to a fae artifact, I would have assumed I was in the seelie realm.

I shrugged off the claustrophobia as a demon walked toward me. Blonde curls exploded from his head, and he shoved his hand through his hair as I watched. His face was pale, expression resolved, and I gestured for him to approach, glancing around us to ensure we had privacy.

"Teremos. Are you sure you want to do this?"

"I volunteered. It was my idea."

"Understood. But I need to ensure you're fully aware of the consequences. I have a backup plan, and it's not too late to change—"

"I'm sure. A year ago today, Lucifer's regiment attacked my village. They killed my mate. She was pregnant with my son." His voice cracked and I could *feel* his pain and hopelessness. "My beautiful mate would have been disappointed in me if I had simply killed myself after I lost them both. I could hear her voice in my head, urging me to hold on. This is different. This is a chance to go with honor. To make my death mean something."

I had to try one more time. "There is no honor in suicide. Only darkness, loneliness, and grief for your family."

He shook his head at me. "I die today. Whether on that battlefield, raging against the people who killed my family, or on my own terms, ensuring you will kill Lucifer and free our people. I swear this to you, Samael. Whether you use my death or not, I will not walk off that battlefield alive."

What would I do in the same place, if it were Danica and my child who'd been slaughtered? I was surprised he had lasted a year, but understood how vengeance had kept his heart beating, kept his body functioning when his soul had already taken flight, ready to join his family.

"If you change your mind at any point, I will switch our strategies. It is never too late."

"I understand. You're a good male, Samael. You will do incredible things for our people."

He wandered away, and I fought back disgust in myself that I was even considering using a male so entrenched in his own grief. But few demons lasted even close to a year after the loss of their mate. Thoughts of his revenge had been the only reason he'd stayed alive this long. I wouldn't take it from him.

A roar sounded, and I turned my head. At least a

hundred dragons had joined us, and I stroked my hand down Scylla's snout as a huge red dragon curled up next to her.

"Be careful," I ordered her. "You have your daughter to think about."

She snorted at me, and I leveled her with a hard stare. She stared back.

Twenty feet away, the werewolf Alpha paced, his gaze on his own people. Over a hundred of them were gathered and ready to shift. Human mates and children had been left behind, put into lockdown with increased security to deter anyone who had been watching and knew so many of his wolves were away from their territory.

We'd had to transport more food than I could've imagined into the pocket realm so the wolves would be able to shift and fight when necessary.

I walked to the Alpha. "What happened?"

"Danica did something to allow me to see Kyla. My wolf has a matter of hours before she goes completely feral and I'll have to put her down."

Dull pride in Danica's scheming warred with sadness. If Danica lost Kyla, she would never recover.

Finvarra approached, ignoring Nathaniel. The unseelie king sent the dragons a distrustful glance. "You seem less crazed," he told me.

"In just hours, I wage war on my enemies and save my bondmate."

Waiting until noon was difficult. But my generals were working with Finvarra's as they strategized. Lucifer had been gathering his people from every corner of his realm, readying for our attack. We were outnumbered and forced to fight in what had become his territory.

It would be all we could do to make sure this battle wouldn't be a bloodbath. And yet even if Lucifer hadn't taken Danica, even if it was someone else he needed in order to take their power, we would still be marching on him.

Because if Lucifer could travel through portals, worlds would end. He would take the smaller realms first. Then he'd turn to the middleground. His armies would roll over any opposition, and he'd force residents to swear their allegiance and fight under his banner.

Then he would turn to the realm we'd made our home. Danica's realm. I had no doubt that Lucifer had never expected the underworld to keep him confined for so long. He'd thought I would be dead centuries ago, leaving him free to go where he pleased. And he'd been silently stewing, seething, and strategizing ever since.

Finvarra was still studying me, still ignoring the Alpha wolf. Neither of them had spoken more than a single word to each other over the past few days.

"And yet, you're not pleased," he said.

Because I knew my mate. Knew she'd done something that could get her killed.

I could feel Finvarra's eyes on me, filing away any sign of weakness. I turned and gave him a look that dared him to attempt to use that weakness.

He smiled at me and wandered away, heading back toward one of his generals.

And I continued to wait for my witchling. Continued to pray to gods I no longer believed in that she was okay.

Danica

The next day, Pischiel found me in my room. I was staring out the window, watching as the occasional meteor flashed brighter than the rest, burning across the sky. Thankfully, Lucifer was away from the palace on some kind of business today. But it was only a matter of time before he realized I was behind the release of his slaves.

"You seem like you're doing better," Pischiel said.

So we weren't going to talk about our spat last night. Of course, I wouldn't hurt an innocent person based on Pischiel's actions, but I'd known deep down that he'd believe me when I made my threats. Because he'd grown up in Lucifer's court.

"Danica?"

I grunted. I wouldn't say I was doing better. Merely suppressing any emotions that attempted to rise. Not exactly a healthy way of coping, but I couldn't afford to mourn in this place. So I was channeling my sorrow and grief into rage.

At least I was no longer lying on my bathroom floor.

"I'm sorry, you know. That he killed Agates." Pischiel slumped in one of the chairs by my fire, letting his head fall back as his eyes closed. Questioning all your life choices *was* likely exhausting.

"Are you?"

"Am I what?"

"Sorry."

He lifted his head and opened his eyes. "Yes. I remember when he was first imprisoned, you know. The underking allowed him visitors at first, before he learned that those visitors were part of a network of spies and rebels. Still, your father had his ear to the ground."

I didn't doubt that. I turned and stared out the window, my body numb as Pischiel continued to talk.

"Lucifer made a mistake executing your father," he said. "Strategically, it was smarter to leave him alive and allow his enemies to believe that, if Samael failed to take the throne, Agates could one day be a much more benevolent king. By snuffing out that hope…"

"He created a martyr," I said, my voice hoarse.

"Yes."

My father had wanted me to join his rebellion. To stoke the embers of rage into a full-scale wildfire.

I turned to Pischiel. "You can't live in both worlds," I told him. "You helped me free those slaves. You kept your mouth shut about Gloria. You've been sneaking around this palace almost as much as I have. But you need to make a decision. Are you with us, or are you still choosing Lucifer?"

He opened his mouth, and I glowered at him. "I'm serious, Pischiel. Either shit or get off the pot."

His mouth twitched. "Charming. As usual." He sighed, getting to his feet. "I made my decision. It's why I came here to talk to you."

My breath stilled in my chest. I didn't *want* to have to kill Pischiel one day.

"I need a guarantee," he told me.

"What kind of guarantee?"

"The kind that means your bondmate won't kill me, even after he learns of everything I've done."

I opened my mouth, and he shook his head. "Your assurance isn't enough, Danica. You may love him, may think that you've seen the worst of him, but you forget—I've been alive for almost as long as he has. I've seen what happens to those he considers his enemies. And none of *those* people got to touch his bondmate while he was prevented from doing the same. If you think Samael is going to be rational about this, you don't know him as well as you think you do."

He stepped forward, clamping his hands around my upper arms. "*Think* Danica. If he makes it down here, think about just how rational he'll be. He may not want to upset you, may even regret killing me a few seconds later, but I'll be just as dead."

I wanted to deny it, but… each time I saw Samael in our dreams, I could see just how much it was costing him to be apart from me while I was in danger. He tried to hide it from me, but being unable to rescue me until we had all our ducks in a row… it was *killing* him.

Pischiel was right. Samael would get his full powers back. And his fury would know no end.

"What is it you want, Pischiel?"

"I want a bond."

I stared at him. "Expand on that little thought."

"Samael bonded many of his demons to him directly. They pledged their allegiance when they traveled through the portal."

"Yes."

"The bond goes two ways. Those who bond with a

high demon owe him their lives. But that bond also means he will fight for their lives when necessary. And he won't kill them unless they betray him."

"A bond is forever," I said. "Are you sure about this?"

He nodded, and I ran it through in my mind. "There's only one problem with this little plan. I'm not a high demon."

"No. But you're bonded to one." He frowned. "Did Samael never tell you this was something you could do?"

"It didn't exactly come up. What about Lucifer? Won't he be able to feel that you're bonded to someone else?"

He shook his head. "The underking doesn't bond with his people in that way. Not even me. It would mean repercussions if he killed those he believed were disloyal without just cause. And it would also mean he would have to risk his life for his people when they were threatened."

And my grandfather wasn't exactly the type to do that.

"I have a question first."

"Sure."

"Would you have done it? If I'd never gotten my memory back? Would you have one day ruled beside me, knowing I was in love with Samael? And that I would always be an empty-headed shadow of myself?"

He sighed. "I don't think it would have ever gotten to that point. I was willing to play along because I knew deep down that you'd get your memories back. That your bondmate would never stop fighting for you."

I studied his face. "And if that hadn't happened?"

"I would have done whatever it took to keep us both alive. To buy us time. Even if that meant your memories were taken a thousand times."

At least he was honest.

"One more question."

He nodded.

"Did you really think I'd slaughter the kitchen maid?"

He heaved a sigh. "No. No, I was just pissed because you didn't trust me, and pissed at myself because I couldn't blame you for not trusting me. And pissed that you'd even noticed that I have… feelings."

My lips trembled. "Okay. If you think I can do this, let's do it."

Samael would understand when I explained it to him.

Pischiel pulled a dagger from its sheath and my empty hands clenched with a sudden longing for my Nim Cub.

"I've never done this before, and I wasn't exactly in a great frame of mind when Samael first bonded me. You'll need to talk me through it."

"I can do that."

In the end, it wasn't difficult. In fact, a lot of it seemed self-explanatory. We both cut our palms, pressed them together, and the slightest hint of a bond appeared in my mind, like a frayed thread.

"You have to—"

"I know what I have to do." It was instinct. I focused on that thread, bringing my bond with Samael into my mind. I studied our bond, the thick gold rope of it, and attempted to replicate it with the thread.

It slowly began to glow, growing stronger as I watched.

Pischiel cried out, falling to his knees, and I got an echo of that pain. I ground my teeth, holding on through the burn of it, as I pressed that thin strand to Samael's end of the bond.

"It's not working."

Pischiel was now writhing on the ground. Fuck.

My mind raced, and I traveled back down our thick gold bond, until I found the spot where it joined to me. My pain was turning to agony, and I had no idea how Pischiel was still conscious. Crossing mental fingers, I pressed the thin thread leading to the spot where Samael's bond connected to me.

It stuck. And it grew thicker. Nowhere near the coiled rope that represented my bond with Samael, but thick enough that I wasn't worried that it would suddenly snap. Huh. I'd thought I had to connect him to Samael, but instead, he was connected to me, and Samael *through* me.

At that moment, I felt Samael, felt him down at the end of *our* bond. Whatever power Lucifer was using to keep me from feeling him was weakened at this very moment.

And Samael roiled with fury.

Uh-oh.

I sent him a caress down the bond, wishing I could stay here for longer. But without my power, I was too weak to fight against Lucifer's spell.

The connection slammed shut. I opened my eyes to find myself on my knees. I could taste copper in my mouth, and I raised my hand to find my nose bleeding. Pischiel lay on the ground, his face ashen.

"Did I kill you?"

He groaned, cracking open one eye. "Almost. I'm guessing some of it was because you can't instinctively reach for Samael while Lucifer is suppressing your bond. And because you don't have access to your powers. The rest of it was just plain incompetence."

I scowled at him, and he was obviously feeling better, because he gave me a weak grin. "Don't worry, princess. Now you know how to do it, it'll be easier next time. If anything, I'd be more concerned about the rage I could feel from your bondmate. And let me tell you, I'm exceptionally glad for our new bond, since he would *love* to kill me."

Danica

Thanks to the pain I'd put my body through earlier in the day, it didn't take me long to fall asleep that night.

As soon as I opened my eyes, I found Samael standing in front of me, his gaze burning into mine.

"Have you been waiting for me?" It wouldn't surprise me if Samael could dip in and out of sleep as he willed it.

He ignored that. "Tell me the truth," he said silkily. "Do you have feelings for him?"

I blinked. "What?"

His expression turned feral, and his hand came up and caught my chin. I allowed it, since it seemed like my demon was a man on the edge.

"It's a yes or no question, Danica."

That was quite enough of that.

I yanked my chin free and slammed my hands into his chest. The bastard didn't even have the decency to move an inch. Instead, his eyes shone with a predatory gleam. He was one hundred percent domineering demon male.

"Of course I don't have feelings for Pischiel. But you better check your tone, because—"

His hand was buried in my hair, and his mouth was slamming down on mine before I could get out another word.

He'd been pushed too far. Being away from me for so long, knowing I was in danger, and now feeling like Pischiel was encroaching on his territory...

It had driven his instincts wild.

"Mmph," I muttered, and my mind went blank.

Then the world spun around me, and my stomach hit the arm of a chair as he bent me over, my clothes disappearing.

"Samael," I began, but he was already leaning over me, biting my nape, licking the shell of my ear. One hand slid to my waist, holding me in place, and his other hand found my core.

"Already wet for me," he growled as I clenched with a gasp. "As you should be."

He pushed against my entrance, hard and thick in this position, filling me up, thrusting deep, until he was buried inside me.

His hand moved from my waist to my neck, gently

encircling my throat. His teeth found the sensitive spot where my shoulder met my neck, and I groaned as he bit down.

"Samael," I gasped out, but he was driving into me now, again and again as I writhed beneath him.

"Tell me you're mine," he demanded, gently squeezing my throat. I clenched around him so hard I saw stars.

He laughed. "You like that."

My cheeks burned, but he was right. This was Samael at his most dominant, and I reveled in that dominance.

Heat lashed across my ass, and I let out a sound somewhere between a groan and a yelp at the feel of his hand on my skin. "Again," I demanded.

"Tell me," he said silkily, spanking me once more.

"I'm yours," I moaned, my body trembling as my climax tore through me. Samael growled behind me, continuing to thrust, his hand pinching my nipple and drawing out my pleasure until I was limp.

And he was still hard within me.

"We're not done," he purred, still thrusting steadily, his hand slipping down to my clit.

I opened my mouth to insist I was too sensitive, but a strangled groan left my throat, and my demon let out a rough laugh as his fingers danced along my slick core.

"Who do you belong to?" Samael growled, and I could hear in his voice that he was close, too.

"You," I gasped out, and the hand around my throat slid to my breast, tweaking my nipple while his other clever hand circled my clit.

"Come for me, little witch."

This time, when the pleasure overtook me, I couldn't make a sound, my teeth snapping together as my hands clutched at the fabric of the chair beneath me.

Samael thrust into me with a low growl, his arms coming around me as he gasped into my ear, both of us silent for a long moment as we came back to ourselves.

My eyes had slid closed at some point. When I opened them, we were lying on a bed identical to the one in Samael's penthouse, and my demon was slowly stroking my hair as he dropped kisses over my face.

"Forgive me."

"There's nothing to forgive, Samael." In fact, I'd have to insist we did that again. There was something to be said for angry sex. "But let's talk about this."

I felt him nod, but his body was tense beneath mine.

"I bonded Pischiel to *us* as part of a deal I made with him," I said carefully.

I explained Pischiel's train of thought, and Samael listened carefully. When I finished, he was silent for a few moments, slowly stroking my hair while he was deep in thought.

"He wants to prevent me from killing him."

"Yeah. I explained that you absolutely would not do such a thing, and he informed me that you were likely to be having a little problem with control."

"A little problem with control," he repeated, and I grinned. Relief unfurled its wings in my chest at his dry tone. Because Pischiel was right. Samael *was* finding it difficult to hold on to his control. And when a demon as powerful as Samael lost that control, people died.

"I know how difficult it's been," I said. "I experienced

it first-hand while you were turning to ash in that bed. And *my* only true enemy was time. But Pischiel's reasoning made sense, Samael. You'd regret it if you killed him. Sure, he was raised by Lucifer, but, in spite of that, there's good inside him. And now he's loyal to you."

Samael's chest rumbled. "He's loyal to *you*, Danica. But that is also acceptable. I can feel the bond, and you're correct. It will prevent me from killing him without prior thought."

My lips twitched at the "without prior thought" stipulation. "Do I need to make sure Pischiel is hidden away when you get here?"

"No. If he's willing to bond to you, he's willing to die for you. I'd prefer for him to be clamped to your side until I arrive. If all else fails, he'll be useful as cannon fodder."

I poked him in the side. "Very funny."

"I wasn't joking."

We were quiet for a long time. Finally, Samael spoke, his voice drowsy. "I was jealous," he admitted. "He gets to see you. To be there for you when you're scared or sad. He gets to hear your voice. To watch you plan your vengeance. And yet I can't help but be grateful to him for everything he's done so far to protect you."

My possessive demon. "Being able to see you in our dreams is the only thing that has kept me going. Without you, I would have given up."

I felt him shake his head. "No, you wouldn't. But I'm glad I could help you even a fraction."

"I will see you in a few hours," he pressed a kiss to my mouth. "All you have to do is stay alive until then."

I trembled, and he raised himself until he was leaning over me, his expression intent.

"I swear to you," he stared into my eyes, "no matter what happens, even if you lose your memory every single day, even if you're powerless for the rest of your life, even if it takes me the rest of *my* life, I will never stop fighting for you."

I attempted a smile, but I'd prepared for this. Deep down, I'd known.

He wasn't going to make it in time. Wasn't going to be here before the peak of the meteor shower. Taraghlan had cost him time. Time we'd needed.

I leaned up and brushed my lips over Samael's. Soaked in the scent of him, the feel of him.

"I love you," I told him.

CHAPTER
NINETEEN

Danica

My bedroom door burst open, and I sat up, heart racing. Lucifer stalked into my bedroom, his face a mask of rage.

Oh fuck.

I leapt out of my bed, backing toward the window, but I knew damn well there was no escape out there.

"Did you think I wouldn't know?" Lucifer hissed as he advanced on me.

"Know what?"

"No one would dare free those slaves. No one but *you*."

Worth it. It had been worth it, even if he killed me right now.

"I don't know what you're—"

"Silence! You worked with the black witch. How you must have laughed when I killed her."

I mean, he wasn't *wrong*.

The expression on his face was chilling. I didn't regret what I'd done—thousands of lives had been saved, their misery ended. But from the look on Lucifer's face, he was counting down the moments until he could end me.

Lucifer gestured at Daimonion, who sauntered toward me, grabbing my arm.

"Follow me," Lucifer ordered.

Daimonion pulled me out of the room after him. "You'll die too," I hissed at him.

"Strangely, I'm not scared of a halfbreed with no powers."

"*I'm* not the one you should be afraid of." Vas would kill him one day. The only question was how much damage the assassin would do before that day?

"If I were you, I would be focused on the pain and suffering you're soon to experience," Daimonion told me. And from the twisted look on his face, he was wishing he could be the one to hand me that pain and suffering.

They dragged me down to the dungeon, to the cell across from Kyla's. I didn't want to know what they'd done with the creature who'd been in here previously, but I had a feeling it wasn't good.

Daimonion threw me into the cage. I landed on hard stone and my knees barked with pain.

Kyla rammed her body against the bars of her cage again and again, howling her vengeance. I mentally begged her to shut the fuck up. The last thing I wanted was for her to attract Lucifer's attention.

But it was too late.

He turned, and I caught the sick pleasure in his gaze as he took in the wolf.

As he smiled at my friend.

The hair on my arms and neck stood at attention. Time slowed to a crawl, and I lunged, as if I could break through the bars holding me back.

Lucifer clicked his fingers and Kyla's neck broke with a loud *crack*.

"No," I choked out. "No, no, no."

"Everyone," Lucifer hissed. "I will kill everyone you love until you're broken. You brought war to my door, granddaughter. You undermined me every second you were in my home. And now you'll pay."

I tuned him out. Kyla was a werewolf. She could heal a broken neck. She could. I knew she could.

But could she?

She was so broken, so thin and weak. She had nothing left.

I shrieked, and this time I was the one to throw myself at the cage, swiping out with my nails in a useless attempt to do anything I could to hurt him.

Lucifer merely tutted, lifting his hand. I knew what that meant.

He was going to set Kyla on fire.

I threw my head back and screamed. My cuff burned as I felt my power once more, buried deep and useless. But there was something else there, too.

I sobbed through my teeth as it seemed to notice me. Ancient. Cruel. Sentient.

"Help me," I begged, reaching out to whatever it was. I could feel it watching, silent but interested. It reached a tendril toward me, and I almost passed out at the vastness of it.

It was... amused by me. I wasn't sure how I knew

that, but I could feel that it found me… interesting.

And it found so little interesting.

The palace shook beneath us. I held onto the bars as Daimonion stumbled back, narrowing his own eyes.

Lucifer's head snapped up. One of his demons appeared at the end of the corridor.

"We have a problem," he said, and Lucifer bared his teeth at the interruption.

The palace shook once more, and a flash of… fear crossed Lucifer's face.

Whatever had caused that fear, I needed more of it.

Lucifer stalked away without another word, his mind clearly on whatever had made the palace tremble like an earthquake.

I panted, my gaze glued to Kyla, but she didn't move. Might never move again. A sob clawed up my throat as I fell back, landing heavily on the stone floor. My heart beat so hard it seemed to rattle my ribs as the world spun around me.

No. I didn't accept this. Wouldn't accept that I'd be stuck in this cage while Lucifer killed my friends one by one.

I closed my eyes, battling fury this time instead of terror. And I reached out for one of the tendrils of that sentience, yanking it toward me.

It fought, something like alarm rolling through it, but I pulled harder.

"What are you?"

It didn't speak, but a picture formed in my mind. The palace, the grounds.

"You're the palace?"

Impatience, annoyance. Then it seemed to zoom out, and I saw Samael's kingdom spread out in front of me like a blanket. There was the mine, still smoldering away. Towns and cities and a river that sparkled like a jewel. To the east, ships waited at a dock, ready to cross an ocean.

I blinked. *"You're the underworld."*

It seemed to nod. Speaking with it was trippy. It could understand me, but it seemed almost childlike, yet infinitely wise, ancient and old in a way nothing else was.

"You just saved Kyla's life." Lucifer hadn't enjoyed that little earthquake.

I got the feeling the underworld was preening. I focused on it.

"You're the reason Samael doesn't have his powers down here."

It sent me an image of a child, curled up, pulling blankets over its head. Was the underworld attempting to tell me it felt shame?

"So do something about it. Please. I'm begging *you."*

Another image. This time of a person with their hands out in a "what are you gonna do" gesture.

Was it telling me it couldn't do anything? Or that it *wouldn't?*

I took a deep, steadying breath, and the underworld sent me an image of Lucifer walking through a portal. That's right. The deal he'd made with the underworld meant that he had to stay here as long as Samael was powerless. If Samael got his powers back...

Lucifer would be free to stroll through the portals and go wherever he liked.

I ground my teeth. If the underking had his way, he'd be able to do that, anyway. I had no doubt that my days—perhaps hours—were numbered. Lucifer was planning to level up by taking my powers before he faced Samael. And according to that fucking prophecy, he'd be unstoppable.

"*Do it*," I demanded. *"Give Samael his powers back."*

The underworld retreated, as if it was a teenager stomping away from me.

Fuck.

Danica

I paced my cell, running through our plan, over and over. That plan required me to be in Lucifer's palace, not in his dungeon. Despite the freezing temperatures down here, I broke out in a cold sweat. Time had no meaning, but I was guessing it had been at least ten hours since I'd been thrown in here, likely longer. I was so thirsty I was almost shaking with the need for water.

Lucifer would have to come for me to take my power. But I'd counted on having a chance to—

Footsteps on the stone. I froze, took a deep breath, and turned.

Pischiel appeared. For a moment, we simply stared at each other.

"Are you okay?"

"Fine. What's happening?"

"We're under attack," he said.

I swallowed. They were here. Samael was here, fighting for our people, and I was in this fucking cell.

Keys rattled as Pischiel pulled them from his pocket and opened the cage door.

"You're free," he told me. "But you have to move now. Lucifer will know I'm the only one who had access to these keys."

I was shaking as I wrapped my arms around him. He stiffened, but stroked his hand down my back.

"You need to get to Samael," I told him.

"I'm not leaving you here alone."

"Lucifer will kill you. Please, get to Samael. He'll know how to use your powers, where to put you in the front lines. He knows you're bonded to us."

I pulled away in time to see the desolation on Pischiel's face. Even though Lucifer was evil, the underking was still the closest thing he'd had to a father. He was turning traitor against his own people.

"I can't imagine how hard this is," I murmured. "But thank you."

"You made me stop hoping and start acting. I may hate you for it, but I'll get over it." He attempted a smile. "Get moving."

I nodded. "Don't fuck around, Pischiel. Get the hell out of here." I slipped the ring off my finger and offered it to him. "This will get you past the sentries."

He shook his head. "Even if I was enough of a coward to leave you undefended, your bondmate would make my death last for days if he learned I took that ring. Use it and get to the spell for your cuff, Danica. Lucifer made me search your rooms, so I hid it under my bed. I couldn't risk being caught with it if someone knew I was visiting you down here."

"Thank you."

"What's your plan?" he asked.

"Blow some shit up. Find my bondmate. Kill my Grandfather."

He shook his head at me, then glanced at Kyla and handed me the keys. "So you can get her out later."

If she was able to heal. I nodded, and he stalked toward the stairs.

"Danica."

Keigan's voice was low. I attempted to tune him out, but I couldn't. I turned, running my gaze over him. "You look like hell."

A faint smile. "I'm not the only one." He sighed. "I just wanted to say I'm sorry. I know it doesn't mean anything to you, but I'm sorry. Being a part of your life, being your friend, even under false pretenses... you taught me how wrong I was to hate paranormals. Taught me that there was much, much more to life than trying to even the playing field for humans."

I stared at him. "What you did, I don't know if I can ever forgive you."

"I know."

There was nothing else to say.

My father's words ran through my head.

"It sounds like he was the closest thing you had to a father as an adult. I can hate what he did, but still feel gratitude for the way he was there for you. People aren't merely black or white, Danica. Even my father was once both."

I stepped forward and slipped the key into the lock, turning them until the cell door opened. "Get gone."

His eyes were wide with shock, but a dull pride quickly replaced it. Pride in me. "Why?" he asked quietly.

"No one deserves to rot down here. Even you."

"Thank you."

We didn't hug it out or anything. He merely nodded at me and walked toward the stairs, his shoulders hunched.

I couldn't help myself. I went to Kyla's cage, where she was crumpled next to the bars. And I stroked the edge of her soft fur. "I know you can come back," I whispered. I could barely reach her, couldn't feel if she still had a pulse. Didn't know if she was unconscious or…

I refused to entertain the thought. "I'll be back for you," I swore. "I'll make sure you get out of here."

Even if she was all wolf. Even if Nathaniel wanted to put her down. I'd never allow him to. She could roam in the forest here, wild and free for the rest of her life.

Tears dripped down my cheeks and I forced myself to my feet. Then I slipped the ring into my mouth and slowly crept upstairs.

The palace shook again. This time I knew it wasn't the underworld, distracting Lucifer from killing my friend. No, it was the bombs Garadiel planted after my father convinced him this was the rebels' chance. Human technology that would never be suspected, created with demon fire which would ensure a lethal explosion. They were planted at key points that would draw attention, splitting the guards' focus and killing anyone who was loyal to Lucifer. Although the worst of the explosions would happen soon…

I panted as I made it up the stairs, weak with hunger and shaking with adrenaline.

Pischiel had poured the spell into a flask and hidden it under his bed. Obviously, he was hoping if anyone found it, they'd simply assume he had a drinking problem.

I opened the flask, dunked my thumb in the liquid, and touched it to my cuff. The cuff fell off my wrist, and I suddenly understood what the demoness at the mine had said. My power felt like a whisper.

But I could feel Samael now.

"Hey," I reached for him and felt him lift his head, eyes wild.

"Danica."

The word was almost neutral, but I could feel the all-consuming relief that swept through him.

"I'm here. And I'm ready to kick some ass. Tell me where you are."

He did something down the end of the bond, and suddenly I was through his shields, looking out through his eyes.

I instinctively knew that Samael had given me an incredible gift. Had allowed me into the inner cavern of his mind. If I wanted to, I could see the worst things he had ever done. His greatest shame, his darkest moments. It was an act of incredible trust.

"I love you."

I blocked out the core of him, focused on what he could see. And my heart stuttered in my chest.

I was looking at a war camp.

Thousands of demons were packed into the palace grounds and beyond. They stood at attention, in straight lines, ready for their orders.

Behind the palace grounds, row after row of tents waited, where soldiers would rest and recover before heading back to the front lines.

And in front of the palace grounds…

At least a hundred thousand demons. Dressed in gleaming silver armor, armed to the teeth, and moving like a well-oiled machine.

Lucifer had been quietly calling his armies together. I knew damn well this was the tip of the iceberg. He'd have more on the way, marching from various parts of his kingdom. But he'd kept these demons hidden, invisible and undetected—obviously suspecting I could still somehow communicate with Samael.

The sheer power it must have taken… I wondered if Pischiel knew. If he did, he had some explaining to do. If he didn't… Lucifer wouldn't have let him live unless he had some plan for him. Some way to pay him back for choosing us.

My breath sawed in and out, burning my suddenly dry throat. Samael stayed silent, letting me see our doom.

I'd failed him. I'd been so cocky, so sure Lucifer had no idea…

"I knew," Samael crooned. *"I've studied Lucifer for centuries, my love."*

I swallowed. *"Why didn't you tell me?"*

He hesitated, and I got it. When it came to deception, I was a novice compared to Lucifer. If I'd learned of this, Lucifer would have immediately known. He would have read the terror on my face, in my eyes. Then he would've had his proof that I could still communicate with Samael, and I would have been locked in the cells this entire time, with no way to help.

"I'm sorry," Samael said.

"Don't be. I need a few centuries before I'll be able to lie as well as you old timers."

A low laugh.

Samael surveyed the camp spread out before him and I examined it through his gaze. The closest portal had been too heavily guarded and would tip off Lucifer too early, so they'd used a portal to the west, close to the mountain chain in the distance. Their own temporary camp was set up beneath the plateau Samael now stood on. From there, he could see not only his own army, but Lucifer's forces spread out, surrounding the palace on three sides.

"He has his sentries in the forest, many of them hidden from sight. And, of course, we know about the wyverns which he will be deploying to finish us off when he believes we are broken."

"The pocket realm?"

"As soon as I believe our army is ready here, I will step into the realm. The rest of our people are waiting inside, and it will be smuggled as close to the palace as possible. Finvarra is currently already waiting with the majority of our forces."

I took a deep breath. The thought of him being stuck in that realm scared the shit out of me. Samael could likely feel just how terrified I was, because an invisible hand stroked my cheek.

I forced myself to inhale. Then exhale. Samael wouldn't turn back now. At least we had this element of surprise. Lucifer would think he'd already won, would be preparing his army to march on our people.

"Promise me you'll protect Evie." I hadn't expected him to attempt to keep her home. Evie would never have stayed behind.

"We'll guard her with our lives. She's been banned from entering the pocket realm. Everyone knows to keep an eye on her. Trust me to keep her safe, Danica. Now get out of there. You know what you need to do."

I did. Slipping the ring into my mouth, I hit the sentries I knew were still loyal to Lucifer, the spots where our forces would end up trapped if I didn't use the packages I'd left, carefully hidden.

Just the thought of using them made me nauseous. This was murder.

No, this is war.

It was both. And I didn't have time to come to an understanding with myself about it. These actions would haunt my nightmares for the rest of my life, but I had to create these distractions, had to clear the way for our people.

I trembled as I checked the servants' quarters. All evacuated. Good. The palace gates rose in front of me, a beacon of hope. I just had to slip past the guards, and I'd return once we'd taken down Lucifer's people, my bondmate at my side.

I took a deep breath and strode toward the gates.

And straight into an invisible ward.

A ward so well-crafted that I hadn't even felt it in front of me.

An alarm wailed, ripping through the air. Heads turned, guards aimed crossbows in my direction, and

Lucifer appeared with his faithful Daimonion, by his side. The assassin held Yusilin in his arms, his eyes lit with pleasure at her fear.

Lucifer smiled in my direction. "I suggest you reveal yourself, granddaughter, or else watch this poor, innocent girl die."

I hesitated. That poor innocent girl had been spying on me since I arrived. This could all be a trick. There was an empty space between the guard on the left and the gate. If I could crawl past him...

Daimonion pulled out a knife and slowly pulled the pointed tip down Yusilin's face. Her skin split open and her expression went blank with terror.

I had to do this quickly. Couldn't let Lucifer see exactly how I'd managed to hide from him. With a deep breath, I spat the ring into my hand and slipped it into my pocket, where I shoved it back onto my finger.

Lucifer gave me a satisfied smile. He gestured, and Daimonion shoved his knife into Yusilin's chest, letting her slump to the ground. I launched myself at her, and the assassin caught my arm, his knife now at my face, the tip of his blade inches from my eye.

"I can cut out her eye," he offered, and Lucifer shook his head.

"Not yet. The shock could disrupt the power transfer."

Lovely.

Lucifer turned and walked away, and Daimonion dragged me after him until we were in the throne room, now empty.

"Close the doors," Lucifer ordered, his voice echoing through the huge space. Daimonion dropped me, my bruised knees howling at me as I hit the ground. I barely noticed, my eyes on the long, wooden table that had been set up in the middle of the room. Restraints hung from the side of the table, and a single grimoire sat on top. Waiting.

Everything else had been cleared away.

My face went numb. I didn't bother getting to my feet. I didn't think my legs would be able to hold me.

BOOM

Daimonion went still next to me. Across the room, Lucifer glanced over his shoulder at me. "You dared—"

BOOM

BOOM

BOOM

The explosions happened again and again. Even from here, I could hear the screaming, the shock. Long nights spent hiding bombs for Garadiel, and it was all paying off.

"Where did you get this power, granddaughter? The power to hide yourself from me?"

I finally made it to my feet. "I didn't hide myself all that well if you knew to put the ward in place."

A cold smile, sharp as a scalpel. "And yet it took me far too long to learn just how you were undermining me at every turn."

"What did you expect?"

He gave me a look of such disdain, I almost shivered. But he was already turning away, opening the grimoire.

Lucifer hummed a little while he read. Psychopath.

Daimonion walked to the throne room doors again and again while Lucifer read. I watched the assassin as he spoke in hushed whispers to whoever was keeping him updated about the battle. If everything was going as planned, Samael would be in the pocket realm right now. We'd agreed that we wouldn't speak unless necessary. I didn't want to distract him, and I could still feel him, alive down the end of our bond.

I reached for the underworld, crooning to it desperately.

"Please, come to me."

Since it had disappeared in a temper tantrum last time, I half expected it to ignore me, but this time it seemed as if it had been waiting for me. I could sense its eagerness.

And it showed me, flying my consciousness high above the palace, until I had a bird's-eye view of two armies marching toward each other. Our army was much, much smaller, the majority of our people hidden in the artifact currently being smuggled into Lucifer's front lines.

The demons advancing on the palace were a distraction, but they would be heavily outnumbered. Many of them would likely die, waiting for Samael and Finvarra to pull their people out of the pocket realm.

I squinted, and the underworld took me closer until I could just make out Bael's face as he stood on the front lines. He roared something at his people, who roared back with a fury that seemed to make the ground tremble.

Lucifer's army wore steel gray. Ours wore obsidian black. Some of Finvarra's people were stationed on the front lines, which Lucifer would have expected. Demons were dotted amongst them, their wings out, ready to take to the air.

Every soldier was armed with swords, knives, and

a shield. I guessed even the most powerful paranormals would never rely solely on that power, which would be drained during the battle. It was why I'd watched Samael's demons train so hard, keeping their bodies in peak condition.

"Thank you," I told the underworld, hoping it would keep me updated. I got the sense it was smiling, and then it was gone, leaving my consciousness back in the throne room.

"My spies have reported that Vassago will be amongst Samael's army," Daimonion announced, practically shuddering with eagerness. I went still. I hadn't seen Vas. I wasn't sure where Samael had ordered him stationed.

Lucifer stared at him, and Daimonion's face hardened. "Your majesty... you promised."

Sick fuck. My expression must have displayed exactly what I thought of him, because Lucifer smiled at me. "You may go," he said, his gaze still on me. "Kill him while my granddaughter is still alive and bring his head to me."

My chest screwed tight, until it felt like it was a knot of dread inside me.

No. Vas would be protected by our people. I had to believe that.

I managed to keep my expression bored as I stared back at Lucifer, dimly aware of Daimonion leaving guards outside the door to the throne room.

The fact that Pischiel wasn't here spoke volumes. Lucifer must know by now. Must know that Pischiel had joined us. And yet, he hadn't said a word. The ball of dread expanded, until it felt as if I'd choke on it.

"Why leave Pischiel alive?"

I knew Lucifer, and if he'd killed Pischiel, he'd have strung him up somewhere public.

Lucifer gave me that look that said he was amused by my ignorance. "Believe me, granddaughter, Pischiel is exactly where I want him to be. And when you learn why he is where he is, you certainly won't be whispering secrets to him anymore."

Pain stabbed through me. Pischiel couldn't be betraying us. I refused to believe it.

Lucifer turned away, busying himself with setting up everything he needed to take my power. Ice cold knowledge stabbed into my gut and twisted. If I didn't do something soon, I was dead.

The doors opened and Lucifer turned his head. I recognized the general, one of Lucifer's most powerful demons.

"Speak," Lucifer hissed.

The general swallowed, but stood tall to give his report.

"We know where the artifact is," he said. "Our people are ready to destroy it as soon as you give the word."

Lucifer smiled. His eyes met mine, and the world receded around the edges.

He'd known. He'd known about the artifact this entire time. And now almost everyone I loved was trapped inside, along with thousands of other demons, dragons, and unseelie.

Stuck in the pocket realm with no warning that they were about to be trapped for eternity.

CHAPTER TWENTY

Samael

Forty thousand men and women were at my back, all standing in formation, all ready for battle.

No one spoke.

Some of them shifted on their feet, likely attempting to release some of the adrenaline and fear that would be creeping up on them now.

Waiting was the worst part.

I trusted Bael—was keeping in regular contact with him. But knowing so many of my people were facing Lucifer's army on his own territory…

I ground my teeth.

"What is taking so long?" Finvarra snarled under his breath.

A strange disquiet took up residence in my gut. I had made allowances for each step of this plan. But I'd kept the details very, very quiet. I wouldn't risk another betrayal.

"Everything is going according to plan," I said, not bothering to look at him. Guilt stabbed at me for what would happen soon, but I saw no other choice.

If Teremos was caught, we had others watching, ready to take over, to do whatever it took to get the candlestick holder where we needed it to be.

Lilith had managed to turn some of Lucifer's most loyal people, instructing them to be ready to say the incantation if our people were unable to get the artifact close enough to Lucifer's palace. This was the most dangerous part of our plan, and we'd prepared accordingly.

But it had been too long.

We were so close. So close to the palace, to Danica.

Bael knocked on my shields and I allowed him enough entrance to speak to me.

"Ah... boss, what's going on?"

I could feel him, swinging his sword, fighting for his life, for the lives of his men.

"How close are we to the peak of the meteor shower?"

Silence. As if Bael was trying to find the right words.

"If this isn't the peak, it must be soon. The sky is filled with shooting stars, lighting up everything in sight. The sun is about to set. It would be beautiful if it wasn't such bad timing."

Danica's terror slammed into our bond, sweeping through me, until I could practically taste it on my tongue.

That smile, that strained fucking smile she'd flashed the last time I saw her.

She'd known. Known we wouldn't make it in time. And she'd planned for it. That last kiss had been her goodbye. Because my witchling would never want our people to march unprepared. Wouldn't be able to live with herself if they were slaughtered attempting to save her.

And so I paced. And planned. Ag was my second, would take up the mantle if I was gone. Because I would never live without my bondmate. Refused to. If Danica were taken from me, I would kill Lucifer, and then I would curl up and die.

Hopefully, I would see her in the next life. If the fates decided I was not to go to the place where Danica was destined, I would slaughter those fates as well, until I found my little witch once more.

A few feet away, Mere stood next to Vas, her lips bloodless as they waited for our signal.

"If I don't live through this, it was nice knowing you," she told him.

He smiled. "Oh, you'll live through this, baby. You promised me a kiss and I intend to collect."

She gaped at him. "I told you to kiss my ass. Not the same thing."

"And that little order has been keeping me going through all of this. You wouldn't want to take that hope away from a man about to march to his death, would you?"

In spite of the situation, my lips twitched. I memorized the moment to show my little witch later, when I finally had her back in my arms. Where she belonged.

Nine books. We just had to get nine books close enough to Lucifer that we could start the spell. Danica had sworn she could take care of the rest.

But first we had to get out of this fucking pocket realm. Frustration threatened to tug me under, threatened to send me into a dark abyss.

This was taking too long.

Danica

"Get out of the pocket realm, Samael!"

"It's okay, Danica."

"No, it's not."

Oh god. Oh god. Lucifer turned from the table and smiled coldly at me. He'd known about the pocket realm this whole time. And we'd served up everyone who could ever be a threat to him in one place where he could take them out with a single blow.

"Show me. Please," I begged the underworld.

The underworld complied, and I was suddenly looking down at Lucifer's people, where a sentry was slowly slipping through the forest and toward the palace, a blue glass candlestick holder in his hand.

That was the artifact? The light fae could be incredibly weird.

I recognized the sentry by his blonde curls. I'd seen him before. This was the guard who'd argued with Garadiel in the garden. Now, though, he was shaking like a leaf, so consumed by his task that he didn't notice every demon around him, watching him like a hawk as he made his way deep into Lucifer's front lines.

Time stretched. The sentry dropped the artifact to the ground, opening his mouth to say the words to free our people.

A sword slashed out of nowhere, and his head rolled to the ground, his body slumping next to it.

Oh my God.

Blood rushed in my ears as the world seemed to recede. Without him to speak the incantation, our army was trapped. And the moment that artifact was destroyed, everyone in the pocket realm was dead.

My breath stilled in my chest, and I sucked in air as the underworld prodded at me, focusing on one man.

Pischiel. He was in the front line, next to our enemies. He was supposed to go to Samael. Had he betrayed us?

He looked sick to his stomach, his face ashen. Rage poured into me, and I realized I could feel him faintly at the end of that thread.

I had bonded him. If he had betrayed us, I would make him pay.

Samael could communicate with those he'd bonded with. I had no time to learn how he did it, desperation clawing at my chest and cutting me open. I forced my mind to go blank and focused on Pischiel's face.

"Pischiel," I attempted, and felt him jolt. *"You have to get them out. Before Lucifer's people destroy the realm. Please."*

"It's going to be okay, Danica." His expression was blank, and his voice was cold. My entire body went numb, horror sweeping through me.

My attention faded slightly as Lucifer paced back and forth, screaming at one of his generals.

"Destroy that artifact!" he roared. "Now!"

I was helpless to do anything but watch as one of Lucifer's commanders turned to Pischiel with a nod.

Pischiel lifted his sword.

"No," I begged Pischiel. *"Please, please don't do this."*

He swung his sword, cutting the artifact in two, and a scream ripped from my throat. In front of me, Lucifer laughed and laughed. I fell to my knees, too numb to cry.

The bond was still there. They were trapped for eternity but not dead. I would find a way to get them out. If it took the rest of my life, I would—

"Little witch."

Now I sobbed, hearing Samael's voice in my head. Knowing I might never get to touch him again. He sent reassurance down the bond, but I was too distraught to feel it.

"Danica, I need you to trust me."

Lucifer's army began marching toward Bael's soldiers. Bael's eyes gleamed with anticipation, and he screamed out an order that had his front lines crouching, ready.

They were about to be slaughtered.

The battlefield receded as the underworld made me focus on what was happening in Lucifer's throne room. My body was leaving the ground as Lucifer used his power to float me through the air, dropping me on the table. I'd never seen him look so happy, his eyes practically glowing with triumph.

He smiled at me, leaning close enough to strap down my restraints himself.

"Hey grandfather," I gasped out. "Fuck you."

I reached for the chain around my neck and snapped it, feeling the invisible rowan in my palm. I'd only have one shot at this.

Lucifer grabbed my arm, ready to tie me down.

And I shoved the rowan into his chest.

Nothing happened.

Lucifer threw back his head. Then he laughed and laughed. "You believe you can kill *me*?" He ripped open his shirt and displayed the thin armor molded to his chest. I couldn't see the rowan, but I heard it snap as Lucifer pulled it free with a smile, heard it fall to the ground as he dropped it on the floor.

"I know every move you make before you even think to make it, granddaughter. Your lack of foresight is a humiliation to my bloodline."

His arm swung, and I rolled off the table with the force of his backhand, my vision dimming as I hit the ground. My eyes slid shut, and I forced myself to open them to slits. If I passed out, I was done.

Of course, I was done anyway.

I'd had one shot. One chance to kill him. And I'd lost it.

The doors slammed open, and two guards sprinted into the throne room, obviously hearing Lucifer's raised voice.

"Get out before I kill you!" Lucifer roared, and they turned, hauling ass straight back out. They left the doors open, and I could hear their footsteps disappearing as they sprinted from the throne room.

My cheek throbbed. Had Lucifer broken my cheekbone? Pain seemed to spread over my entire face, and it immediately began to swell.

Lucifer didn't bother hauling me onto the table again.

"I'll rip your power from you and use it to kill everyone you love," he vowed. His hand raised, and I threw up a ward. My power was still sluggish, but I would slow him down any way I could.

He *grinned* at me. "You have more fight than your father."

I ignored him, stumbled to my feet, and sprinted toward the door.

It was a fight-or-flight reaction that would do me no good, and my ward dropped for a split second as my head spun dizzily. Lucifer's power crept out, holding me in place. He strolled toward me, and I shuddered, nothing but prey as he grabbed my hair, spinning me toward him. I used the momentum, raised my arm.

And backhanded him.

My bone bracelet smashed into Lucifer's eye, and he howled as if he'd been gutted. The bracelet burned, and I had a single moment to mentally thank Hannah before Lucifer held out a hand and my entire body was engulfed in agony.

I dropped to the floor and shrieked. Distantly, I could hear Samael roaring through the bond as Lucifer used his power to do something that made it feel as if acid was eating through my skin and muscle and bone.

I went away, leaving my body behind.

"Thank you," I sobbed to the underworld as the pain dimmed. *"Thank you."*

Was that… *surprise* it was sending back? For my gratitude?

Once again, I was overlooking the battle. Overlooking my people as they bled, killed, died.

Gnomes were positioned in Bael's army. Where had they come from? Short and viciously fast, they slid into Lucifer's ranks, cutting tendons and distracting his soldiers long enough for Bael's soldiers to take their heads. Above them, demons clashed in the air, blood and feathers splattering those fighting below.

The underworld focused its attention on one gnome. Gary.

No. No no no no no.

There had to be a hundred gnomes on the battlefield, and while most of them were distracting the soldiers, the other half were slowly integrating themselves into their ranks, sliding beneath swinging swords and sprinting, all of them, toward the palace.

What the hell were they doing?

Gary was holding something, and he ducked a swinging sword, throwing the object at a gnome next to him, who rolled beneath a lunging demon. The gnome threw the object back to Gary, who caught it just as his friend was engulfed by demon fire.

Gary's expression turned terrible, but he kept running.

One after the other, the gnomes were killed, until I could barely force myself to keep watching. They were so much smaller than the demons, and most of them weren't focused on fighting, but instead on getting beyond the front lines, close to the palace.

The pain was eating my muscles like acid, but I held on to what the underworld was showing me. I would give anything to be able to throw a ward around Gary, to protect the gnomes from Lucifer's demons.

Ten gnomes surrounded Gary now. All of them keeping him safe. Now they were deep in Lucifer's ranks, close to the palace, and Gary's friends fought savagely against demons who were unprepared for them.

Then Gary stopped. Scanned. A demon shot into the air in front of him as demon fire lit up his hand.

Oh God.

But Pischiel was suddenly there, and he slammed the demon to the ground. Gary's gray face was pale, his jaw set, and he barreled down the battlefield and straight into Lucifer's front lines.

What the hell was he doing? Did he have a death wish? I wanted to scream at him, wanted to warn him, and my breath caught in my throat as one of Garadiel's men grabbed Gary by his arm.

"No, please!"

But he wasn't killing him. The demon shot into the air, spread his wings wide, and *threw* Gary toward Garadiel.

Garadiel caught the gnome, his teeth bared. Gary handed him the object, and a sob ripped from my throat as Garadiel took the blue candlestick from him, throwing his head back.

I couldn't hear him over the sounds of the soldiers, but I read his lips.

"Mors vincit omnia!"

It took a moment before one of the generals on the front lines cocked his head, a dull realization filling his eyes as the man they'd fought beside betrayed them to their enemies.

To us.

One of the soldiers lunged at Garadiel, swinging his sword, but Samael was there, burying his knife in his throat.

I hiccupped, tears flowing down my face.

My brutal, vicious bondmate. Of course he'd been the first to leave the pocket realm. The first to step into the unknown. But our people flooded out behind him, popping out of the artifact as if they'd appeared out of the ether. Demons immediately took to the skies, followed by the dragons. On the ground, light fae were dotted amongst the demons. A few thousand maybe, all of them wearing gleaming green helmets.

Together with Finvarra's unseelie army, the seelie swung enchanted swords and fought like they were possessed, protecting each and every gnome on the battlefield. Gnomes who were constantly ignored, continually underestimated. And who had just saved the lives of over forty thousand high demons, high fae, werewolves, and dragons.

My head snapped to the side, and the underworld receded, leaving me staring up at Lucifer as my cheek burned.

He'd taken a risk, planning to use our strategy against us. Worked with the seelie king who'd told him all about the pocket realm attached to the artifact disguised as a candlestick holder.

Samael had known Taraghlan betrayed him, but he'd been out of time. And he'd somehow arranged for an exact match of the artifact to be snuck toward the palace. One that would fool the demons who were expecting it.

If not for the duplicate candlestick, Lucifer would

have won this war with one fell swoop.

And the only reason he hadn't, the only reason his people were now dying in droves, was because he'd been outplayed.

I choked out a laugh. "There's only room for one vengeful, overpowered demon in this realm, grandfather. And that's Samael."

Lucifer hit me again. He was really losing it now if he was lowering himself to physical violence. He seemed to realize the same, because he took a deep breath, and his expression turned blank. Then he grabbed me by my shirt and began to drag me back toward the table.

"You're terrified. I can feel it. Stay alive for me, little witch." Samael's voice in my head. I attempted to calm down, knowing that for him to be distracted while powerless, while he could only fight with a sword and shield...

Outside, the sun was setting. Soon, the meteor shower would be at its peak.

Lucifer began to chant, and my whole body went cold as icy fingers slid up my spine and traveled along each of my limbs.

The power drain felt like death.

My power was depleted, most of it still buried far beneath my shields thanks to the cuff that had been on my wrist for so long. But according to the prophecy, it would be enough.

Enough for Lucifer to kill Samael.

Enough for him to slaughter our armies.

Enough for him to stroll through a portal and lay waste to my world.

I threw up a shield. Lucifer knocked it down as if it was paper. My wards were far too weak. *I* was far too weak. I'd been foolish to think I could go up against Lucifer. Blind to think I'd be able to hold him off long enough for our people to get into the palace.

"I'm sorry, Samael."

"I'm coming, little witch. I'm almost there. Just hold on."

"Don't come. You need to retreat. He'll kill *you."*

The only hope we'd had was for Lucifer's death to give Samael back his powers. And that hope was gone, because he'd known about the rowan arrow the whole time.

"Please show me them again," I begged the underworld. I wanted my last sight to be of my friends, my family, still furiously alive and fighting.

I blinked, and I was once again looking down at the battle. I could feel my powers, my life, draining away, but I watched as Samael fought at the front lines, cutting his way through Lucifer's army. He moved like a nightmare, like his bones were fluid. It was as if he had an extra sense, one that told him exactly where his enemy would attack, and the maneuver they would use.

Next to him, Ag fought with grim determination, moving with centuries of experience. Vas barreled through soldiers next to Ag, his expression hard, and something cracked in my chest. He was okay. Okay, and surrounded by our people.

On Samael's other side, Sathanas and Sitri swung their own swords, sending out blasts of their demon fire when necessary. And Lilith… my mouth went dry.

She raged down the battlefield as if she'd been born to fight on it. She may not have the muscle of the guys, but she was so fast, it was almost difficult to keep track of her.

Lilith had spent so much time lounging around like a cat that I'd never realized just how quick and deadly she could be. As I watched, she ducked past a swinging sword, her movements so fast the demon swinging it looked like he was in slow motion. The demon shoved his power at her and it bounced off her shield, leaving him wide open as she cut him down with demon fire of her own.

But it wasn't just the high demons that fought for Lucifer. He'd ordered lesser demons to join the ranks, and they snarled, giving into their own bloodlust as packs of them aimed for individual soldiers in our army.

On the left flank, Nathaniel and his wolves ripped demons apart like they were made of fabric, the wolves' claws and teeth dripping blood. A wolf went down and was instantly dragged away, replaced by a wolf I recognized. Liam.

In the air, dragons raged, spitting fire and setting Lucifer's soldiers alight.

Bael's soldiers advanced, no longer outnumbered by Lucifer's. Hannah's laugh rang out, hoarse and wicked. Someone had sat her on a horse, and she was feeding on the fear and pain of Lucifer's soldiers as they died. She raised her hand and sent her death magic into their lines, laughing again as ten or twenty soldiers dropped to the ground.

A roar sounded, and the underworld showed me more.

Lucifer had released his hellhounds. Seven of them.

Selina fought them like a wild thing, cutting at one of them with both her magic and the longsword she swung as if it was an extension of her arm.

Aubrey strangled a hellhound with long, thick vines. His smile was feral, his eyes hard, and he moved as if he was dancing. Meredith fought on Aubrey's other side, a dagger in each hand. She wasn't as fast, but Aubrey was keeping an eye on her, stepping in when she seemed to falter. More of Samael's demons had joined them, keeping the hellhounds from creating devastation in their right flank.

And there was Virtus. The gentle griffin plowed through the hellhounds with a roar, looking for all the world as if he was frolicking through a field of daisies.

My gaze shifted to the palace gates.

Somehow, the demons and unseelie had cleared a route to the wall. They held off Lucifer's soldiers now, preventing the guards stationed at the top of the wall from slaughtering the witches down below.

Gemma stood in front of the huge stone wall encircling the palace, her eyes narrowed on the lethal flowers of the garthia plant. Her coven stood behind her. Behind them, more witches waited, standing in some formation known only to them. I spotted Siobhan, Riona, and Maeve amongst them. The Allen coven was here, along with a witch I recognized as belonging to the Jefferson coven.

At least six other covens were gathered behind them. The witches had united. At least for this one battle.

Evie approached, and my hands began to sweat. She

reached for the bag Gemma held out. Then, with a small smile, she pulled out a single bone.

Each coven leader had their own bag, their own witchbones. One by one, they reached into their bags, handing out bones to all of the witches in their covens.

More of the wolves pushed close. There was Nathaniel, roaring as he cut into a demon who attempted to send demon fire barreling into the witches. Any of Lucifer's people who came close were ripped apart. Behind the witches, even more werewolves waited to get into the palace grounds, trembling with anticipation.

Evie spoke a single word, and the witchbone she was holding burst into flame. She threw it at the wall, and it blasted a hole the size of a gnome. The witches spread out, throwing their bones, one after the other, taking down the wall, and the garthia plant with it.

Fire spread, crackling against the stone, until the garthia plant was engulfed. Above the palace wall, Scylla appeared, inhaling once, and the fire was gone. All that remained of the plant was ash and embers.

I could feel the black books. Hidden on our people, approaching the palace from all angles, as people bled and killed and died to guard them, to keep those holding them safe.

They'd come. All of them had come. For me. For us. In an effort to free the demons, and to save my life.

I was aware of everything. *Everyone.* Kyla was pacing down in the dungeons, her wolf yearning for her pack. Oh God, she was alive.

Pischiel had joined Samael now, swinging his own sword with our people. Even Keigan…

I ground my teeth. He was supposed to sneak out. To run like hell. So why was he still in the palace?

Lucifer screamed, falling away from me, and I crawled backward, gasping for air as I had a brief reprieve from the drain on my powers. His blood had been used to keep the garthia plant strong. Now that the plant was dead, was Lucifer weakened somehow?

Seeing the people I loved was enough. Enough to give me hope. Enough to make me strong.

I'd tried killing Lucifer with the rowan arrow, but in my heart I'd known. I had one more card to play.

Even if I couldn't kill the psychopath, I could sure slow him down.

CHAPTER TWENTY-ONE

Danica

I t hurt to breathe. Whatever Lucifer had done to me had ripped at my insides, and I could no longer remember a time without pain. But since Lucifer was also groaning in pain instead of driving his power into me, I could now think well enough to function. To plan.

Lucifer shuddered and I let out a hoarse laugh. His pain pleased me on a deep, dark level.

I glanced out the window. I wasn't sure how much time had passed while I was burning from the inside out, but the sky was lit with meteors, scorching the night sky.

I rolled my shoulders. There were worse things to see as I took my last breaths.

No. I couldn't think like that. I climbed to my knees, my head spinning. Walking wasn't possible, so I began to crawl.

"My home," Lucifer raged as he stumbled to his feet. I glanced over my shoulder at him, but kept crawling, achingly slow. Each movement stabbed at my muscles like thousands of tiny knives.

Lucifer's nose was bleeding, and I let out a rusty laugh. Looked like the plants were more connected to him than we'd imagined.

"I bet that hurt," I managed to gasp out.

"The least you can do, granddaughter, is face your death with dignity," he snarled.

Yeah, yeah.

Lucifer glanced out the window with a look of elation. The sun had set, and the night sky was lit up with radiant streams of light, streaking through the darkness. He advanced on me, raised his hands.

And began to chant once more.

Above the throne, the words carved into the wall blurred and changed. *Do ut des. I give so that you might give.*

I know. I get it.

It wasn't the *rowan arrow* I was supposed to keep hidden from all.

It was as if I was in slow motion as I crawled toward the table, where I was pretty sure the rowan arrow had fallen. The invisibility spell on the rowan was holding, so I could only hope I could manage to snatch up one of the pieces.

Lucifer laughed, and my body began burning from the inside out once more. I screamed, writhing on the ground. The last time I'd died, it had been almost peaceful at the end. My mom had been waiting for me.

This? This was what hell felt like.

Samael was linked tightly to me, and I felt his dread like it was my own. Something was very, very wrong.

"Please," I said, reaching for the underworld again.

Lucifer laughed. He resumed his chanting, and the world began to dim at the edges.

The underworld showed me.

And I screamed.

Daimonion had found Vas.

Samael had gotten separated from him, and was fighting his way back, desperation and determination warring across his face. He moved like lightning, dodging and leaping, ducking and weaving as he roared at Vas to *move!*

None of Lucifer's people dared interfere with Daimonion's kill. He stood a few feet from Vas, his own sword in his hand, a sick pleasure in his eyes.

My body began to turn cold once more, my power draining faster now. I held onto the underworld, unable to look away from Vas. My friend. The brother I'd never had.

His eyes were lit with retribution, his face covered in mud and blood. I smiled as he dropped his left shoulder. I knew that movement. He was leaving himself slightly open, practically daring Daimonion to attack. When he did, Vas would bury his sword in his gut. Then he'd finally take his head.

The assassin didn't hesitate. Whatever had stilled his hand and left Vas breathing the night he slaughtered Vas's parents…

It was gone now.

Knowing what I knew about Daimonion, I had a feeling he'd seen something in that infant, and had decided he would be a worthwhile opponent one day.

These old, murderous creatures did so have a tendency to get bored.

Daimonion raised his sword to swing. Vas stumbled, a little move I liked to call "the uncoordinated bear." Bael had fallen for it three times before he finally realized Vas was messing with him.

But Ag... I saw the moment he moved as if it was in slow motion. It was the first time I'd ever truly seen fear in Ag's eyes, and he lunged toward Vas, threw himself in front of his nephew, shielded him with his own body.

He didn't know. Didn't know Vas was luring the assassin closer.

The blow cut across Ag's shoulder, deep and vicious. Ag snarled but didn't move, determined to protect Vas.

Daimonion's face lit with a dark fury at being denied the kill he'd aimed for.

Vas threw back his head with a roar that seemed to make the entire battlefield pause. I felt Samael freeze. Felt him swing his sword with even greater desperation as he fought to get closer to his friends, his family.

Daimonion used the confusion, used Ag's sudden inattention and determination to protect his nephew.

And smiled as he lit Ag up with demon fire.

Vas's howl was chilling. Distantly, I felt Samael, and through him, all of his demons. They were thrusting their power into Ag in an attempt to keep him alive. But they'd been fighting for hours. They were mostly drained themselves.

A scream ripped up my throat as Ag fell to his knees. Then he slumped fully to the ground, and I knew. He was gone.

Vas charged at Daimonion, his own sword swinging. The assassin had likely used a good chunk of his power to kill Ag, but he still had centuries of killing compared to Vas.

"Do something," I begged the underworld. It stayed silent, but once again, I could feel it watching, weighing.

Vas sliced at Daimonion. Again. Again. Again. The assassin laughed, ducked, but I'd been forced to spend enough time with him that I could see the strain on his face. He raised his sword to block Vas, but he wasn't fast enough. Wasn't driven by the cold fury that drove Vas.

Vas's sword bounced off of Daimonion's. But he used that motion to twist. To thrust his sword into Daimonion's gut.

"More," I silently urged Vas. I'd stabbed Daimonion myself, and he'd healed it within a couple of hours. No healer required. *"More, Vas."*

That's when his hand lit up with demon fire.

I almost choked. Pischiel's words running through my head.

"It takes centuries before a demon is powerful enough to use demon fire. Samael was the only exception."

Something had cracked open inside Vas, and he'd up-leveled. Face stunned, he raised his hand, examining the bright glow.

Daimonion's eyes widened, and Lucifer's assassin, who had slaughtered countless people, who had rampaged up and down that battlefield…

Turned to flee.

He launched himself into the air, ducking and twisting, but Vas snarled, lifted his hand higher, and let his power loose. Demon fire engulfed Daimonion's arm, but he kept flying, his scream filled with cold fury and a promise of vengeance.

Vas screamed his own rage. Then he dropped to the ground, next to what was left of his family.

My throat ached. Ag had become something like a disapproving father-in-law over the past few months. I mentally reached for Vas, wishing I could wrap my arms around him. But the underworld was already showing me more.

Showing me Taraghlan, marching toward our people with an army of seelie dressed in white.

His soldiers were armed. They were fresh. They practically burned with eagerness and power.

He hadn't just delayed Samael. Hadn't just told Lucifer about our plan with the pocket realm. No, he was here to join forces with Lucifer, to attack us from behind.

The knowledge slammed into me. We were going to lose. We were all going to die.

Samael

Ag was dead.

Dead.

Vas was still on his knees, seemingly incapable of moving. Our people surrounded him, keeping him in the center of a rough circle as they killed with cold fury. I had to get to him. Had to get him up.

My fault.

I'd turned, stepping too far away, unable to resist slaughtering one of Lucifer's top commanders. I should have known Daimonion was waiting for his chance to kill Vas.

I buried my sword in the chest of the closest soldier, beheading another. Then I whirled, making my way toward Vas. My hand found his armor, and I pulled him to his feet.

"Get up," I roared down at him.

He stared up at me, unblinking.

And the back of my neck burned with awareness.

I turned, and dread unraveled in my gut. Taraghlan's army marched toward us. Not all of his people. No, he was smarter than that, would never risk all of them. He'd brought just enough to cement his alliance with Lucifer.

More than enough.

I shot into the air, sliding in front of one of my demons, who'd taken a heavy hit to one arm and could barely hold his sword. He slashed out at Lucifer's soldier with his power, but like all my people, it was weakened just as his body was weakened.

I sliced through his opponent, and he fell to the ground, choking on his blood. But I was already watching Taraghlan's people. They were fresh. Powerful.

Lucifer must have promised to immediately war with Finvarra in exchange for a pact with the seelie king.

And we were now sandwiched between Lucifer's army in front of us and Taraghlan's behind us.

Bael had turned his ranks to face Taraghlan's, and Bael's front line shot into the air, providing a distraction for the seelie, who would be forced to watch for attacks from both the air and on the ground.

But it wasn't enough.

I burned for my power, could practically feel it, just beyond my fingertips. A few feet away, Lilith launched into the air, slitting a throat with one hand and turning one of Lucifer's soldiers to ash with the other. She still fought with a cold fury, but even she was tiring, her face covered in blood from a cut to the eye. The cut had healed, but her face was black and blue beneath her helmet, her body too depleted to heal her as fast as it should.

Our eyes met. She knew. Knew it was hopeless.

I only wished I could have seen my little witch one last time.

I could feel her, down the other end of the bond. Could feel her horror and terror. She knew. Somehow, she knew what was happening here.

Frustration shot through me as I slashed at another soldier. One of Lucifer's. Except they were all mine.

Several thousand of his soldiers had fled once they realized I was fighting within the ranks. Several thousand more had turned to our side, just a couple of hours ago when they'd thought we were here to save them. When they thought I would take back my throne.

I dodged around a group of demons fighting in the air, drops of blood spraying over those fighting below. And I aimed at Taraghlan himself, leading his army.

My vision narrowed until all I could see was his face.

"No," Lilith screamed at me. She'd dropped down and managed to rouse Vas, who was fighting once more with grim determination. "Go to Danica."

She was right. Here, while I was powerless, Taraghlan

could kill me with a thought, and I would likely take my witchling with me. But if I could get to the palace, could ensure the black books got close enough…

I arrowed toward the castle.

And I could have sworn I felt Ag behind me, guarding my back.

Danica

The pain was endless.

Dying this way felt as if it would take years.

Ancient words poured from Lucifer's throat, and I could feel him, feel his satisfaction, feel him growing stronger.

He bared his teeth at me in a feral grin as I lay writhing on the black marble floor, my agony too sharp to scream.

I fought with everything in me to turn my head toward the door. Toward freedom. My last sight wouldn't be Lucifer taking my life.

It would be Keigan's face.

What?

I blinked, and the scream I hadn't been able to let loose bubbled in my throat.

His eyes met mine, dark with sorrow.

No. No, no, no.

We both knew he had no chance. He was buying me a few seconds at most.

He launched himself at Lucifer.

The spell draining my power disappeared with Lucifer's inattention as he felt Keigan's approach.

I made it to my knees, a sob fighting its way free from my throat. Keigan's eyes gleamed at me, and he smiled—the gentle smile that had felt like coming home from the moment I'd met him.

Lucifer turned.

I forced myself to move.

Slowly, painstakingly, I began to crawl once more. Toward the two halves of the rowan arrow.

A crack sounded. Keigan's neck. And I knew. Knew he'd never look at me with those dark eyes again. Knew he'd sacrificed himself to buy me time. Just a little time. But maybe… maybe it would be enough.

Because it wasn't the rowan arrow I was supposed to keep hidden from all. It was Angelica's ring. And I'd been careful—oh so careful—not to let anyone know exactly which ring it was, and what it did.

Sure, a few people knew I could use the ring to become invisible. But they didn't know it broke enchantments. And they didn't know it could be used in the Spell of Three.

Gloria squinted at me. "Nothing else. I'm not your witch to command, Danica Amana."

"Not even for the chance of a clean slate with Samael once this is all over?"

She studied me. "Speak."

I filled her in. Gloria shook her head. I begged, cajoled, and turned to horrific threats that made me nauseous to even speak them. Finally, she agreed that it could be done. I handed her the ring in my pocket. And she did what I wanted.

There was one way out of the sacrifice required for the Spell of Three.

If the person was voluntarily choosing to have it placed on them with a blood sacrifice of their own.

And if they were wearing Angelica's ring.

The ring that could break the spell of three also allowed Gloria to place it on me.

And because I'd voluntarily bled for the spell, choosing to place it on myself, it would ensure that when Lucifer killed me, he would be weakened.

Hopefully weakened enough that the black books would help. And then Samael could kill him.

I made it close to the table before Lucifer turned. Close to where I was pretty sure the rowan arrow had dropped. The invisibility spell on the rowan was holding, so I could only hope I'd manage to snatch up one of the pieces.

"Tell them to chant," I ordered Samael.

I felt his attention, felt the moment he could sense my resolve, when he figured out what I was about to do next.

He roared at me, his rage and pain so deep, it would have terrified me if I hadn't seen the beautiful heart of him.

"Now," I insisted. *"They have to use the books now."*

His fury was endless. But I heard him give the order, felt it be passed on.

Lucifer's hand wrapped around my hair as I swept my hand along the floor for one of the pieces of arrow. My palm pushed it further away, and I lunged, scalp burning, as Lucifer laughed.

Time slowed to a crawl. Keigan's face flashed in my mind. Yusilin, dropped to the ground like trash. Kyla, at the mercy of her wolf. Samael's parents. Ag. My father. The slaves. Everyone in this realm.

I turned and plunged the arrow into Lucifer's thigh.

He screamed, his hand raising to hit me.

But it was too late. I'd ripped the arrow free, and I shoved the rowan into Lucifer's own hand, squeezing his fingers tightly around it. I felt his confusion, but he was too busy focusing on the wound in his leg.

Lucifer wasn't used to pain.

I was accustomed to constantly getting my ass kicked. To giving pain and taking it. But Lucifer? These days he was soft. And it would be his downfall.

Above the throne, the words carved into the wall blurred and changed.

"I give so you might give," I screamed. "*Do ut des*."

I threw myself at Lucifer's hand.

And the arrow plunged into my chest.

CHAPTER TWENTY-TWO

Samael

Nine books, held by nine creatures of power, all of them channeling the remainder of that power into the spells in the black books. I could feel each one, knew their exact location as they used the grimoires to harness that power. Could see their faces as if they were standing a few feet away.

Gemma, her old face twisted in disgust as she read from the grimoire in her hands.

Evie, tears dripping down her face in a way that told me she *knew*. Knew what her sister had done, but she sobbed out the words anyway.

Aubrey, one hand absently ensuring his vines continued to hold a hellhound trapped beneath them as he chanted.

Meredith, her face covered in splattered blood, eyes on the grimoire as she screamed the words.

Next to her, Selina's expression was almost serene as she gazed toward the palace, the words flowing off her tongue as if she was born to say them.

On the opposite side, near the palace gates, Hannah chanted, the black witch's power streaming from her. Her face was gray with exhaustion, but her eyes were like two black coals as she spat each word.

Lilith had taken up the book Ag was supposed to use. Tears dripped down her face as she filled in for him.

Vas chanted from the eighth black book. He looked like he was half dead himself, but he'd managed to pull himself together long enough to read the words he'd memorized earlier.

And the ninth book…

I'd almost expected Finvarra to abstain. Thought he'd take this opportunity to go after Taraghlan. But unlike the seelie king, Finvarra was capable of playing the long game. He knew he needed Lucifer dead almost as much as I did. His power seethed around him, joining with the others as they chanted as one.

And at the center, Danica.

Danica, who'd shoved that rowan arrow into her own chest. Who'd given the last of herself, everything that she had left, to save her people. My people. *Our* people.

Danica, who refused to let Lucifer win. Who had vowed to make him pay for what he did to our families.

My beautiful, brash bondmate.

My lips moved. I directed the others, wishing with everything in me that I had my own power to give to the spell. But my every conscious thought was with my little witch as I felt her, lying on the floor of that throne room, bleeding out.

For a moment, I could have sworn she surrounded

me. Could have sworn she was right above me, watching.

But all I felt down the bond was agony. Agony and determination.

Danica

I was screaming.

No. A faint smile hovered around my mouth as I tasted my own blood. No, that screaming was Lucifer.

He wasn't dead yet, but I could feel the spell from the black books, feel it coming from each point, feel the power from our people spearing into Lucifer, keeping him screaming as they chanted the spell. The spell Cyprianus had created before he was killed. The one he'd dispatched in pieces, hoping he'd be able to take his revenge from beyond the grave.

I'd be lying if I said I didn't enjoy the sound of Lucifer's screams.

But I knew. If he wasn't dead yet, from the death of the garthia plant, the Spell of Three, and the grimoires...

It wasn't going to be enough.

The underworld showed me everything.

One last look. It was giving me one last look at my friends and family before I died.

The underworld felt almost... curious as I sobbed, my vision dimming at the edges.

Evie... she was in the gardens, her ward protecting the witches as she dropped the black book, the spell finished.

But on the battlefield…

It was a slaughter.

Our people had taken the chance. Had gotten close enough to use the black books. But Lucifer wasn't yet dead. And the seelie were too fresh, too powerful.

As I watched, Taraghlan directed his gaze to where the seelie in green helmets–were fighting on our side. They took orders from Aubrey, and Taraghlan snarled, screaming at his people to kill the traitors.

Then he turned to where Mammon was fighting like a madman. He'd held back his power and was using it to cut his way through Lucifer's army until the lines broke, and some of Lucifer's more cowardly soldiers took to the skies to escape. Others cut and run.

Taraghlan lifted his hand. The ground trembled, a jagged opening forming beneath our right flank.

The ground opened, swallowing hundreds of them whole. When it slammed shut again, the silence was eerie.

Mammon was gone.

A female demon I hadn't met began screaming, falling to her knees. She tore at her hair and then fell unconscious. I knew without being told that one of the demons who'd died was her mate.

I screamed as one of Lucifer's soldiers leaned down and beheaded her unconscious body.

Finvarra's power felt endless. Even now, after so many hours of battle, he wielded it like it cost him nothing as he took down swathes of Lucifer's demons with the wave of his hand, cutting through his army as he stalked toward Taraghlan.

But I saw him turn, saw some sixth sense warn him.

Saw his eyes widen as his people were struck by black, oily magic, falling to their knees.

Black witches. Somewhere, Lucifer had stashed his own black_witches, and like Hannah, they were growing even more powerful with the blood and death and fear.

Then came the wyverns. As expected, Lucifer's commanders had waited until the last minute to let them loose. Their eyes were crazed as they shot into the sky, insane with bloodlust after being forced to hear the battle. At being chained up while they could smell blood and death.

They struck in packs, aiming for the dragons. The dragons spat fire, but they were tired too, and I heard Scylla's roar as a bright green dragon faltered, its huge body covered in black wyverns who were attacking as a pack.

They tore out the dragon's throat, and the ground shook as he landed, creating a crater in the earth.

I closed my eyes. I was a coward, but I couldn't watch.

The underworld prodded at me, as if *I* were annoying *it*.

I sent it a vision of my teeth bared in a snarl and it paused. Then it poked me again.

I opened my eyes, and my sharp inhale made the arrow jostle in my chest. More blood trickled up my throat and into my mouth.

I was staring up at the ceiling of the throne room, but it blurred in front of my eyes as the underworld showed me something else.

There, in the distance, an army marched toward us.

Toward where the unseelie were being killed by Lucifer's witches.

Thousands upon thousands of demons marched. All dressed in black, weapons in their hands.

Slowly, slowly, they came into view. And there was nothing I could do about it. The unseelie had two choices—leave the demons to their fate, or stay and be slaughtered.

Finvarra had held up his end of the bargain. There was no way he would allow his people to die for nothing.

I saw the knowledge on his face. Saw him open his mouth to order his people to retreat. Some part of me knew he would stay himself. Would fight to the death and take Taraghlan with him.

And then he went still.

Some of our people seemed to have a kind of sixth sense, because their heads turned. Then they swung swords harder, their power burning brighter. And they roared with elation.

The demons advancing on the palace were marching.

I let out a dry sob. They were *all* marching, because many of them still had no wings.

They were likely still malnourished. Likely wanted to be anywhere else but here, where Lucifer could kill them all. Could turn them into slaves once more.

I froze as I recognized the leader. Kazbiel. I'd watched as his wings were ruthlessly cut from his back, and now he led his people back, to help us fight.

Tears slipped down my face. I hadn't expected it. Hadn't even entertained a shred of hope. After everything that had been done to them, the slavery and hardship they'd endured—losing their wings, watching the people they loved die, being cut off from their power and weakened day after day.

They'd still come.

And behind them, roaring through the skies...

Nacheran. With his people at his back. His face lit with a feral grin. And sprinting in front of his army, looking for all the world like a gamboling puppy...

No way.

The creature had to be fifteen feet tall. I mentally cataloged its features. Four feet. Dark fur. Three heads. Each with a mouthful of fangs, and an unmistakably canine imprint.

Cerberus. That was fucking Cerberus.

All of this, everything the underworld had shown me, had flashed through my mind within a few seconds.

Someone was roaring orders, and I spotted Bael, still swinging his swords as if he would never tire, his shield held strong against incoming arrows. He'd somehow funneled what remained of his power into that sword, and it cut through the enemy like a knife through butter.

He looked up and roared another order.

As one, every dragon dropped to the ground. Wyverns shot after them, roaring with rage.

And out of nowhere, a thick, black net appeared in the sky.

I gaped. Who was responsible...?

Hannah. The witch was smiling up at the magical net, which had likely only been possible thanks to the pain and suffering on that battlefield.

It engulfed hundreds of wyverns, holding them in the

sky, frozen in place as they raged, attempting to break the net with teeth and claws. It hadn't trapped all of them, but enough that the dragons had a fighting chance as they arrowed back into the skies, screaming their fury.

Lucifer let out a snarl on the ground next to me. We were both trapped in a limbo, somewhere between life and death. Lucifer had harnessed the Spell of Three to cause havoc, almost killing Samael. Now he was learning what it meant to love people enough that you'd do anything to see them live.

"Show me Samael," I begged the underworld.

Oh God.

Samael was on his hands and knees, several of his demons surrounding him, keeping him safe.

But they couldn't keep him safe from this.

The older and more powerful the demon, the more the rowan would hurt them.

The rowan was roaring through our bond now.

And Samael had no power to fight with. I was risking taking him with me.

I reached for the underworld once more.

Please, I begged, desperation clawing at my chest and tearing into my lungs, my heart. *I'll do anything. Name it.*

The underworld seemed to consider it.

"He's dying!" A sob ripped through my body as I felt Samael. Could see him, almost unconscious, still struggling to drag himself toward the palace. To me.

"I'm sorry, Samael."

"Don't you give up, little witch. Fight. You fight... like hell."

Agony ripped through me. I was dimly aware of my body still writhing on the floor, as if I could claw my way out of my skin to escape the wildfire that raged through every inch of my body.

But Samael was getting weaker. And my pain, the arrow sticking out of my chest… it almost didn't register in comparison to watching him die.

"Please," I gasped out again as blood bubbled up between my lips.

Next to me, Lucifer let out a wet laugh.

"I knew you'd beg in the end," he mumbled.

He was dying. I knew he was. But if anyone could shake this off, it was Lucifer. The underworld seemed to come to some decision, showing me a picture that made my mouth drop open.

The underworld felt my instant denial, and I felt it begin to drift away.

"No. Come back. It's a deal. If, on the slim chance I live, it's a deal."

That was all I needed to say.

Power roared through the other end of the bond, and the world dimmed at the edges of my vision as I felt Samael's shock.

Felt him get to his feet with a jubilant roar.

Felt him lift one hand and kill every single enemy in the palace gardens.

Lucifer's army dropped their weapons, immediately kneeling. Our people didn't stop killing until Samael took to the skies.

"No more," he ordered, and his voice boomed across the battlefield. He turned his gaze to the wyverns who weren't trapped, who were aiming for the soldiers fighting below, the beasts still out of their minds with bloodlust. Sorrow crossed his face, but with a tilt of Samael's head, they turned to ash.

I must have passed out, because the next time I opened my eyes, he was in the throne room with me, his hand cupping my face.

His expression was frantic, fear like I'd never seen in his eyes.

Oh yeah. That arrow was still in my chest.

"You let… me think… you were trapped… for eternity. You son of a bitch."

His gaze took in my sorry state, and then he climbed to his feet. I instantly missed the feel of his hot hand on my cheek. I wanted to feel his skin on mine as I died. He must have felt that longing, because he hushed me.

"Soon, little witch."

He turned to Lucifer, who was still choking and writhing. Even after the rowan arrow, the black books, he was still holding on.

Samael looked at me, a question in his eyes, and my gaze met Lucifer's.

"Please," Lucifer said.

He'd turned Kyla into a shadow of herself. He killed my father. Then he killed Keigan. He slaughtered Samael's family. The people I loved wouldn't be safe until he was dead.

And yet, some small part of me mourned for the grandfather he'd pretended to be when he was playing with me. When he stole my memories.

I pushed that away with a choked laugh. "I knew

you'd beg in the end," I managed to get out. If I could kill him myself, I would. But it only seemed fair that Samael get his vengeance after all these years. "Mors vincit omnia," I mumbled. "Death always wins, motherfucker."

Samael nodded at me and sliced his sword down, beheading Lucifer in one stroke. Then he lifted his hand, engulfing both parts of my grandfather in demon fire.

I was the one who screamed. My chest burned and burned, until I would have done anything, given anything for the pain to stop.

Samael dropped onto his knees next to me. I was dimly aware of demons pouring into the throne room, our people crowding around us, likely so they could say goodbye.

Evie was suddenly next to me on my other side, breath hitching as her hot tears rained down on my face.

"Please don't leave me, Dani," she begged.

I opened my mouth to tell her that I wasn't, but another scream tore free from my throat.

Samael roared for a healer, then buried his face in my neck.

The arrow twisted again and I lost consciousness.

When I came back, the rowan arrow was still twisting, but I was surrounded by healers, Eldan holding my hand.

"My God," he breathed, and I forced myself to look. Forced myself to stay conscious as the arrow pushed its way out of my chest.

And the wound began to close.

Light filled the throne room, spearing from every inch of my skin. I was pulled into the air, and Samael reached for me, only to be knocked back by whatever strange power was playing with me.

I had a feeling I knew what that power was.

The underworld was no longer tied to Lucifer. Would likely never make such a deal again. I had a feeling it had learned its lesson.

Something shot out of my back as I continued to rise into the air, before the underworld gently placed me on my feet.

I caught a flicker at the corner of my eye and turned, but the flicker moved with me.

I turned again.

"She's like a cat chasing her tail," Bael said, and several people laughed.

I froze. The light and color *was* moving with me, because those were my wings tucked close to my back.

My… wings.

The underworld had embraced me as one of its rulers and decided I needed wings of my own.

They weren't feathered like the high demons, or even made of membrane like the lesser demons. No, my wings they were made of light and power and color and…

It took me a moment to figure out how to spread them experimentally.

And every demon in the room dropped to one knee.

Even Samael, who reached for my hand, brought my palm to his lips. "My queen," he murmured.

"Don't even think about handing this off to me," I hissed at him. "I'm not doing this by myself, so sit your ass on that throne."

He threw his head back and roared with laughter. Then, as our people watched, he lifted me into his arms and strode toward the throne, sitting down with me on his lap.

His mouth slammed down on mine, and time stopped. Slowly, he drew away, his eyes smiling down at me.

"Together, little witch. Always together."

Danica

We sat on the throne for about thirty seconds, just long enough for our people to see that we had claimed it.

Then we stood up and got back to work.

Nathaniel was already in the dungeons, Finvarra lurking a few steps behind him. Both men studied Kyla, who was still in her cage. I still had the keys Pischiel had given me, but from the way Kyla was growling, lips peeled back to expose sharp white teeth, it wasn't exactly safe to free her.

"We take the cuff off from around her neck," I said. No one argued.

I stepped forward, and a hand clamped onto my shoulder. "I don't think so," Samael murmured, gently pushing me aside as he strode toward the cage.

I didn't bother arguing. Both of us were now the rulers of the underworld, which meant both of us could use our blood to set the prisoners free. No spell needed.

Samael held Kyla in place with his power. She let out an enraged howl that made the hair on my arms stand up, her eerie pale blue eyes promising death to anyone who came closer.

Unfortunately for her, Samael was back at full strength. He held her close to the bars and sliced his dagger down one palm, pressing it to the metal encircling her neck.

The metal fell away, hitting the ground with a thunk.

Samael released Kyla, and she immediately snapped at him. He was lightning fast, but even he nearly lost a finger to the furious wolf.

Nathaniel advanced, crouching down. He leveled Kyla with a hard stare, and she fought it, growling at him. Eventually, she lowered her eyes. Nathaniel kept his gaze on her as he spoke to us. "Even a feral wolf will bow to an Alpha. It's biological, a dominance contest they have no control over. But when I reach for her... she's not there."

The Alpha glanced at me, and his eyes were grief stricken. "She's gone, Danica. There's nothing left for me to hold on to. The kindest thing—"

My knife was in my hand before he finished his sentence.

"Don't even fucking think about it."

Samael tensed and I knew he'd take my side no matter what. Even if it meant Kyla truly was feral. Even if it meant we had to carve out a piece of our territory for her to roam in, somewhere she couldn't hurt anyone.

Finvarra chose that moment to stalk toward the cage. For some ungodly reason, Nathaniel allowed him close to Kyla.

I jolted forward as the unseelie King's hand darted through the cage, dodged Kyla's snap and grabbed her by the scruff of the neck. Even as weak as she was, she slashed out with him, her claws cutting open his face and neck, blood dripping down his skin.

The unseelie king merely gave her a shake, and I gaped as his wounds began instantly knitting together.

"Is that all you've got?" he purred.

Finvarra had a death wish. Kyla watched him out of cold eyes, then swiped out again. He responded with another shake.

Nathaniel growled. "Enough. You won't torture my wolf."

Finvarra ignored him. "This is how you're going to go out, wolf?" He smiled darkly. "I don't think so. Shift. NOW."

She ignored him, growling and twisting in his hold. He got right up in her face.

"We have a bargain. And you're going to complete your end of it. Shift, or I'll take you and keep you as a werewolf pet, chained to my throne."

Snarls sounded from everyone in the dungeon, including me. Finvarra ignored us.

I'd kill him before he made Kyla his pet.

Samael was shielding my body with his, but I felt his stroke along our bond. Finvarra may be powerful, but this was *our* territory, and together, both of us could take the dark fae king down if we had to.

Nathaniel had gone still, and I saw the moment he decided to kill the unseelie king. His claws slid out, and he crouched, muscles quivering, ready to leap...

This was about to be a bloodbath.

And then Kyla shifted.

Finvarra still held her, although his other hand found her waist. Her eyes burned into him, silently vowing retribution.

They were still the icy blue of her wolf.

Then those eyes rolled up in her head and Finvarra lowered her to the ground as she passed out. I elbowed past the guys and shoved the key into the lock as Nathaniel roared for a healer.

Finvarra cast Kyla one satisfied look and then turned. Nathaniel let out a long, low growl. The hair on the back of my neck stood at attention at the promise of death in that growl.

"How did you do that?" I managed to get out.

Finvarra raised one eyebrow. "Feral or not, she still owes me."

And their bargain had overridden even an Alpha's call.

I glanced at the bronze mark on the back of Kyla's hand. Nathaniel didn't seem to care how it had been done. The Alpha may have been known for his control, but he was shuddering with the urge to tear into the unseelie king.

"Threaten my wolf with captivity again and I'll slaughter you," Nathaniel snarled.

Finvarra merely smiled, and it promised death right back. "You're welcome to try. Now, I believe I have a scroll to find." He nodded at me and Samael. "Majesties."

Then he was gone.

CHAPTER TWENTY-THREE

Danica

The next day, I stood outside the palace gates, enjoying the feel of the sun on my face, even as I stifled tears. I'd been saying my goodbyes to my friends all morning, and it wasn't getting any easier.

Samael was busy organizing meetings, checking on the wounded, and preparing for our first council session in a few days. He'd already said his own goodbyes, and I doubted he'd said them around a lump in his throat. My lips twitched at the thought.

Lucifer's army may have surrendered, but Samael wasn't content until every single one of them swore their fealty to him. Most of them were more than ready to do just that. Others were convinced by the fact that Samael had given them the opportunity to live, when many who had fought against him expected instant slaughter at his hands.

Of course, there would be some that were unhappy. Some who would be a threat to us, who would fan the flames of rebellion.

We would deal with that when it happened.

Healing tents were set up throughout the battlefield. Samael called in favors from every realm, ensuring that their healers were sent to us to save as many lives as possible.

Aubrey had decided to go back to my realm, but he may not be there for long. By fighting on our side, he'd defected from his court. He'd known he would be branded a traitor, and he'd joined us anyway. The seelie dotted amongst our army had been loyal to him, and there would be repercussions.

His king? As soon as Taraghlan had felt Samael get his power, he'd fled, ordering his people to follow him. Samael had taken some of them prisoner, but it was unlikely the seelie king would negotiate for prisoners of war.

But Taraghlan *would* want his ring back. The ring that had saved our asses. I'd used it for the third time, which meant, as far as I was concerned, it was likely a dead artifact. But I had no doubt that the seelie king would want to determine that for himself, and the white slash on the back of my hand made it clear our deal was not complete. That meant he'd have to face me one day.

I was looking forward to it.

Gary had immediately returned to our realm to be with Cil and Zip. But he'd promised to bring them for a visit soon.

Meredith had also left earlier today, and I'd thanked her for using her power to ensure Lucifer couldn't call in any reinforcements.

She'd hit it off with Selina, and apparently they were planning to 'do lunch.' Mere had placed herself in danger by revealing her unique power, and while Vas had known it needed to be done, Samael had told me he was livid about it.

Now, I was watching as Nathaniel prepared to leave with his pack. They wanted to get home, back to their forest where they would bury their dead, mourn, and move on with their lives.

Nathaniel leaned close and murmured something to Evie, his wolves waiting close by. Whatever Nathaniel said got a reaction from my sister, and she made a sound I'd never heard her make—a growl more wolf than witch. It seemed to please Nathaniel, because his eyes glowed, satisfaction radiating from him.

Kyla was back in her wolf form. She waited with her packmates, her gaze distant. It had taken her hours to wake, and when she had, she'd seemed confused, still half-wild. Nathaniel had assured me that he'd keep her close and wouldn't let her wolf take over.

I strolled toward them, dropping to my knees in front of her. Her pack tensed and I knew it was because they worried she'd lose control and tear out my throat.

I ignored them and looked into those icy eyes.

"I'm sorry it took me so long to get you free."

Kyla snapped at me, but it was... playful. For the first time... I felt true hope.

Nathaniel stepped closer, laying his hand on her head. I saw it in her eyes, the sudden urge to tear that hand from his body, but she managed to retain control. Then she lay down, placing her head on her paws with a long sigh.

My heart ached. "Are you sure you don't want to stay here?"

"She needs to be surrounded by her pack. She'll be okay," Nathaniel assured me. "I'll keep you updated."

"Thank you. And thank you for everything else."

He nodded. With a last glance at Evie, he turned to lead his pack home. Kyla chuffed at me, leaning close to my neck. I laughed as she licked my nose, and then she was gone.

Virtus stayed behind for a long moment, staring into my eyes. The griffin had enjoyed fighting the demons. And he loved being a part of a pack which didn't think he was a liability. Although he still wanted to be able to take a snooze on my bed occasionally.

I raised my hand and stroked his soft mane. "It's a deal. Visit whenever you like. But for now, look after Kyla, okay?"

He nuzzled my neck, nudged Evie playfully, and then trotted after the wolves.

"I'm moving out of the tower when I get back," Evie announced as we watched them go.

I got to my feet and blinked at her. I hadn't expected her to stay in the underworld, although a small part of me had hoped… "Why?"

"I need my own space." Her expression was stubborn, and I tamped down the hurt that instantly rose.

"We won't be visiting for a few weeks, and even then, we won't stay for long," I said carefully. "You'd have the penthouse to yourself."

While we would be returning to Durham periodically,

and my goal was eventually to be able to live there part time, for now we had too much to do in the underworld to leave for long.

Evie glanced at me. And she must have seen the hurt because she rolled her eyes, throwing her arm around my shoulders.

"I love you, but I know damn well you'd have all the demons in that tower watching over me. I need... freedom, Dani. I've never lived alone, never had to buy cheap, crappy furniture and go to work to pay the bills."

Her face lit up in a way I couldn't understand, given that I'd eked out that exact existence. It definitely hadn't been anything to write home about. And yet, I got it. She wanted independence for the first time in her life.

"I'd offer you my apartment, but Rose is still staying."

She shrugged. "I'm going to find my own place. But I want to work for you."

I glanced around and she laughed. "Not here. I know you, and I know you're not going to close your business. You'll try to do it all, and you'll burn yourself out. You and Samael will argue, you'll get drunk at Meredith's, and then you'll finally have to admit that it was always ridiculous to think the queen of the underworld would be able to dabble as a private investigator slash bounty hunter."

I scowled at her. Then I burst out laughing. "You asshole. You want to take over."

She shook her head. "No, but I want to help you create something while I figure out what I want to do. Besides, I need a flexible job that keeps money coming in while I hunt down the assholes who call themselves

Humans for Equality. Equality," she snorted. "Can you believe that shit?"

I'd told her everything Keigan had said, and we'd both held each other and cried. But fear flashed through me at the thought of Evie in another realm, going after killers without me.

I blew out a long breath. "Two conditions."

She frowned at me, but I gave her a look that said my conditions were non-negotiable.

"What conditions?"

"I want you to train with Edward. Even just for a month or two."

Interest flickered in her eyes. "You think he'll do it?"

"He will if it means I owe him a favor. I don't want you relying on your power, Evie, especially since you don't really know how that power works, or even what it is. You're fast, and you can shoot, but you need more training."

Evie mulled it over for a moment, but finally shrugged.

"Fine. What's your other condition?"

"You keep Kyla on. When she's... feeling better."

She rolled her eyes at me. "Duh. We've already talked about it. Well, I talked, and she nodded, so it's a done deal."

My eyes heated, and I blinked several times. If anyone could help Kyla regain her humanity, it was Evie. And if I was feeling the *slightest* FOMO, I would get over it.

I'd made my deal with the underworld, right before it had given Samael back his powers.

It showed me a vision of myself, sitting on an obsidian throne, a crown on my head. Samael sat beside me on his own throne, but the underworld had been clear. I was to stay and rule this place. It had also communicated a few things to me: Lucifer had made an agreement with the underworld all those centuries ago, but he hadn't kept to his side of the bargain. He'd been doing everything he could to lose his tie to the underworld while still keeping Samael powerless.

The underworld had been watching. It made that much obvious by the glimpses it showed me of myself, and everything I'd done since I'd arrived here. I sure as shit hadn't been my best self, but the underworld had decided I had more honor and integrity than Lucifer.

Which admittedly, was a low bar.

I hadn't wanted to end up in the underworld. But a deal was a deal and I was looking forward to exploring this strange realm. I couldn't wait to learn more about my people, to find ways to improve their lives.

Besides, I would never make Samael rule alone. Would never be parted from him again.

Not that *he* would allow such a thing.

It was difficult, though, knowing that–with a single word–I'd given up any hope of a normal life.

Evie had been studying my face, and she was as astute as ever. "We'll call you if we're facing anything super dangerous," she promised.

I knew my sister. Knew she didn't want that at all. Knew she wanted to learn and grow and kick ass, without my shadow over her shoulder.

"No," I said. "You want this business, you have it.

Train with Edward, take Kyla with you for the scary stuff, and figure it out on your own."

My words sounded harsh, and I almost took them back as Evie's eyes filled with tears. But she threw her arms around me once more. "Thank you," she sobbed. "I won't let you down, Dani."

I smiled. She knew she could come to me for advice, but this was the best thing for her. I opened my mouth, about to tell her, to warn her that Nathaniel was her mate. But my conversation with Nathaniel ran through my head.

"Tell me, Danica, how do you think your sister will react to learn that, even in this, her choices would be removed? That she would be destined to be mine?"

"She would run. And she'd never return."

"Your sister is many things, but she's not a witch. Or at least, not just a witch. She's going to need to be protected, and yet, if she learns I am her mate, she will leave. She knows we're watching over her right now, but if she wanted, she could take steps to end that. I have no doubt that if your sister put her mind to it, she could leave without a trace."

I didn't know if I was making the right choice. Didn't know if Evie would ever forgive me for not telling her something so important. And yet, I hoped Nathaniel would play the long game. Would let Evie grow into herself and enjoy her freedom.

Even if that freedom included Liam.

I winced at the thought. The wolf had been seriously injured in the battle. That's where Evie had been while we were freeing Kyla. She'd been by Liam's side, helping the healer prevent his intestines from sliding out of his body.

Evie pulled away, her expression serious. "They came, Danica. Gemma and the coven. Samael managed to convince her to work with the other covens in Durham. History was made with this battle."

"Screw history. How do you feel about it?"

"I don't know how to feel. They left before I could thank them."

I nodded. "Gemma didn't want any fuss. She's dying, Evie."

"I know." She sighed. "I need to get back. But I'll visit in a couple of weeks, before I go to Edward. Deal?"

"Deal."

She wandered away, and I turned as Selina approached, somehow looking like her usual put together self.

"Tell me you use some kind of spell to always look so good."

Surprise flashed through her eyes, and she laughed. "Now that's a nice compliment after a difficult few days."

"I saw you fighting the hellhound. You know how to swing a sword."

That was an understatement. She'd also been lightning fast, dodging poisonous claws with ease.

Selina smiled at me. "Now that is a long story."

"I didn't get a chance to talk to Aubrey before he left. I don't understand why he did it. He's always said he was loyal to his king. Now he'll be a pariah."

Selina frowned. "I asked him the same. He merely said life had become boring, and this would liven it up."

I rolled my eyes, and she laughed. I knew Aubrey well enough to know that wasn't it at all. He'd infused the fake artifact with his power, enough that it fooled the demons who were watching the sentry "sneak" it close to them. Samael had told me that the demon had *wanted* to die, but the sight of him losing his head still played in my mind over and over again whenever I closed my eyes.

I sent her a sidelong glance. "So, you and Aubrey, huh?" I was *sure* I'd picked up on vibes last night over dinner.

She raised one eyebrow. "I think you have quite enough to do without needing to spend time matchmaking, your majesty."

I smirked. "Aubrey once told me the same thing about playing kingmaker." And yet, I was ready to help him take down his king whenever he decided to make his move.

"I need to get back." Selina raised her hand and clasped my shoulder. "It hurts you, that everyone is leaving."

"Yeah. I missed everyone while I was down here, but I'm reminding myself it's much different when I can walk through a portal at any time."

"Other than that sadness, how are you?"

"I'm... hopeful. And grateful. So many people came, Selina. They came to fight with us, to join with us. I never could have imagined..." my voice broke, and she wrapped an arm around my shoulders.

"You will be an incredible queen, Danica."

"Thank you."

I'd be learning on the job, but things were going to change for the demons who lived in the underworld. Our council would introduce the first whiff of democracy to this place. Everyone here would have a voice.

"Will you show me your wings?"

I concentrated, narrowing my eyes in a way that I was sure made me look constipated. But my wings appeared, splaying wide behind me.

"They're beautiful."

"I know," I said. "I want to fly, but Samael insists that I'll need practice and refuses to let anyone else teach me."

She laughed. "And what did you say to that?"

I shrugged, tucking my wings away. "I get it. We haven't had enough time together, you know? We bonded when Samael was hit by the Spell of Three, and then, not long after he woke up, I was taken. We need time to ourselves. Time to fight and snark and laugh and all the things normal couples do. So if he wants this to be just for us, I understand, and I'm fine with it."

"That's lovely." Her beautiful blue eyes shimmered, and she wiped away a tear. "I better be going. Look after yourself and let me know if you need anything."

I nodded, throat tight, and watched as she walked away. Then I took a deep, steadying breath. It was time to find Vas.

Samael had allowed him to hunt the black witches. Lucifer had kept them hidden out of sight, but close enough to do some damage. The last I'd seen of Vas, he'd been stalking away, face blank and eyes promising death to anyone who got in his way.

He hadn't returned once they were all dead. But I had a pretty good feeling I knew where he was.

I made my way to the dilapidated building behind

the palace, clomping down the steps. I found Vas standing where I'd stood just days ago, his eyes dark as he stared down at the wyverns who'd been caught in Hannah's net.

They roared, furious at being chained once more. Samael was already speaking to experts to determine whether they could be rehabilitated and set free. If we allowed them their freedom right now, we had no doubt that they would destroy towns in their rage, and hunt innocent civilians.

If they couldn't be rehabilitated, Samael would at least grant them a quick death. No more would they know that the sky was so close and yet lost to them.

Vas shifted his wing so I could step up next to him. "How are you doing?"

He shrugged. I didn't press, merely leant into him. He'd talk when he was ready.

"I'm okay," he said finally. "How are you doing?"

I turned and buried my face in his chest, wishing my father were here. Wishing he could see his people freed.

"I'm okay," I managed to get out when I was done wetting his shirt. His chest shook with silent laughter, and I pinched him.

"I need you to tell me before you go after Daimonion."

He stiffened. "Is that an order?"

I took a careful step away from him. "No. It's a request from a friend." Hurt stabbed deep into my stomach, so deep that I dodged him when his hand reached out for me.

He used his wing to corral me closer. I scowled at him, but he'd already thrown his arm around my shoulder.

"I'm sorry. I'm not the most fun to be around right now. I got my uncle killed, Danica."

"No, you didn't."

He opened his mouth, and I shook my head. "I was watching. The underworld allowed me to see what happened. Ag… he hadn't spent enough time with you on the streets. He didn't know that you were daring Daimonion to come closer."

He was silent, and I sighed. "It was an accident, Vas. A terrible accident. But it wasn't your fault. Ag left himself wide open because he loved you. Because he couldn't stand to watch you die. Don't destroy his memory by blaming yourself. He'd hate that."

"I'm going to kill Daimonion, even if it means he takes me down, too."

"I know."

He studied me. "Where are your wings?"

I grinned. Everyone wanted to see them. Eventually, I was sure it would get old, but for now I enjoyed showing them off. I stepped away from Vas and concentrated. They appeared, beautiful and new.

"You always wanted wings," he smiled at me, and there was a shadow of the old Vas in that's smile.

"As soon as I figure out how to use them, I'm challenging you to a race."

He rolled his eyes, but his hand darted out, stroking along the edge of my wing. "Can you feel that?"

"Yup. Feels weird."

I shifted my balance, leaning forward and overcompensating. They looked like they were made of light, but they felt like they were made of tendon and muscle, heavy on my back.

"Just wait until you try to fly," Vas said.

"Pffft, I'll pick it up in no time."

I wouldn't, but some of the tightness had disappeared from around his eyes at my cockiness, so I counted that as a win. With a final hug, I left him in the stables, still watching the wyverns.

My head was aching, so I slowly made my way to the gardens, nodding at Sitri. Samael had obviously decided I needed a guard, and he fell into step behind me. I wasn't going to argue. I had a feeling Samael had wanted to give Sitri something to do. He'd been close to Mammon.

So much blood and pain and death.

I glanced up as Lilith flew overhead, low enough that I caught her nod of greeting. As long as I lived, I'd never forget the sight of her storming toward Lucifer's front-lines, her face covered in blood.

Taking a deep breath, I stepped into the walled garden, where I found Hannah sitting in a quiet corner, her face calm as she soaked up the warmth of the sun.

I nodded to her, about to leave and find my own spot, but she waved me over as Sitri leaned against a concrete wall nearby.

Hannah studied my face. "You're sad, halfling. While I thank you for the meal, it's not what I expected after such a victory."

I rolled my eyes at her, and her lips trembled.

"I am sad," I said finally. "There's been so much death. So many from both sides."

"And you miss your father most of all."

"Yes. Well… I miss Keigan too. Does that make me a traitor?"

It was her turn to roll her eyes at me.

"From what I heard, he laid down his life to save yours. He gave you the time you needed to save all of us. If there's one thing I know about negative emotions, it's that berating yourself for feeling them only makes you feel worse."

I took a deep breath and slowly let it out. I would mourn. But we would rebuild, and we would ensure the people in this realm never had to live in fear again.

"Ah, halfling. Something tells me I won't be getting many meals from you in the future."

I smirked. "You know, you could be happy that I won't be drowning in rage and misery."

"Humph."

"I have a question."

"Ask it."

"You once told me my power wouldn't save me. And it didn't. But you said I'd need to rely on the 'things I keep hidden from all.' I'd assumed you meant the rowan arrow."

"Ah." She'd closed her eyes again, and she cracked them open. "It's stupid to assume things."

I scowled, and she shook her head at me.

"You went through your life hiding many things, halfling. Your vulnerability. Your courage. But most of all, the sheer love you had for those you cared for. You refused to let it make you weak. And yet, by using it to make the ultimate sacrifice, it made you strong." She smiled. "And of course, you had the ring. Thanks to that tricky wolf."

My scowl deepened. "And you couldn't just have told me that?"

"What am I, your personal seer? You've always defied most of my visions. Now leave me in peace."

I rolled my eyes but left her alone.

Samael

I waited for the ferryman, attempting to find some patience. It had been three days since we took the throne, and I'd cleared my schedule to be here.

Danica had refused to come. She was still too angry. Still too deep in mourning for the relationship she hadn't gotten to have with her father. I continually found her down below the dungeon, in the tiny cell her where father had spent her entire life.

Each time, I'd gather her into my arms and take her back to our rooms, holding her as she wept.

Charon stepped onto the bank of the river, his expression blank.

"You shouldn't have come," he said.

"I want to see him."

He gave me a look, then turned his gaze back to the river. The ferryman's wrinkled hand was still wrapped around the pole he used to guide his craft.

"You know that's not how it works."

"Make an exception."

"Not even for you, Your Majesty."

I leveled him with a hard stare, frustration roiling through my body. The ferryman merely angled his head. "You forget, I knew you when you had barely started walking. You won't intimidate me into doing what you want."

In spite of my annoyance, I rolled my eyes. "I'd been walking for years." And yet, Charon was ancient in a way few things truly were. Even my lifespan would seem to be the blink of an eye to him.

"He's safe," the ferryman announced, his eyes on the water rushing below us. "Your friend knew it was his time. And he would not be pleased if you spent too long mourning him."

My eyes burned hot. Ag was supposed to rule with us. To finally see peace. "Does he know?"

"Does he know you have your crown, and you killed the one responsible for his sister's death? Of course. He knows all."

"I only need a few minutes with him."

Other than with my little witch, it was the closest I'd ever come to begging. Charon sent me an icy look. That look softened as I glanced back at the water, swallowing around the lump in my throat.

"You would call him back from peace and love? Make him leave the other side, leave the people he hasn't seen for so long? To reassure you?"

The disappointment in Charon's voice was heavy. There weren't many people whom I would allow to give me that look of grave consternation, and yet it had been the ferryman who was sent to find me after my family was slaughtered. The ferryman who'd ensured I could grow into the man I would become and one day take my throne. And, more importantly, live to find my bondmate.

I turned to walk away, unable to speak. Behind me,

Charon heaved a sigh.

"You cannot speak to him, but I will pass on a message."

I whirled and caught the hint of sympathy on his face before it went carefully blank.

"Agaliarept says Mammon is with him, and to stop feeling guilty. He asks you to protect Vas. Allow him his vengeance, but do not allow the rage in his blood to make him risk everything. Your friend wishes you a life full of love and happiness, and instructs you to guard that happiness with everything you have. And he says that if you ever become close to being a ruler like Lucifer, he will find a way to take you out, even from the other side. Although he has a feeling your witchling would never allow that to happen."

I opened my mouth, but my throat had closed up. I clamped my mouth shut once more and nodded, but the ferryman wasn't finished speaking.

"Your father says it wasn't your fault. He says you need to release the guilt you have carried for so long. He should never have expected you to be able to keep Alette alive."

I cleared my throat, but my voice was thick. "She was my sister." I was her big brother. It was my job to keep her safe.

"And she wants you to know that she couldn't have had a better brother. She wishes for you to finally let go of the past and embrace the future with your beautiful bondmate."

I shuddered, longing to see her just once more. I opened my mouth, but Charon smiled at me.

"And your mother…" he frowned, then burst out laughing.

"She says you have lingered here too long, and need to get back to your bondmate. And she looks forward to watching over your grandchildren."

My mouth dropped open, but the thought didn't terrify me. No, the thought of my little witch, heavy with my child… it didn't terrify me at all.

One day. When we were both ready.

Charon's eyes cleared, and I knew they were gone. All of them. He gave me a faint smile. "Go, your majesty. Go and rule in peace. I look forward to a time where I will have far fewer souls to take to their final resting place."

I nodded, the fracture in my heart healing, even though a part of it would always remain bruised, always long for those who'd left me too soon.

I turned, and Charon cleared his throat behind me.

"And tell your mate her father knows she is angry. But he trusts that she won't let that anger consume her. He loves her more than he could ever have imagined loving anything or anyone. And," he lowered his voice, "if you make her unhappy, he will find some way to make you pay."

I was torn between laughing and scowling. But I merely nodded at Charon, certain he could see the gratitude in my eyes. He nodded back, and I went to find my mate.

CHAPTER TWENTY-FOUR

Danica

I glanced at my bondmate, who raised one eyebrow at me. We sat on twin obsidian thrones, and I was making a mental note to find a cushion. Samael had ordered the second throne to be found and pulled out from where it had been hidden away in storage. He'd run one hand over it, murmuring that his mother had sat on it the last time it was in use. Other than ten of Samael's demons, the throne room was empty.

And yet there was a huge, yawning space next to Samael's throne. A space where Ag should have been standing. All of us felt them–the people we loved. Still here, but *not* here.

Samael was still pissed about my whole almost-dying thing. I'd explained to him multiple times that since I was only half demon, it had been worth making Lucifer stab me so the Spell of Three would hit him. I hadn't *planned* to die, but at that point, it looked like I was going to die anyway.

Samael had been *displeased* by that argument.

I'd then snapped at him that he should have told me about the fake artifact. We'd agreed to talk about it later, since Kazbiel was currently standing in front of us, his head bowed.

As soon as I told Samael who the demon was, and who had marched behind him, he'd promised we would carve out territory for those who had no one and nothing to return home to.

"You will be rewarded for your loyalty," he said, studying the stumps where the male's wings had been. His face was blank, but I could feel his cold fury.

"We're loyal to her majesty," Kazbiel said. "We will swear to her."

Samael shrugged. "My mate is loyal to me." His expression was arrogant, his tone exceptionally smug. I shot him a look, battling the urge to do something that would remove some of that smugness. My demon gave me a slow, wicked smile that told me he knew what I was thinking, and I narrowed my eyes at him.

Samael still had zero people skills. If he was relying on me to be the voice of reason, we were screwed.

He turned his gaze back to Kazbiel.

"Swear to Danica, and I will accept."

Kazbiel froze, and I caught the shocked gratitude in his eyes. He'd expected that Samael would kill him for the suggestion. But he'd said it anyway, still standing for his people.

Kazbiel knelt, and my mind flashed to the way he'd fallen to his knees, to the sharp edge of the blade as it had sliced through his wings. I opened my mouth to tell him to stand, but Samael reached out and squeezed my hand.

He was right. I could already tell that the demon was proud. Kazbiel wouldn't appreciate me treating him as if he was broken.

"I swear my loyalty to Her Majesty Danica Amana, Queen of the Underworld. I pledge my allegiance and protection for all of my days."

I felt it. A zing between us. A new bond. Thin but strong.

I cleared my throat. "Samael has mentioned that I will need my own advisors. It will take a long time to fix the damage that was done in this realm. I need someone I can trust to manage those advisors. Someone who will always tell me the truth."

He stared at me for one fraught moment. Finally, he nodded, the ghost of a smile crossing his face as he bowed his head once more. "Yes," he said. "I'll take the job."

I smiled at him. "Great. We'll get started as soon as your people are settled."

Because they *were* his people. I hadn't known it at the time, but Kazbiel had led a good chunk of the resistance. When he'd been captured, Lucifer had wanted him killed, but one of his generals had convinced him that more damage would be done if his followers saw him toiling next to them in the mines.

Samael flicked me a glance, and I realized I'd zoned out. Now, Hera knelt in front of us on the black stone, her head bowed as she quaked. She held Samael's bracelet in her hand, holding it up as if in offering, as if she could exchange it for her life.

I sighed. Then I got to my feet and stalked down the stairs, taking the bracelet back. I slid it onto my own wrist and smiled at Samael. "There," I said. "No harm done."

He narrowed his eyes at me. "You can't be serious."

Mercy for Lucifer's concubine. It was unusual, that was for sure. But... I had no evidence that she'd been involved in any of Lucifer's decisions. Everyone I'd talked to—including Pischiel—had told me she was seen as a beautiful trophy to hang on Lucifer's arm. That was all.

"How did you get involved with Lucifer, Hera?"

She cleared her throat, her eyes darting between Samael and me, as if she couldn't decide who was the greater threat.

"There was an... uprising in my village three decades ago. Lucifer decided to make an example of us." A muscle jumped in her cheek. "My father was one of the leaders of the rebellion. Lucifer killed him in front of me. Then he decided I was beautiful enough to keep. I... bargained with him. I'd go with him willingly if he spared my mother's life."

And once here, she'd figured she would never leave this court. Decided she may as well embrace her future.

"Is your mother still alive?"

She shrugged. "I'm unsure. Lucifer swore he would leave her alone, but..."

But Lucifer couldn't be trusted. "You may return to your village."

Dull hope lit up her face, and then it went blank once more.

"What's wrong?" I asked.

"It's... it's nothing."

"Speak," Samael drawled, obviously already bored

with this conversation. I gave him a look, and he sighed.

"If my mother is gone, there will be nothing left for me in my village. The people there believe me a traitor, believe I turned my back on them."

I studied her. "What is it you're asking for, Hera? You know I'm not good at court-speak."

She laughed. A tiny sound that was immediately cut off. A sound that seemed to surprise her.

"If... if my mother is no longer living, I would like to return here. To make myself useful."

"Useful how?"

"Before Lucifer took me, I was studying to be a healer. There are many people here who need to be healed. Both inside and out."

"Done," I said. "If your mother is alive, you may bring her back with you if you don't want to stay in your village."

The color drained from her face, and she swayed on her feet. I glanced at Bael, who stood a few feet away, and he nodded. He'd catch her if she went down.

This was a mixture of relief and shock. She'd expected me to say no. Had been prepared for it. She'd asked anyway, but she wasn't prepared to feel hope once more.

"It's okay," I told her. "Lucifer's dead. It's over now."

Tears dripped down her face and she nodded at me, opening her mouth and immediately closing it once more. With a bow of her head, she backed away, hurrying out the door.

"I know what you're thinking," I glanced at Samael, who was lounging on his throne as if he was a cat lounging in front of a fire.

"Do you?"

His voice was low and wicked, and it made me shiver. "You're thinking I'm a sucker."

He raised my hand to his mouth, pressing a kiss to my palm. "I'm thinking about how lucky I am to be bonded to a woman who is not only brave and bold, but is also compassionate and willing to give others the benefit of the doubt. I have no compassion left, little witch. Our subjects are lucky to have you."

My cheeks heated. Samael still remained the only man who'd ever made me blush.

"And," he lowered his voice until I could only just hear him. "I'm thinking about how I can't wait to bend you over that throne and—"

I let out a strangled sound as the throne room doors opened, and Samael laughed.

The room went quiet as Pischiel walked in. He glanced at me and smiled, but the smile dropped when he met Samael's eyes. They regarded each other silently.

Pischiel had managed to stay alive throughout the battle—thanks in large part to Samael. My demon studied the man who had once been his childhood friend, and Pischiel studied him right back.

Pischiel bowed his head.

"Lower," Samael said, his expression turning predatory.

I leaned over and elbowed him. "Don't be a dick," I hissed.

Samael rolled his eyes at me.

"You spared my life," Pischiel said to Samael,

ignoring our byplay.

My bondmate heaved a sigh. "You kept Danica safe. She told me how you gave her those keys. Without your actions, without Danica being free, we could never have won the war. Not to mention," he said silkily, "you bonded to my witchling before I got here."

I didn't roll my eyes at the stark possession in his tone when he said "my witchling," but it was close. Pischiel merely flicked me an amused glance.

"What will you do now?" I asked him.

He smiled, and it suddenly looked like a weight had been lifted from his shoulders.

"I want to go home."

I angled my head and his smile widened.

"Nacheran is my uncle on my mother's side."

I gaped at that. "You were playing Lucifer this whole time."

He shook his head. "Not like you think I was. I did small things. Things that wouldn't be noticed. Things that could never have been tied back to me."

"You let me think you were Lucifer's bestie."

A languid shrug. "I couldn't afford for you to know otherwise. If you failed, and Lucifer learned that I had anything to do with it, I would be slaughtered, and so would everyone who worked with me."

"But ultimately, you betrayed him. You brought me the keys. And you opened the pocket realm."

"It was time to make a choice. And now it's time I made another one."

My eyes heated. "I don't want you to go."

I didn't know where this was coming from, but it

was just too soon. Everyone was leaving. Everyone. And Pischiel had been a giant, smug pain in my ass for most of the time I'd known him, but he'd also been the one constant I'd had in this place.

Samael reached out and took my hand once more. But to his credit, he stayed silent. Any jealousy he'd felt when I'd bonded Pischiel to us was either gone or hidden.

"I know you have no feelings of lust for him, little witch," Samael said. *"Which is why I'm allowing him to live. Besides, I believe the male will return if you allow him to leave. If you allow him to spend time in normalcy."*

I squeezed Samael's hand. *"You played with him as a child. He saved my life. You'd never kill him. Don't pretend with me, mister."*

"Hush."

Samael had managed to help me contain the sorrow that had almost broken free. Pischiel remained silent, his expression blank, clearly aware that we were talking about him.

"What will you do?" I asked him.

His smile was blinding. "My uncle offered me a position as his advisor. I'm still determining whether I want to take it. If not, I'll figure something out."

My lower lip trembled, and I ruthlessly clamped down on it with my teeth. Pischiel rolled his eyes and stalked up the steps, ignoring Samael as he tensed next to me. Then he leaned down and wrapped his arms around me.

"I'll be there whenever you call," Pischiel murmured in my ear. "I'm proud of you, Danica."

He pulled back, and I took a shaky breath, smiling

up at him. He glanced at Samael, and pride unfurled in my chest as my bondmate held out his hand. Pischiel's eyebrows shot up, but he shook Samael's hand, then turned and strode down the steps.

Garadiel was next. "Your majesties."

He bowed low, clearly more of a fan of the usual formality.

"Rise," I told him, and he straightened, his gaze flicking above our heads. The gold words remained on the wall, still shifting each time someone new walked in. Unlike Lucifer, both of us wanted the words to stay. They were a reminder that we were here to make our people's lives better. To sacrifice for *them*.

I smiled at Garadiel. So much of the tension had left his face that he almost looked like a different man. Yusilin had survived, thanks to some fast-acting by her friends who'd gotten her to a healer, and Garadiel had spent the past few hours clamped to her side.

I was rooting for them.

I felt Samael's attention and shifted on the hard throne. I kept zoning out, and I nodded at Garadiel.

"What are your plans now?"

"To serve in any way I can," he said immediately. He turned to Samael. "I didn't think that you could be the one to save us. But her majesty convinced me otherwise. I will serve and protect her to the best of my abilities."

Samael nodded. "There's a lot of that going around." He shot me an amused look, then glanced back at Garadiel. "I have a task for you."

"Anything."

"The dungeons," Samael said. "I need you to

determine who is a credible threat, who engaged in actual criminal behavior, and who was merely being punished due to their defiance of Lucifer."

I'd already freed the Dearg Due, as per our agreement.

Garadiel nodded. "Gladly." He turned his gaze to me. "I feel I need to apologize for that day in your bathroom."

"No. What you said to me that day... it got me off the floor." I blushed, knowing the demons were listening intently, but I wouldn't hide from the truth. "You were right."

"Your father would be proud."

"Thank you." I kept my voice low. "Do you... do you know what happened to Cellen and his sister?"

Sorrow flickered through Garadiel's eyes. "Lucifer—"

"He killed them both, didn't he?" Nausea made my gut clench. Cellen deserved it. But his sister had been a pawn. I didn't even know her name.

Garadiel nodded, and I took a deep breath. "I don't understand how I have Lucifer's powers." I could feel them, merged with my own, and the sheer amount of power scared the shit out of me.

Garadiel looked like he was deciding whether or not to keep speaking, and Samael gestured for him to step closer. He walked up the stairs and leaned down to murmur to me.

"Will you follow me?"

I nodded, and a small part of me wasn't surprised when he led to the room behind the throne room. Where the scroll lay, still under the glass. Samael stalked behind us, never one to be left out of anything to do with me.

"I can't read that thing," I said. Behind me, Samael had gone very still as he stared at it. He wrapped his arm around me.

"Allow me to read it to you, little witch."

I opened my mouth, but he was already speaking.

"On the night of a hundred thousand stars, the morning star will drink of its bloodline, until even kings will bow to greatness."

I scowled. "See? The morning star is dead."

Garadiel smiled. "Your mother named you well. I'm unsure if she knew the exact wording of the prophecy... however...

"Huh?"

"Danica. Your name means 'morning star.'"

"Well. Shit."

Samael placed his chin on my shoulder, still gazing at the scroll. I pinched him. "What else does it say?"

His breath caressed the shell of my ear, and I shivered as he spoke. "After the war of stars, peace shall reign in the underworld for five hundred years."

I grinned. "Now that's a prophecy I can get behind." My grin fell. "I just wish my father was here to enjoy it."

Garadiel moved in front of me, his eyes serious.

"Your father had a prophecy of his own, Danica. When he was young, he went to a market where an old witch had a vision. She told him he wouldn't meet his daughter until days before his death. The moment he found out Lucifer had brought you to the underworld, he knew his days were numbered."

My chest twisted. "He could have made sure he didn't meet me. Instead, he had you tell me to go to him."

"He would have given anything to see you. And he was done, Danica. Done with being caged like an animal."

"But if I hadn't seen him then, maybe we could have freed him and sent him on his way."

"Attempting to circumvent fate never works well. Your father had made his peace."

I swallowed around the lump in my throat. Samael had told me about his visit to the ferryman. Had told me what my father had communicated.

"Tell your mate her father knows she is angry. But trusts that she won't let that anger consume her. He loves her more than he could ever have imagined loving anything or anyone."

It… helped, knowing my father was somewhere else. Even if it meant he wasn't here with me. I hoped he was at peace. Hoped he could take to the sky, stretch his wings whenever he liked.

I remembered how much he'd hoped to see my mom. I could picture them both there in that garden, slowly getting to know each other once more. Maybe they would fall in love again all over again. I wanted that for them.

Garadiel excused himself, and Samael took me into his arms. I gazed up at him. "How were your talks with Lucifer's generals?"

"Stimulating," he said dryly and I laughed. "Some of them will become threats. But…"

"We'll deal with it when it comes."

"Thank you. For staying. For sitting on that incredibly uncomfortable throne next to me."

I raised one eyebrow. "Would you have let me go?"

"Never. But if you had told me you wanted to rule in

name only, I would have made it happen."

"We're a team. You and me, Samael. Even if I hadn't promised the underworld, I'd never leave you to do this alone."

500 years of peace. It was going to happen. I'd make sure of it.

His hand cupped my face, and I nuzzled his palm. "I cannot wait to spend our lives together, little witch. You are more than I could have ever imagined." He lowered his head and I brushed my lips against his.

This was where I belonged. Here. In Samael's arms. This was what I'd fought for. What I'd always fight for.

"Later," he murmured, finally stepping back.

I gave him a saucy wink. "Later."

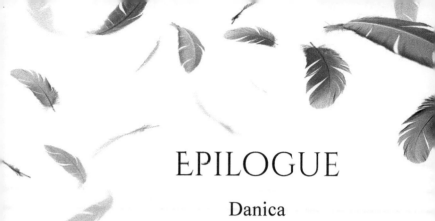

EPILOGUE

Danica

I wandered around the bedroom I shared with Samael. We were having any trace of Lucifer purged before we moved into the royal quarters. But for now, this room was light and airy. Priceless paintings hung on the walls, antiques dotted almost every surface, but most importantly, the furniture was made for comfort. This was a place we could step away from everything and everyone and just be together.

Lia meowed at me from where she lay on our bed. I leaned over and stroked her soft fur, picking her up and carrying her toward the balcony. She already had the run of this wing, and it was likely only a matter of time before she was strutting around the rest of the palace.

Pushing aside the sheer curtains, I stepped out onto the balcony and stared down at our kingdom. Movement caught the corner of my eye and a lesser demon watched me from where he was perched like a gargoyle on one of the turrets. I watched him back, but he seemed content to sit in silence. Apparently, many of the lesser demons had been secretly loyal to my father. All while I'd been handing them over to the Mage Council in my realm. It would take me a while to come to terms with that.

Lia hissed at the demon, and he regarded her with clear interest. Every lesser demon here knew she wasn't to be harmed, but my heart still leapt in my chest as Lia climbed onto my shoulder and then leapt up onto the turret next to the demon. He stayed still while she sniffed at him, swiped out at him with her paw a few times. Then she curled up next to him in the sun, closing her eyes.

My life was so weird.

Samael should be here soon. I'd asked Bael to ensure he had some time off this afternoon. To lure him up here to me.

Because life was short.

And I needed my bondmate.

I looked down at the gold mark on my arm, and my lips curved. It wasn't all that long ago that I was going toe-to-toe with my demon and vowing that I'd make sure that mark was removed. Even when I'd fallen for him, I'd still chafed at the bond.

Now, I'd cut anyone who tried to remove the symbol of our mating.

Funny how coming so close to my own death— right after almost losing Samael–really put things into perspective. Less than a year ago, if someone had told me I'd pine for a demon whenever he wasn't around, I would have stroked my Nim Cub warningly, and dared them to repeat themselves.

I couldn't wait to live my life with Samael by my side. He was still a snarly, possessive demon, and I was still a wily, smart-mouthed half-witch. But the next few centuries were going to be one hell of an adventure.

A door opened, and I could feel Samael step into our room, could feel the power churning around him as a smile played around my mouth.

I turned and stepped through the balcony and into our room. My heart gave one hard thud as my gaze found liquid silver.

There he was. The man who'd come for me, knowing he'd be powerless in this realm. The man who'd fought for his people, who'd been with me every step of the way, even when I couldn't remember his name.

He was dressed in a suit that matched his eyes, and I drank him in, my fingers itching to caress the ridges of his abs, to wander lower, lower, until—

"Well, this is interesting." Samael ran his gaze over my body, and I grinned at him. Those were the first words he ever said to me.

"Take off your clothes," he ordered.

I merely raised one eyebrow, and he smiled.

"Please," he purred, "disobey me. I haven't gotten my hands dirty for weeks."

I blinked at him and burst out laughing. Back when Samael first said those words, he'd been threatening to kill me.

As I watched, he pulled one of my throwing knives from his pocket, placing it on the dresser next to him. He'd kept it as a talisman after I'd thrown it at him–managing to stick him in the calf–and he still refused to give it back.

I closed the balcony door behind me and made a show of glancing over his shoulder.

He took a single step closer. "It won't work, you know."

I angled my head. "What won't work?"

"Waiting for your chance to escape. There are no chances here."

I bared my teeth at him. He bared his back. His teeth were *still* scarier.

He launched himself at me and I was too busy laughing to fight him off. Within a couple of seconds, I was blinking up at him, my back pressed against silk sheets.

"You have two choices," he said, and I raised my eyebrow at him.

"Your first choice? Both you and the traitor die. This Steve dies harder, begging for death for daring to cross me."

I smiled at him. "Go on."

"Your first choice? Submit to me and be rewarded."

"Hmm," I pretended to think about it while he methodically stripped me of my clothes.

I stretched my hands over my head and watched as his gaze dropped to my breasts, the hunger in his eyes making me both languid and eager.

His warm body covered mine, and I gasped as his clothes disappeared from his body.

"And the second choice?" I raised one eyebrow imperiously, and he looked suddenly younger, like the weight of the world was finally off his shoulders.

"You work for me."

"In what capacity?"

His gaze dropped to the demon on the floor. "This

isn't the first death in the past few weeks, although it's a different method. Something is hunting demons, and your reputation precedes you. You'll be my personal bounty hunter."

"You work for me," Samael purred, gently pushing my hair back off my face. My whole body went tight. Mine. Mine for always.

"In what capacity?" My hand stroked down his chest.

"You'll be *my* personal bounty hunter."

Somehow, he'd made the words sound filthy, and my face heated.

He took the opportunity to slide his hand down to where I was already wet for him, and I let out a low groan.

"For how long?" My words tripped over each other as he flicked my clit.

"Forever," he declared, and then he slid into me, making the edges of my vision turn fuzzy as I wrapped my legs around him.

I forced myself to frown, as if I were frantically thinking of some way out.

"I'll make you a deal."

Was there anything more attractive than Samael's eyes sparking with a mixture of lust and amusement?

"What kind of deal?"

I grinned up at him, delighted by this game. He began to move, and I groaned again, all thought leaving my head.

He stopped, and I let out a string of curses that made him laugh down at me.

"What kind of deal?" he repeated.

I smiled up at him, my foot slapping at his thighs in

an effort to make him *move.*

"I'll be your personal bounty hunter, if you'll be my personal dangerous and scary-as-hell demon."

His expression softened. He knew what I was asking. Out there, we had to rule the underworld. But behind closed doors, when no one could ever see us, we would just be Danica and Samael.

He raised his hand to my face.

Then he thrust once more, hitting the spot inside me that made me clench around him.

His mouth found mine, tongue stroking as we moved together. Then he lifted his head, gazing down at me as if he couldn't look away.

"It's a deal."

The end.

I hope you enjoyed Demon's Advocate! I couldn't let the story end there, so I wrote a free bonus chapter for this book, and you can find it at staciastark.com. You're going to want to read this one ;)

While this is the final book in Danica and Samael's story, the final book in the *series* is called **Play the Demon** and features Vas and Meredith.
The spin-off series is also now complete, and Bargains with Beasts features Kyla and Evie's stories.

Thank you for coming on this adventure with me, and I'd love to connect with you in my Facebook group– Stark Society.

ALSO BY STACIA STARK

The Deals with Demons Series

Speak of the Demon
Dance with the Demon
Inner Demons
Luck of the Demon
Demon's Advocate
Play the Demon

The Bargains with Beasts Series

Unnatural Magic
Unbroken Magic
Unending Magic

The Kingdom of Lies Serie

A Court This Cruel and Lovely
A Kingdom This Cursed and Empty
A Crown This Cold and Heavy
A Queen This Fierce and Deadly

www.ingramcontent.com/pod-product-compliance
Ingram Content Group UK Ltd.
Pitfield, Milton Keynes, MK11 3LW, UK
UKHW041854190125
4173UKWH00039B/459

9 781959 293057